Craig Johnson is the *New York Times* bestselling author of the Longmire mysteries, the basis for the hit Netflix original series Longmire. He is the recipient of the Western Writers of America Spur Award for fiction, and his novella *Spirit of Steamboat* was the first One Book Wyoming selection. He lives in Ucross, Wyoming, population twenty-five.

★ ★ ★

Praise for Craig Johnson and
the Longmire series

"[*Depth of Winter*] is a rip-roaring adventure, and if Longmire seems uncannily able to recover from blows to the head and other injuries that would disable a lesser man, well, that's what it takes to defeat this 'monster among monsters.' The sheriff as the spirit of Quixote, riding a mule to the rescue."
—*Kirkus Reviews*

"Crack dialogue, smart humor, mystical realism, strong sense of place, and colorful, complex characters." —*Shelf Awareness*

"This is one hell of a book. . . . *Depth of Winter* is a great new novel by the fabulous Craig Johnson. For longtime fans of the Walt Longmire series, this book will, without doubt, be a true gem to read." —*Fresh Fiction*

"It's the scenery—and the big guy standing in front of the scenery—that keeps us coming back to Craig Johnson's lean and leathery mysteries." —*The New York Times Book Review*

"Extraordinary . . . Delightful . . . Readers are reminded that as compassionate and fair-minded as Walt has become, there remains at his core a ruthless protective instinct for those he loves."
—*Kings River Life Magazine*

"Like the greatest crime novelists, Johnson is a student of human nature. Walt Longmire is strong but fallible, a man whose devil-may-care stoicism masks a heightened sensitivity to the horrors he's witnessed."
—*Los Angeles Times*

"The characters talk straight from the hip and the Wyoming landscape is its own kind of eloquence."
—*The New York Times*

"Johnson's trademarks [are] great characters, witty banter, serious sleuthing, and a love of Wyoming bigger than a stack of derelict cars."
—*The Boston Globe*

"A Walt Longmire novel is like going on a ride-along with an old friend, watching him ferret out the bad guys with wit and humanity (and more than a few bullets), while we swap stories and catch up on old times."
—*Mystery Scene*

"Stepping into Walt's world is like slipping on a favorite pair of slippers, and it's where those slippers lead that provides a thrill. Johnson pens a series that should become a must read, so curl up, get comfortable, and enjoy the ride."
—*The Denver Post*

"No urban crime series is more sophisticated or more amusing than the Longmire novels when it comes to the complicated psychology of criminals and their victims."
—*The Connecticut Post*

CRAIG JOHNSON

DEPTH
OF
WINTER

PENGUIN BOOKS

PENGUIN BOOKS
An imprint of Penguin Random House LLC
penguinrandomhouse.com

First published in the United States of America by Viking,
an imprint of Penguin Random House LLC, 2018
Published in Penguin Books 2019

ISBN 9780525522492 (paperback)

THE LIBRARY OF CONGRESS HAS CATALOGED THE HARDCOVER EDITION AS FOLLOWS:
Names: Johnson, Craig, 1961– author.
Title: Depth of winter / Craig Johnson.
Description: New York, New York : Viking, [2018] | Series: A Longmire mystery
| Identifiers: LCCN 2018023887 (print) | LCCN 2018025790 (ebook) |
ISBN 9780525522485 (ebook) | ISBN 9780525522478 (hardcover)
Subjects: LCSH: Longmire, Walt (Fictitious character)—Fiction. | BISAC:
FICTION / Mystery & Detective / General. | FICTION / Westerns. | FICTION /
Suspense. | GSAFD: Mystery fiction. | Suspense fiction.
Classification: LCC PS3610.O325 (ebook) | LCC PS3610.O325 D46 2018 (print) |
DDC 813/.6—dc23
LC record available at https://lccn.loc.gov/2018023887

Printed in India
9   10   8

Set in Dante MT Std
Designed by Cassandra Garruzzo

For Anna, Greg, and the rest of their lives together.

ACKNOWLEDGMENTS

Come in from the blistering light of Calle Juárez and set yourself down on a stool, gentle reader. Lean your elbows on the room-length bar and glance up at the hand-carved bar-back that was shipped from France back in the mid-thirties. Allow yourself to relax into the calm, peaceful ambiance of the green-tinted lamps and the soft glow of old-world mahogany that belies the belli-cose streets of downtown Juárez, Mexico, just outside.

Opened two years into the American Prohibition, The World Famous Club Kentucky found a ready customer base from across the border and before long celebrities of all stripes were taking up residence at the bar where you now sit. Don't pay any mind to that giant, stuffed hawk above the bar-back, or the trough that runs the length of the bar, harkening back to when patrons used to stand and rather than lose their place, simply relieve themselves in situ, as it were.

Allow me to call Lorenzo "Lencho" Hernandez over to mix you a drink in the home of the original margarita, and don't worry about the price, they're only two dollars apiece, so you can have as many as you'd like.

Behind us there's a very large man in a cowboy hat sitting at a table with a legless hunchback in dark glasses and a porkpie hat, and they seem to be having a very intense conversation, but we'll get to that later. Right now I want to say thanks to you and a few other people the way I always do before we get this story rolling.

If I had my way we'd be circling the place with my usual *compadres*, Gail "Highball" Hochman and Marianne "Mai Tai" Merola. We'd lift a glass to my raft of Penguins, Kathryn "Cosmopolitan" Court, Sarah "Sidecar" Stein, and Victoria "Screwdriver" Savanh. Brian "Old Fashioned" Tart and Ben "Bellini" Petrone will get us one for the road while Jessica "Gin Fizz" Fitzpatrick and Mary "Whiskey Sour" Stone drop pesos in the old Wurlitzer jukebox as the Coasters play "Down in Mexico." I also need to thank Michael "Michelob Ultra" Crutchley and Ry "Rye Whiskey" Brooks for some of the funniest lines in the book.

And lest I forget, though, the one that always quenches my thirst will always be Judy "Champagne Cocktail" Johnson, the top shelf of my life.

In the depth of winter I finally learned that
there was in me an invincible summer.

—*Albert Camus*

Poor Mexico, so far from God and
so near the United States.

—*Porfirio Díaz*

1

I turned my water glass in the slick circle of condensation on the smooth, red lacquer of the table between us and studied the man across from me. I was afraid that if I didn't pay attention, he might disappear. The Seer was like that; it was as if he simply drifted away, giving him access to places without appearing to be there, making other people's secrets his own.

"You should take in some of the culture while you are here south of the border—go to the bullfights." Adjusting his straw porkpie hat to a jauntier angle, the hunchback smiled. "You might enjoy it."

I said nothing.

He looked in my general direction, the smile slowly fading. "My friend, Miguel Guerra, says you are highly motivated, but that if I can talk you out of this, I should."

I still said nothing.

He stared at me. "Do you speak Spanish?"

I wiped the sweat from under my eyes with a thumb and forefinger—I had a hard time convincing myself it was coming up on November. "Very little."

He had taken his cheap sunglasses off and placed them next to his drink. His eyes were opaque, and they wandered past me, toward the knobby hills to the south that rose from the desert like a bony hand, the fingers spreading to make peaks and battlements, as if the mountains were at war with the flat land. "That's not good, because where you are going there will be places where no one speaks English."

The Seer sipped his soft drink and then batted the white cane between the knees of his threadbare pants at the exact place where his legs ended.

"Your English is very good."

He shrugged. "I have lived my whole life here in Juárez, and back before the new drugs, we were just a suburb of El Paso." He glanced down at his truncated legs. "Not the old drugs that did this. My mother traveled to Germany in the sixties and was given the drug that took my legs and my sight and in the process gave me this humped back." He vaguely waved at it sitting there like one of the battlements behind him. "Did you know that hunchbacks are seen as lucky in my country—that we bring good fortune?"

"I hope that's the case."

"Personally, it has never brought me any providence." He paused for a moment and then turned toward the Club Kentucky, seeing it the way it was in his mind's eye. "Juárez used to be Las Vegas before there was a Las Vegas—twenty-four-hour bars, casinos, cabarets, brothels." The Seer sipped his soda. "It is said that this club invented the margarita." He nodded. "Marilyn Monroe sat on that very stool where you sit now."

"How do you know Marilyn Monroe?"

He smiled broadly for the first time, and I was surprised at the blinding perfection of his teeth. "My mother was here."

"In this bar?"

"*Sí*, January twenty-first, 1961. Monroe filed for divorce from Arthur Miller here in Juárez. She was with two men, her lawyers, Aurellano González Vargas and Arturo Sosa Aguilar. They

filed a suit of incompatibility of character." He leaned in confi-
dentially. "A marvelous playwright, but she told my mother he
was hung like a cocktail sausage."

"Huh."

"She also saw your John Wayne drink himself senseless and
walk out onto the sidewalk where he fell face-first like a tree."
Sensing my disinterest, the Seer leaned back against the wall.
"Most tourists love stories about Hollywood celebrities."

"I'm not here as a tourist."

He waved his cane toward me and changed the subject. "Can
you ride a burro?"

"I can ride a horse."

"That does not mean you can ride a burro; there are places
where you cannot go by horse or car."

"Fine, I'll walk."

"It is not enough." He studied the problem for a while and
then shook his head. "Where you are going you will need a
reason to be there, or they will kill you just to hear the sound
of their weapons."

"I guess trying to blend in isn't much of a possibility?"

He smiled and slowly began shaking his head. "Let's see,
shall we?" His face became somber, and his mouth hung open
as if he were tasting the air between us like a snake. "From the
timbre of your voice and lung capacity I would say you are at
least two hundred pounds, and from the way the floorboard
creaked when you walked in I would say two-fifty."

"I am."

"From the angle of your voice, I would say you are six-foot-
four or five."

"Five."

"Facial structure also affects the voice—you are of Northern
European descent so I am guessing blondish, but considering

your age possibly gray, and with blue eyes—but not pure blue, more likely blue with either green or gray."

"Gray, no blue."

"Ah, eyes are difficult. . . . But you will have to forgive me in that I have never actually seen blue or gray or any other colors for that matter." He glanced toward the bar where he knew without seeing that the entire staff of four aged bartenders were watching and listening to us. "And from the deference of the staff, I am guessing your persona is formidable."

I sighed. "Lately."

"You are armed?"

"Yep."

"With what?"

"Colt 1911."

He shook his head at the antiquity of my sidearm. "Why the .45?"

"Because they don't make a .46."

He smirked and allowed his sightless eyes to rest on the surface of the small table between us. "I regret having to ask . . . but can you shoot?"

"Yep."

"How well?"

"Well enough for whatever needs to be done."

He paused for a moment and then nodded. "Maybe we use this." He tipped his head to one side. "There have always been men who come here from your country mostly for money and women, but other things, too. I propose a safari, but not for animals."

"For what then?"

"There were men like yourself who came to Old Mexico in search of antiquities. Even now. There was a good friend of my cousin's, a Mr. Guzmán, who was here searching for a particu-lar Russian Model P made by your Colt company."

"José Guzmán." I smiled. "Although I think his friends call him Buck."

"I believe that is his name, *sí*. He was a lawman like you—you know him?"

"A legend."

"My cousin was with him when he bought the single-action pistol from a fat policeman who was directing traffic in the mid-dle of the street in Nogales." He sipped his Guayaba Jarritos. "What kind of lawman are you?"

"Absaroka County Sheriff, Wyoming."

"We don't see many sheriffs." He warmed to his purveyor of antique armaments idea and nodded more vigorously. "This will provide us with an excuse for being in areas where we might not normally be, and it gives us a bargaining reputation without the hazards of drug money." He finished his soda. "I will begin spreading the word that there is a gringo in town looking for vintage armaments and that we will be traveling around the area south of here."

"We?"

He lowered his eyes. "Yours is a good cause, and I would like to help you."

I shook my head but then spoke, realizing he couldn't see my response. "I can't let you do that. I appreciate your help, but if you go with me you're likely to be killed."

"I am half dead now, so what does it matter?" He folded up his cane and reached out his arms like my granddaughter Lola did when she wanted to get out of her high chair. "We will need a driver."

I finished my water and pushed the old wheelchair, which

was painted a vibrant turquoise and orange, toward the door, the cane across his knees. "You're not going, and I don't need a car—I have a truck parked on the other side."

His turn to shake his head at me. "A new truck?"

"I don't know, a rental. It's blue, I think."

He took charge and wheeled past me down the bar toward the front entrance. "Too new for our purposes, and the US plates are too conspicuous; we will need something that blends in, along with a driver who knows the roads."

Hastily, I tossed a few pesos onto the table before following after him. "I thought cars couldn't go on the roads where we are going."

He called back over his shoulder. "Eventually, but first we will need a driver and a vehicle that will not arouse suspicion."

One of the old bartenders opened the glass door for him and then assisted me in getting him over the rubber threshold with a demeanor that read happy-to-be-rid-of-the-both-of-you. Blinking from the bright sun and pulling at my sweat-soaked shirt collar, I joined the Seer on the streets. "Does it ever cool off in this damn place?"

"It snowed here thirty-seven years ago." He replaced his inside sunglasses for the oversized ones that he used outside. "In the winter at night it gets colder." He grinned. "Sometimes."

We had reached the curb when a large, honest-to-God pink, 1959 Cadillac convertible pulled into view and slid up in front of us like a pulsating puddle of Pepto-Bismol, oozing to a stop. A young man with long hair and amazingly thick glasses got out and came around, opened the door, and saluted me. "*Hola, Capitán.*"

The Seer gestured toward the young man. "My nephew, Alonzo—our driver."

I gave him my hand. "Walt Longmire."

"Good to meet you." He lifted his uncle from the wheel-chair, carefully placed him in the passenger seat, and then put the conveyance into the cavernous rear.

I leaned forward, but the Seer stopped me with his cane. "We have not discussed the fee for our services."

"I figured we'd get to that."

He gestured toward his nephew and stuck a hand out. "One hundred US dollars apiece per day, plus expenses."

"Driving this, gas alone should be another thousand." I shook his hand and noticed how strong his grip was, then reached out and tapped the Longhorn steer horns mounted on the hood. "So is this the inconspicuous vehicle we'll be taking south?"

Alonzo gunned the motor. "This sonless, goat-fornicating, godforsaken, flat-beer-tasting beast will carry us as far as the equator if need be." He grinned, and you could tell that he and the Seer were from the same genetic corral. "We will see you tonight at Our Lady of Guadalupe Cathedral." He threw an arm over the side of the Caddy and pointed down the street. "I will meet you inside a little before nine p.m." He turned his head. "Any questions?"

"Yep." Running my eyes over the glossy flanks of the hot pink Caddy and the outrageous tailfins, the largest ever produced, I stuffed my hands in my jeans and glanced at him. "How much Mary Kay did you have to sell to get this thing?"

On the long trip back to the Avenue Benito Juárez bridge, I thought about what I was doing. I was a stranger in a strange land, and my backup was a legless, blind humpback and his Coke-bottle-lensed, Caddy-driving nephew, neither man instilling a great deal of confidence.

The sidewalk became more crowded as I approached the

Border Patrol building on the right, and I was reminded of the cattle chutes we used in Wyoming as I took the general entrance back into my country instead of the one to the left for Americans with documents.

I had to remember to get a passport.

Standing in the long line, I looked around me and figured that the Seer had been right about my blending in—I was going to have to lose about eight inches, forty pounds, and investigate a pigment transplant.

Behind the Plexiglas, a bored-looking young woman gestured for me to step forward. "American citizen?"

"Yep."

"ID?"

I pulled out my driver's license and handed it through the opening at the bottom. She studied it for a moment, and I watched as her left hand slipped beneath the counter. A moment later another uniformed individual was standing beside her and motioned for me to go to the unmarked door to the right, not the general one to the left.

"Is there a problem?"

"Not really, except that you're supposed to have a passport to enter Mexico, even if you don't really need one to get back in the US." The older man who was stationed behind the young woman motioned again, and she turned back to me with a practiced smile. "Just a routine check—you're the lucky one-millionth customer of the day." I nodded and followed my license; the heavy door buzzed, and I pushed it open and entered a short hallway. The Border Patrol guy appeared from the other side and pointed toward the door at the end of the hall.

"Do I get a prize or anything?"

"Oh yeah, it's in there."

I walked down the hall and just as my hand touched it, the door buzzed and the lock sprang.

FBI Special Agent-in-Charge Mike McGroder sat reading from a file folder at a metal table with his loafered feet on its surface. "I told you not to go by yourself."

"Your socks don't match." I sat in the chair opposite him. "I was just doing a little sightseeing. Did you know that Marilyn Monroe got her divorce from Arthur Miller in Juárez?"

"No."

"Did you know he was hung like a cocktail sausage?"

"Walt." He glanced at the camera in the corner of the ceiling behind him. "You were reconnoitering in a foreign country, and you're lucky I've got pull and can get you back in this one."

"As far as I can remember, I'm an American citizen."

"An armed American citizen in Mexico, which means you get the nicest corner cell in the shittiest maximum-security prison in the Free and Sovereign State of Chihuahua."

"I just wanted to get the ball rolling."

"Okay, Sisyphus." He put his feet on the floor, tossed the file onto the table, and ran a palm over his crew cut. "I've got you a meeting with the AIC and the DEA guy here in El Paso tomorrow at four-thirty."

"I'll already be gone."

"Walt." He placed his elbows on the table, lacing his fingers as a chin rest. "They know you're coming. Hell, they're planning on you coming, and they're going to have a very warm reception for you."

"I figure."

"I'm just trying to give you a fighting chance at survival."

"Doesn't matter."

"Look, let's set ourselves up for success here. I think getting your daughter out of Mexico and you surviving it is what we're shooting for."

"Me surviving would be nice, but I doubt it'll happen." I sat back in my chair with the image of a five-year-old girl with reddish hair dancing through a pasture as the horses looked on. "He knows I'm here, he knows I know he's got her, and he'll kill her if I don't play by the rules." I reached under my lightweight jacket and pulled the aforementioned .45 from the small of my back and placed it on the table between us. "That's what I've got. Now I know I'm going into a fight, so I'll gladly trade it for a rifle, a shotgun, an RPG, a Sherman tank, or an atomic bomb—but that's what I've got."

"Not anymore." He reached across the table and slid my Colt back toward him without looking at it. "You wait until tomorrow afternoon for the meeting with the authorities, and then we'll formulate a plan to save your daughter."

I coughed a laugh. "You think those guys know what's going on down there?"

"More than some jumped-up sheriff out of Wyoming, yes." He waited a moment and then added, "You arrived last night, what the hell is the hurry?"

I stood, and for a lack of anything else to do, took a few short steps. "My daughter, Mike. It's like I'm walking around with a hole in the middle of me, and all I can do is listen to the wind blow through. I'm going to do something, and I pray it's not the wrong thing, but I'm going to do something." I made the next statement to the camera lens in the corner. "I'm not waiting. He'll know we're planning something and then will fold up the tents along with Cady and they'll disappear, and I can't have that."

Mike came around the desk and sat on the corner. "You don't know what you're doing, and you could set off a cartel war that might wind up killing thousands of innocent people." His turn to glance at the camera. "I need your badge."

"You didn't give me this badge, the people of Absaroka County did."

"Let's not make this any harder than it is, okay?"

Turning my eyes back to him, I pulled the badge wallet from my shirt pocket, holding it for a moment, and tossed it on the table. "You're arresting me?"

"We're not letting you back into Mexico."

"Try and stop me." I walked toward the door where I'd come in, but the latch held fast. I turned to look at him.

He picked up my sidearm and wallet, placing them together in one hand and stuffing them under his arm. "I just did."

It was a waiting room, but both doors were securely locked, so it might as well have been a cell. There were three chairs and the desk where McGroder had had his conversation with me. I'd seen a lot of those desks in federal buildings—somebody must've had a sale.

I sat behind it and looked for the button McGroder must've used to unlock the doors but couldn't find it. Opening one of the drawers, I discovered two paper clips, a busted Swingline stapler, and a thumb-worn biography of Ambrose Bierce so old that he might've owned it himself before disappearing into Mexico all those years ago.

By chapter five, I'd decided that the book was actually pretty good and only lowered it when an elderly gentleman in coveralls opened the door through which Mike had disappeared.

The custodian was holding a mop and kicking a commercial bucket in front of him as I stood. He saw me and started to close the door, but I recognized an opportunity when I saw one.

"Hold on, I'll get out of your way." He paused for a moment, and I gestured with the book. "I can find somewhere else to read."

"Are you sure?"

I clutched the door in one hand and looked out past his shoulder to the empty hallway behind him. "Oh yeah, it's about time for me to get out of here anyway."

Truer words having never been said, I slipped past and then turned and held the door. "This thing sticks, so I'd just leave your bucket in the doorway if I were you."

It had sounded as though McGroder had gone straight down the length of the hallway, so I tried the corridor on the right and discovered a bathroom with a window just big enough to pass a house cat through.

Abandoning that path, I tried the other side and discovered another holding cell—so, my old cell, which was being mopped, a new one, the bathroom, or door number one. I crossed back to where the old guy was mopping and carefully moved the bucket so that the door quietly eased shut.

Clutching my trusty tome, I marched down the hall and swung open the door at the end, only to be confronted by an armed private first class in his battle dress uniform, who pushed off the wall and looked at me questioningly.

Hanging on the door, I made sure he saw the book. "Hi."

He pushed off the wall. "Hi?"

I threw a thumb over my shoulder. "Hey, none of my business, but I think there's a janitor locked in that waiting room at the end of the hallway." I gestured with the Ambrose Bierce. "I was headed to the bathroom and heard some pounding."

"Can't you let him out?"

"I think the door's stuck, and like I said, I'm headed for the bathroom."

The private nodded as he brushed past me. "With the amount of holdees we've got daily, they sometimes use those waiting rooms as cells and they don't have passage locks."

"Yep, somebody ought to do something about that." As he strode down the hall, I slipped up another passageway and turned a corner where there was a glass wall connected to another, more elaborate conference room. I was close enough to see the back of Mike McGroder's head along with a couple of other guys in suits going over what looked like a long list of items being pointed out by a young man whom I didn't know.

Since he was the only one turned toward me, I smiled, waved the invaluable Bierce, and mouthed the words, *it's really good . . .* And kept walking.

He paused for a moment, somewhat perplexed, and then waved and went back to his agenda.

There were two large glass doors past what looked to be the public reception area and a counter where two more Border Patrol agents were talking to a long line of people. I knew the drill by now, so I pushed open one door and headed for the outside without pause. I was through and on the sidewalk when I heard someone behind me.

I turned the corner of the building and headed for my rental truck that was parked in the four-dollars-a-day parking lot. The FBI man hadn't taken my keys, so I popped the doors with the remote and wheeled out onto Sixth and then Santa Fe up to East Franklin, where I took a right and parked in the alley beside the venerable Gardner Hotel.

I'd checked in late last night having just discovered the Gardner on this, my first trip to El Paso. With a wink, the nice lady at the desk asked if I wanted room 221.

I didn't see why not, and she'd handed me the key.

It had been a cold, wet evening in 1934 when the front desk

clerk at the Gardner had checked in a large party who had re-
served a number of rooms under the name of John D. Ball and
Company. They drank a little bit, danced a little bit, but all
things considered, had behaved themselves pretty well that
night. They had checked out without incident, and it was only
when their luggage was saved in an Arizona hotel fire a week
later that they were arrested by the Tucson Police Department
and identified as John Dillinger and gang.

Unlocking room 221, I went in and was greeted by a tall
Hispanic individual sprawled on my bed with pointy-toed boots
on his feet and a black Stetson parked on his head, the business
end of a .357, which was pointed at me, in one hand, and an old,
linen postcard, which he was studying, in the other.

"Stick 'em up."

It was not Dillinger.

I turned my back to him, picked up my duffel, and went
about gathering my things, including the badge I'd palmed from
my wallet, Henry Standing Bear's stag-handled Bowie knife, and
my real Colt .45, which I'd left in the dresser of my room—I
wondered how long it would take McGroder to realize I'd
handed him a paintball gun in a pancake holster and an empty
badge wallet.

"I'd ask how it went, but since you appear to be checking
out, I'll guess not so good?"

I rested the duffel on the bed and progressed into the bathroom where I gathered up my toiletries. "I need to get out of
town—out of the country, actually."

"Well, shee-it." He threw his long legs off the bed and stood,
shoving his big revolver into its holster and his sun-bronzed
hands into the pockets of his faded Wranglers. "That bad, huh?"

I took the postcard that he had left on the blankets, stuffed it in my shirt pocket, and dropped my dopp kit into the bag. "Bad enough. They find me, and they're going to hold me; already did for an hour and a half."

"How'd you get away?"

I pulled the book from under my arm and tossed it to him. "They aren't going to let me across the border, either."

He studied the cover. "What, you threatened to teach 'em how to read?"

Slipping the strap over my shoulder, I gestured toward the door. "I've got to get going."

He glanced up. "I can see that." He tossed the book back and then walked past me and turned the corner toward the stairs. "C'mon, we'll take my truck 'cause I'm sure they're going to be looking for that rental of yours."

Stuffing the Ambrose Bierce into my duffel, I followed and started down the steps after him, but he stopped suddenly, and I almost sent him the rest of the way airborne. He turned his head and motioned for me to go back, which I did, as he retraced his steps in slow motion like a Peckinpah movie.

In the safer confines of the hallway, he turned. "Two ol' boys in suits, and I don't think they're sellin' Amway."

"Only two? I'm insulted."

He pushed me down the hallway and grinned. "Well, you ain't exactly Dillinger." He gestured toward the window at the end of the hall. "Take the fire escape but go up not down, and I'll keep 'em busy for a while."

"Then what?"

"There's three bars behind this place, the Tool Box, Briar and Hyde, and the Epic, all with sloping roofs that lead to East Missouri Avenue—turn right, and there's Chiquita's Bar. Go in there and tell Juan Carlos that Buck sent ya, and he'll put you in my special booth, so you can face the door and have your back to the wall. You just wait there till I catch up. I'll be along directly."

"Why that bar?"

"'Cause they don't piss in yer beer if yer a cop."

As I pulled up the window, I whispered back at him. "Guzmán, how is it I get the feeling you've done this before?"

"Oh, and don't go the other way because that's the El Paso County Probation Department offices." He gave me a thumbs-up, the end of the appendage missing, the result, I was betting, of a roping accident, and booted open the door to Dillinger's room, while unbuttoning his shirt and singing in a very loud and somewhat off-key voice. *"I had a friend named Ramblin' Bob, he used to steal, gamble, and rob. He thought he was the smartest guy around. Well I found out last Monday, that Bob got locked up on Sunday—they've got him in the jailhouse way downtown. He's in the jailhouse now . . ."*

Stooping, I crawled out the hall window, lowered it shut behind me, and swung onto the metal steps. Quietly ascending them, I popped out on top of the Gardner just as somebody threw open the window below me.

I picked up my duffel, thumbed the strap onto my shoulder, and made my way around the air-conditioning units, which looked down at the one-story inset at the back of the hotel. I was about two doors down from what had been my room, and I could hear a lot of thumping, singing, and crashing as Buck Guzmán *kept 'em busy.*

It was a quick straddle over the side and onto the adjacent building where it was so hot that the patched portions of the roof stuck to the soles of my boots.

The next roof was a little bit steeper, so I tossed the duffel down first and then rolled over the side to land on my feet. I got across to the next one, walked to the edge, and squinted at a colorful mural just in front of a twenty-foot drop.

I looked around. There was an escape ladder toward the alley, so I tripped the latch and it ratcheted to the parking lot below. Climbing down, I threaded through the cars and headed for the opening in the fence at the north end, expecting a black SUV or a Lincoln Town Car to slide in front of me at any moment.

Safely making it to the sidewalk, I turned right as instructed, skimmed behind a tree, and pulled open the door of Chiquita's Bar to step into the cool darkness.

My eyes adjusted from the glare outside, and I could see the place was mostly empty except for a large group of noisy young people in a corner booth and an elderly bartender who was polishing glasses.

I stepped toward the bar and asked, "Are you Juan Carlos?"

He gave me a quizzical look. "Yes."

"Buck sent me."

A moment passed. "Sent you for what?"

"Well . . . He said to put me in his special booth and that he'd be along." Juan Carlos looked toward the corner where the young men, recovering from my entrance, were talking loudly again and laughing. "I'm sure any place will do."

He gestured toward the booth on the other side of the narrow building. "You want something to drink?"

I nodded. "Um, water?"

He stared at me.

"A beer, please."

Nodding a hello toward the gang, I made my way to the other corner booth in the back, threw my duffel on the seat, and slid in after it. I tried to ignore the group who were looking at me and then whispering and laughing as the bartender approached with a paper napkin and a Lone Star.

"Dollar seventy-five."

"I might be here for a while—do you want to run a tab?"

"Dollar seventy-five."

Realizing that things get expensive when you're on the lam, I pulled my wallet and plucked out a few bills. "Keep the change."

I sat there and thought about my situation and how I'd possibly made it worse. Buck had been the one who had set up my meeting with the Seer, but I wasn't sure if he'd been aware of how quickly things could accelerate when dealing with federal government agencies. I glanced up at the clock behind the bar and could see it was already three in the afternoon, so I had a little less than six hours to get to Mexico and get started saving Cady.

I tried to breathe regularly, but there was a pain in my chest that wouldn't let up, a pain that had nothing to do with my physical condition. A million versions of my daughter haunted me, memories that sometimes appeared in sepia tone and others that were so clear that I felt as if I could almost reach out and touch her. They were not epic moments in our lives together, but rather small looks, brief exploits, or quiet words, like the time she'd confronted me when I was driving her to school at the wizened age of six. "I like it better when Mommy drives me to school."

I pulled up to Clear Creek Elementary. "And why is that?"

She climbed out of my unit, pulling her backpack onto her shoulder. "It doesn't look like I just got out of jail."

I looked up through my memories—the kid on the end with all the tattoos was staring at me. "Hey, Poppy, how you doin'?"

It was dark, but I could see the number 155 under his do-rag and the words KNIGHT TEMPLAR at his throat. "I'm good. You?"

He glanced at his friends and shook his head. "I'm confused . . . Um, did you think this was a cowboy bar?"

I adjusted my hat. "I'm just waiting on a friend."

He spoke again as the others snickered. "I mean, I don't see John Travolta or no plastic bull in here."

I turned the beer on the napkin. "I'm having a kind of rough day. . . ."

"Me too, I was sittin' here having a few drinks with my friends and suddenly this cowboy comes in like he owns the place."

I thought I saw a few flashes of metal under their table, and my hand drifted to the bag at my side.

"I think maybe you should go sit at the bar like a good little cowboy."

I was losing my patience but figured a gunfight was likely to end with me once again in the hands of the El Paso Police Department and subsequently the FBI. "Look, guys . . ."

"Guys?" He glanced at the others. "We look like guys to you?"

I was silent.

"Oh, I get it. You're looking for guys. Well, you got the wrong bar for that, my friend. You're looking for the Tool Box around the corner—that's more your kind of place."

I sighed and slowly began unzipping the bag and feeling for my Colt. "I just want to drink my beer."

He slid from the green Naugahyde, and I watched as his hand snaked to the waistband of his elaborately stitched jeans. "No, I think maybe you should go suck on a longneck somewhere else. Get it, Poppy?"

It was at that point that a great deal of sound and fury came from the front of the establishment, and Buck Guzmán slung open the door. He strolled by the bartender, snagging the beer he held out for him before continuing toward us, still singing. *"He's in the jailhouse now, he's in the jailhouse now. Well I told him once or twice, to stop playin' cards and a-shootin' them dice. He's in the jailhouse now!"*

Stopping between the booths, he looked at the young men,

especially the tattooed one standing in front of him and then at me as he pointed with the bottle. "I thought I told you that booth."

"It was occupied."

Pivoting, Buck drew a thumb across his beltline, pulling back his canvas jacket and exposing his basket-weave gun belt along with the massive, stainless S&W Model 19-5. He cocked his head at them. "What the hell are you wetback *pendejos* doing in my booth?"

As quick as a flock of roadrunners, the corner emptied, and they climbed over each other as they hurried for the door without looking back. Guzmán turned and grinned, his teeth shining, touched with the gold inlays that were a specialty of the dentists from down Mexico way, the gold US Customs and Border Protection badge in plain view.

He chugged his beer, his Adam's apple bobbing as the bottle quickly emptied. Gesturing toward the bartender, he shouted, "Juan Carlos, *dos cervezas, por favor!*" Wiping his mouth with the back of his hand, he sat across from me, cocked his head to one side and belched. "United States Border Patrol, puttin' the panic in Hispanic since 1924."

2

"Took my clothes off—there's hardly anything that'll put pause in a lawman quicker than some naked guy wavin' his taquito in their face." He shrugged. "Thirty-three years on the job, I've had enough of 'em waved at me."

I watched as Buck drifted through a turn in the road, billowing dry red dirt like an angry cloud behind us as we headed southeast. "I thought you and Dillinger were more burrito size."

"Well, we are, but I can't let those federal boys get too good of a look at it 'cause they might want to haul it back to DC and try and fold it in two and put it in a quart-sized pickle jar at the Smithsonian or somethin'." Guzmán sipped one of the beers from the Yeti cooler that sat on the floorboards of the sparklingly new GMC three-quarter ton. "You sure you don't want a beer? You gotta keep hydrated down here."

Glancing to the right, I kept looking for some landmark that might show me where my country ended and another began. "No thanks."

"Dry territory where you're headed—so hot and dry there a grass widow wouldn't take root." He took another swallow. "Told those federal boys I was borrowing your shower but that I hadn't seen you, even though your damn truck was parked right outside."

"They're not going to let me go back over."

"Oh, hell, gettin' into Mexico is no problem, it's trying to get out that's a little tough." He gestured with his beer. "Have one."

"No thanks."

He eyed me. "You're kind of a serious feller, aren't you?"

"Lately."

"McGroder says they took your daughter."

I watched the sun dropping to the west and was stunned by the colors that were so different from my part of the high plains, the purples and yellows fading to ochre like an old bruise. "Yep."

There was a long pause before he spoke again. "Somebody's got to say it."

"Don't."

He nodded and drove on in silence for a while before turning to the right and slowing the big truck.

"What?"

"Running lights, where there really shouldn't be any." He kept slowing down and edged to the side of the road as one of the trucks, pointed in the other direction, pulled up beside us. "Put your hat over your face like you're takin' a nap."

I did as he instructed and waited as he killed his engine and the whir of his window became the only sound. "What the hell are you silly bastards out here doin'?"

A younger voice answered as another man laughed. "Snipe hunting. How 'bout you, Captain?"

"Oh, havin' a beer and enjoying the cool of the evening."

"Looks like your buddy might've had one too many."

"Yeah, he's a lightweight from over in San Angelo. Hey, no shit, you guys out here whistlin' around with just your running lights on and you're gonna have a head-on with some drunk."

"Like you?" There was a pause. "They've got all of us out

here hunting for some sheriff from Wyoming; I don't know what it is he's supposed to have done, but they brought in two extra shifts to look for him—sounds like one bad hombre."

"Oh, I don't know . . . Sometimes those *federales* can't see the monkeys for the palm trees." Guzmán hit the ignition on his truck and left them with a final warning in a different tone of voice. "Turn your headlights on before you run over some poor unfortunate."

There was a chorus. "Yes, sir."

His final words squeezed out as the window came up. "Nobody wants that paperwork."

They laughed and pulled out as I raised my hat a bit. "Safe to come out?"

He threw the lever in gear and roared away. "Boy, they want you bad."

"McGroder's going to know I'm with you after the scene at the Gardner."

"So?"

"Don't you think those guys will report you being out here?"

"Those men work for me, and if they don't want to be checkin' peckers at the lowest bordello in southern Juárez, they better not be tellin' anybody where I am anytime soon—especially the F. B. of I."

I glanced at the clock on his dash. "Am I going to make it?"

"Oh, yeah. My man will get you to mass on time." He grunted. "He's pretty serious about his religion, to the point of carving crosses in his cartridges."

Guzmán took an old dirt road, swerved right, and we pulled to a stop. Shutting down the motor and opening his door, he climbed out and dragged a vintage Dallas Cowboys gym bag from behind the seat. I pulled out my duffel, and we walked through a few scrub oaks and bushes scattered with trash to the end of a tall fence as the last rays of the sun disappeared below the desert floor. "Where are we?"

"You see that swale into the creek down there?"

"Yep."

"That's Mexico, and as you might've noticed, the fence ends twenty feet that way." He turned to look at me and pointed. "And it doesn't pick up again for another quarter of a mile that way."

"So, it's not contiguous?"

He laughed, bumping the gym bag against his leg. "Hardly. Some places it's I-beams twenty feet tall, some places a single strand of barbed wire, and in others it's like this—nothing."

I stared out into the darkness, looking at the faint, greenish glow to our right that looked like some special effect from a bad fifties science-fiction movie.

"Juárez—the streetlights look green because of a lower voltage."

I nodded.

He shook his head. "Stupidest idea I've heard in my life."

"What's that?"

"A wall. Hell, almost fifty percent of the illegals in this country arrive by plane; they get a work visa or a tourist one and then they just stay." He walked to the edge of the small bluff. "They been shooting the drugs over the wall with T-shirt cannons, using remote-control planes, digging tunnels. . . ." He took a few more steps, still looking at the lights. "The cartels and assassins I'd just as soon shoot on sight, but I can understand the immigrants. Most of these poor people are just looking for a little hope, a chance at a better life picking lettuce twelve hours a day at less than minimum wage—now how can you hold that against 'em?"

I said nothing.

"Found a nine-year-old girl about three-quarters of a mile from here." He gestured behind us. "Leg swole up like a salt-cured ham where she'd got hit by a big diamondback and then to add insult to injury, the damn thing curled up next to her to stay warm and sleep through the night."

"She live?"

He huffed a laugh. "No, and neither did the buzz worm once I got done with him." He glanced toward the green lights on the horizon. "Hell, my family came from Mexico."

"When?"

"February 3, 1848, when we brought Texas with us—five generations in this country and Spain before that." He laughed. "Now, don't be too put off by my man."

I glanced around. "He's here?"

"Oh, yeah, watching us right now. I can guarantee it." He turned toward me and dropped his voice. "He's part Apache and part Tarahumara, a tribe known to be some of the best long-distance runners in the world, at least when they're not obliterated on corn beer."

"I'm not going to have to run, am I?"

"I wouldn't rule it out, but I'm betting if there's a fast way to get from A to Z anywhere in Mexico, he knows it." Buck took a few steps forward and peered into the semidarkness. "Besides, he's got other talents."

"Like what?"

"Let's hope you don't have to find out." He pointed into Old Mexico. "He's there."

It was as if he simply appeared. I'd been looking across the creek only seconds before and he hadn't been there, but an instant later, he was. Standing quietly amid the rushes and a few cattails, a thin young man stood with a vintage rifle cupped in both hands, a weapon almost as long as he was with a braided piece of rope as a sling.

His hair was very thick and long, pretty much covering his face; he was dressed simply—huaraches, canvas pants, and an orange T-shirt with a cotton poncho to guard against the thin chill in the air.

"C'mon, I'll walk you over."

He started off, and I followed. "Are you sure there's nobody else around?"

"Nope, but he is."

We walked across the slope and then picked a few flat rocks to ford the three-inch deep creek, and in a few minutes we were standing in front of the skinny young man. "Walt, meet Isidro."

"Does he have a last name?"

"Not that I know of."

I extended a hand to the wiry young man. "Walt Longmire."

His strong hands stayed wrapped around the M1C Garand that looked like it had seen lots of better days. Etched in the wood of the stock with what had probably been a horseshoe nail was a single word—EPITAFIO.

"He doesn't talk much, but he can do bird calls like you never heard." Buck glanced back at me. "What's the state bird of Wyoming?"

"What?"

"The state bird of Wyoming, what is it?"

I took a moment to readjust my head. "Um, western meadowlark."

With Guzmán holding a hand out in presentation, the young man raised his head and in one of the most exact replications of a western meadowlark call, he trilled the end and looked at me.

"Well, I'll be damned."

"Maybe." Buck smiled and then stepped to the side and

spoke in hushed tones to the kid, finally pointing toward me. As far as I could tell, the Indian nodded his head once.

Guzmán slid the gym bag into the crook of Isidro's elbow, reached over and squeezed my shoulder. "I wish I felt better about where you're headed and who you're goin' up against, but at least you've got a good team to die with."

"Thanks."

He stiffened. "I'm not kidding. They're gonna kill you, and the guy that does it will probably still have the smile on his face from saying *buenas noches*." His eyes searched for mine. "I know you said not to mention this, but . . ."

"Then don't."

He shook his head and stripped the bag from his arm. "It's a suicide mission, that's what you're on."

I nodded and tried to smile. "Wish me luck."

"I'll do better than that." He held out the bag with the Dallas Cowboys football helmet printed on the side. "Trade me."

Curious, I handed him my duffel and took the bag and unzipped it, and it was filled with handguns in differing states of condition. "What the hell is this?"

"Collateral. The Seer said the two of you are gonna use the old gun trader ruse, and in that case you're gonna need guns to trade." He slipped the strap of my duffel up onto his shoulder, but in an act of kindness drew out the Bierce biography and handed it to me. "You're not going to need a change of underwear or a toothbrush where you're going, but a book is always handy."

I took it and then tilted the vinyl bag and started counting. "There must be ten guns in here."

"A singular haul for a weekday in El Paso but don't get caught with 'em in Juárez or it's ten years in a Mexican prison." He reached over and tapped a bulging, zippered compartment at the end. "There's a little ammo for some of 'em along with something else in there in case things get really hairy." I began reaching for the zipper tab, but he brushed my hand away. "Later, if you need 'em." He looked around and palmed me a tarnished but hefty set of brass knuckles.

"You've got to be kidding."

"Just in case somebody takes all those guns away from you, or you need a little stealth. I figure you're big enough that if you hit somebody with those, it'll kill 'em."

"I'm not looking to kill anybody."

"Whoa, hold up there, hoss." He dipped his head, looking under the brim of my hat. "You better be ready to kill anybody that comes at you. There ain't no court of law over there where you're going, not even the bullshit law they got in Mexico City. It's the real-deal Wild West where you're headin', and the only law they've got is survival of the meanest son of a bitch standing. You got me?"

I nodded.

"That Las Bandejas country is the home of some of the worst drug cartels in Mexico, and that fella Bidarte waltzed in there a little over a year ago and carved himself a piece of the kingdom. He's badder than they are, and I didn't even know there was such a thing." He smoothed his mustache with a wide hand. "I can't think of anything worse than having somebody I care about in the hands of a creature like that. I'm gonna give you a piece of advice to go along with those guns and knucks. Don't trust anybody, not the police, not the military, nobody. They are rabid animals, and you've got to be ready to put them down in an instant if you're gonna get back what's yours."

I slid the strap onto my shoulder and thrust my hand out to him this time. "I don't know how to thank you."

"Come back in one piece, and then you can buy the beer."

"I'll come up with something better than that." When I turned, the wiry kid had already started off at a brisk walk along a path heading to Juárez. Hurrying to catch up, I glanced back and could see Guzmán waving to me like a ship he would never see again.

Isidro was walking, but it was the fastest walking I'd ever attempted, and after a while I was lightly jogging just to keep him in sight. There were thorn bushes on all sides of the path, a little higher than my head, but after a while the bushes left off and we were on a dirt road that I could see led into the sprawling outskirts of Juárez.

I was glad the sun had gone down, but I was willing to bet that it was still a good eighty degrees. I was starting to get winded when I saw Isidro wrapping his rifle in the woven cotton poncho he'd been wearing. He was standing on the broken curb of the first sidewalk we'd seen, his expression impossible to read.

"How much further is it?"

He remained silent and looked up the street to where a spectacularly painted bus sat idling with about thirty advertisements for dentists plastered on the sides. He gestured toward it.

The door was closed, but when he knocked on it, it opened, and we were treated to the driver, who looked like he must have been sleeping, extending his hand for the fares. Not sure how much we needed, I gave him two pesos, which seemed to satisfy him, and Isidro and I took a seat about halfway back.

Every couple of blocks the ancient diesel would grind to a stop; people got off and people got on. Two women sat in the front; the older one who was on the left turned and looked at me, so I tipped my hat. She immediately turned back and never looked at me again. A few more passengers got on, the women got off, and before long we were in the more populated areas near the center of the city.

After a few more stops, Isidro got up, and we moved to the side entrance.

As we stood there, I became aware of a charm hanging from his neck, a kind of devil with horns and a pointed beard, but handsome and if possible, kindly looking. I reached across and pointed toward the charm, using one of my three words of Spanish. *"Diablo?"*

He studied me and then shook his head and covered the charm with his hand. Speaking in a mutilated voice I could barely understand, he said, *"Riablo."*

He offered nothing more, and I followed him out onto the sidewalk into an alley in front of us. He didn't hesitate and started off into the darkness; I had little choice but to follow.

From the way Isidro traveled the alleyways and avoided the lit main streets, I had the feeling he wasn't unfamiliar with the back doors of Juárez. There were a couple of times he pasted himself against a wall and I followed suit, figuring there must've been someone whom we weren't supposed to meet.

On one occasion a couple of Policía Federales in their open half-tons with heavy guns mounted in the beds slowed and glanced up the alley we had occupied, but they either didn't see us or if they did, didn't care and continued their slow roll through town, looking for all the world like an occupation force.

Under the shadow of the spires, we crossed a plaza and got to a gate underneath a tree alongside a hand-laid brick wall where Isidro punched a code into a modern-looking keypad. We heard a faint click, stepped into a garden full of flowers, and began moving quickly across another open area where a number of decorative archways looped underneath the cathedral and the Misíon de Nuestra Señora de Guadalupe. A man in a light-colored shirt with a collection of pens in his front pocket seemed to be waiting for us.

As we got closer, I could see that he was actually dressed in vestments and that the man was a priest. He held the door open for us, and we hurried inside and down some steps into an area with books lining the walls and heavy tables arranged in an impressive symmetry.

The priest spoke in quiet tones with Isidro and then turned to me and spoke in English. "We are so pleased to be able to assist you."

"Thank you."

"I am Father Rubio—any friend of Señor Guzmán is a friend of ours." He gestured toward one of the tables, indicating that I should sit. "Please—Isidro will communicate with your friends, and then you will join them."

I sat at the nearest table, careful to place the NFL bag on the floor, out of sight. "Again, thank you."

"Would you like a glass of water or something?"

"I'd love anything to drink." He disappeared for a moment and then came back, placing a doily and a glass in front of me. I took a sip as he sat in the chair on the other side and whispered, "I've noticed that Isidro doesn't talk much at all and when he does he seems impaired?"

He leaned forward, his soft, dark eyes studying me. "They cut out his tongue. The drug dealers, they cut the tongues of the children years ago at the place where he is from, the place where you are going, Estante del Diablo. Isidro survived."

"*Estante?*"

"Shelf. Shelf of the Devil—it is a small mountain village near an area called Las Bandejas south of here near the Médanos de Samalayuca Nature Preserve."

"Sounds beautiful."

"It was—kind of like Eden before sin arrived." He glanced behind him. "The Tarahumara, some of them relocated from the west to escape the cartels, but the evil followed them. The farmers in the area were forced to give up their legitimate crops and began growing drugs. Isidro's father refused, and they killed him and his wife—she was an amazing woman, her mother was involved in the Spanish Civil War, a Republican Loyalist fighting against Franco and the Fascists. You have seen the rifle Isidro carries?"

"Epitafio?"

"It was his grandmother's." He sighed and studied me some more. "Do you know how he and Guzmán first met?"

"No."

"The Policía Federal were first making up their tactical squads, you know, SWAT, Terrorist Response, and others, and Guzmán was down here at a firing range to teach with a number of other specialists from different countries when this young man comes riding over the dunes on a mule, a battered Garand rifle hanging from the saddle horn by a piece of rope." He stood and walked to the kitchen behind him to refill my empty glass and placed it on the doily again. "The men, they began laughing, but Guzmán took the boy aside and set him up on a platform and told him to shoot the thirty-yard target, which Isidro does, three bullets. Guzmán looks through the binoculars he has and shakes his head, telling the boy that he only hit it once. Isidro disagrees so Guzmán has him shoot the fifty-yard target, same three times, same result."

"Only one hole?"

"Only one hole. So the other men come over, and Guzmán instructs Isidro to shoot the hundred-yard target, which he does—same results." He smiled. "By this time, Guzmán has figured it out and has the young man shoot the old Garand at the hundred-yard target but this time asks him to grade his shots, one in each surrounding circle, which he does." He laughed. "Now, no one is smiling, and Guzmán says the boy is the finest natural talent he has ever seen."

"Beware the man with only one weapon, for he surely knows how to use it."

The priest patted the table. "Amen."

"How come he's not working for the police?"

"He was trained and joined the force but was asked to make a shot that he would not take."

"He wears an interesting charm around his neck."

"Riablo. In the beliefs of the Tarahumaras, the Riablo aligns himself with the devil but is not wholly evil; he works with God in aligning the balance of things in a sacrifice."

"Seems to me Isidro has sacrificed enough."

"*Sí*, he now works freelance, and whenever Guzmán calls."

I sipped my water. "The place where I'm going . . ."

"Estante del Diablo—a village near an old sulfur mine, a rugged and beautiful place. I began my service there, but things became worse and worse, things that now must go unnamed. It was one of the central villages for the auctioning of livestock, but now they auction other things. . . ."

There was some movement from across the room, and Isidro reappeared with Alonzo, the Caddy driver I'd met earlier in the day. "Are you down here listening to old wives' tales?"

I stood. "Some."

Alonzo turned to Father Rubio and spoke in Spanish, the conversation becoming somewhat heated.

Finally turning to me, the priest explained, "He wants you

to accompany him to the cathedral proper, because it would be easier to transport his uncle back through the main entrance to the car, but I have warned him that the *policía* and others have been here on the church grounds, and I think you would be safer going out the way you came. I would say it is likely that they are looking for you already."

I turned to Alonzo. "We're going to kind of stand out, don't you think?"

"My uncle has a plan. C'mon, we don't have a lot of time."

I glanced at all of them in turn and started after Alonzo but then noticed that Isidro was still standing by the priest. "He's not coming?"

"He's Tarahumara, he'll run." Without another word, Alonzo turned and started up the steps.

The interior of the cathedral was surprisingly modern, and the warm glow of the oak pews and amber stained glass made it seem like more of a communal area than a place of worship, although a few of the faithful were scattered in the front with one or two older women seated in the rear near the main entrance, their heads covered with mantillas.

Alonzo and the priest led me down the side, Rubio stopping to speak with one of the women. The Seer was seated about two-thirds of the way back, leaning forward on the pew in front of him, his hands clasped in what seemed fervent prayer.

I slid next to him and placed the gym bag on the floor between us. I couldn't help but close my eyes in the calm and quiet of the place.

"Take off your hat, you are in the house of God." I opened my eyes to see that the legless man was finished praying and now was sitting back and staring at me with his sightless eyes.

I slipped the palm leaf off and held it in my hands. "What, you can hear it on my head?"

He glanced up at the vaulted ceiling of the nave. "Do you believe in God, Sheriff?"

"I guess . . ." I smiled, feeling pretty much ambushed here in the cathedral. "You could say I've had my doubts lately."

He grinned back, probably sensing my smile from the way I spoke. "In the face of all the miracles celebrated in this cathedral, how can you doubt?"

"Well, I would balance them with all the sorrow and pain."

"*Sí*, but the pain and sorrow are there to remind us that we are alive."

"Uh huh."

I could feel his dead eyes on the side of my face. "You do not believe in miracles?"

"Nope."

He nodded. "You should—it may be the only way you get your daughter back."

There was a noise in the vestibule, and my eyes followed the priest as he hurried toward the back where a group of *policía* appeared dressed in their black BDUs and helmets and carrying automatic weapons. The officer in the front was a tall man and the only one to remove his helmet, revealing a thick shock of silver hair.

Father Rubio was having an animated conversation with him as I tried to slip down in the pew, but the officer took a hard look at us before he motioned for his men to retreat, giving me one last glance as they departed.

Alonzo met the priest as he walked through the aisle, the two of them leaning down in front of us, both of them speaking at once, the priest in Spanish and Alonzo in English. "It's the PF, and they're looking for you."

"Did they see me?"

"Yes, and they are waiting outside, because Father Rubio says they cannot enter the church with their weapons."

I posited a suggestion. "How about we go back out the way we came in?"

"They will have someone at all the doors."

"Did you admit that the gringo is the sheriff?"

We all turned to look at the Seer, who appeared deep in thought.

Alonzo was the first to speak. "No, but he is the only gringo in the place."

The Seer smiled. "Father Rubio, are you in possession of your marvelous pen collection, and in it, do you have a blue marker?"

Rubio glanced around at the absurdity of the question. "*Sí, pero . . .*"

"Give it to Alonzo, please."

The priest plucked a large marker from his pocket and handed it to Alonzo.

"Now, get the bag you told me about."

Exasperated, Alonzo reached down and picked up the heavy blue and gray duffel from the floor and balanced it on the back of the pew between us. "Now what?"

"Carefully write the initials *B* and *L* in capital letters on the bag, both sides, please."

"Uncle, this is no time for games."

"Do as I tell you."

Alonzo did as he was told, carefully blocking the letters on the light panels of the bag. "Do you want me to put periods after the letters?"

"Artist's discretion; if you think it helps in the design, feel free to do so."

The young man grumbled but decided to make the addition. "If I knew what the hell I was doing, it might help."

"Don't blaspheme in the House of God." The Seer turned to look in my direction. "Are you ready to go?"

"Um, yep."

"Then if you would be so kind as to place me in my wheel-chair?"

Glancing at the others, who seemed as perplexed as I was, I lifted the man from the pew and seated him in his chair, which was at the end of the aisle. "What now?"

He glanced around as if it were obvious. "We leave, but first place the gym bag in my lap."

I reached over and took it from Alonzo, lowered it into the space between the Seer's half-legs, and figured it was about two centuries of incarceration in the bag. Turning him around, I slowly pushed him toward the door as the others fell in behind. "Whatever this plan is, I sure hope it works."

The Seer nodded and motioned toward his nephew. "Alonzo, it would be best if you were pushing and the sheriff was be-side me."

Father Rubio called after us. "I will pray for your safety."

The young man muttered under his breath, "For all the good that will do."

I took my place alongside the wheelchair as we closed in on the large double doors at the front of the church, and I won-dered what in the world the Seer had cooked up.

I pushed open the door, and there must've been twenty cops standing just outside and another dozen on the plaza below leaning on their vehicles or hanging off the heavy guns mounted in the back of the half-ton black pickups. I figured we were go-ing to be spending the night in a Mexican jail, and then I would be handed back over to the FBI—and that was the best-case scenario.

The tall man with the silver hair stood at the front, still holding his helmet, and studying me as I held the door open for the Seer and his entourage. He stepped forward and extended his hand, careful to brush the old man's fingers so that he could easily find them. "It is good to see you in church, my friend. You are changing your ways?"

"Ah, Colonel Hernández." The Seer laughed. "Just making bigger deals."

The head Fed motioned toward one of his men, who sneered as he came up the steps and took my arm. "Will you introduce us to your friend?"

The Seer looked embarrassed and then shoved the gym bag in his lap a little toward Hernández. The blind man thrummed the bag where the initials *B.L.* were evident, as if in an attempt to tip him off. Then in a low voice he murmured, "This is no time for jokes, *Jefe*."

Then the Seer threw an arm out toward me with dramatic flair, his voice mimicking that of a sports announcer. "Do not tell me that you do not recognize the great number seventy-four, All-American defensive tackle, eleven-time Pro Bowl and Super Bowl champion, Mister Cowboy, Bob Lilly?"

Every once in a while, when all the chips are down and you don't stand a chance, a moment arrives where you have the opportunity to do something so erratic, so outlandish, so stupid that only an innocent person would even think of doing—and for me that moment was now.

Yanking my arm away from the heavyset policeman, I crouched slightly, put my shoulder into his chest, and heaved him up and away just like I had as an offensive lineman with the tackling dummies back at USC all those years ago. I had caught him off balance, and he flew backward, crashing flat onto the concrete, handily saved from concussion by the padding of his bulletproof vest and helmet.

Whether it was the shock of the action, the braggadocio of the act, or possibly the suspicion that he wasn't the most well-liked man in the unit, I was immediately relieved when the colonel began slowly clapping and the entire group joined him and cheered.

3

"My hand hurts."

Alonzo put his foot in the Caddy, and we rocketed through the velvety night like a pastel panther. "From hitting the policeman?"

I readjusted the blue Sharpie in my shirt pocket, making sure the cap was on. "From signing autographs."

The Seer smiled at me. "I must admit that I had a moment of genius, Mr. Lilly."

"It was an act of desperation."

Alonzo passed the slower-moving traffic while dodging the potholes and the southern Juárez buses. We were driving through a neighborhood made up of old industrial buildings, which looked like a great place to get killed. "How did you know he'd go for it?"

"The colonel is a great fan of American football, and I knew he would not pass up an opportunity to meet a celebrity, even if he had small doubts, no?"

"Does this mean we're dropping the gun-buying ploy?"

"Perhaps. Being a football star might work better, given your size."

"Fine with me—I'd just as soon not spend the next two

hundred years in a Mexican prison." I glanced around at the large warehouses along the road and could see young women walking the dimly lit streets. "What's going on here?"

"*Maquiladoras*, assembly plants along the industrial zone, which allow duty-and tariff-free manufacturing between borders. My people work for about one-sixth of their counterparts in los Estados Unidos because they have to. When the program started in the mid-eighties it was a workforce mostly comprised of men, but then they found that young women had better manual dexterity and would work longer hours, so they are mostly girls now." He lowered his chin onto the back of his hand. "It is where *Los Perdidos*, the Lost Ones, mostly come from, the women who go missing and are killed in the city." He adjusted his hat. "The young ones come from the country, girls with little or no experience in the world but are drawn here by the promise of wages." He gestured to the surrounding area he could not see. "Tell me, does this look like a nice place to work?"

"No."

"They have no money, so they walk or take public transportation where there is little police protection."

"How many go missing?"

"Hundreds, possibly thousands."

I sighed. "Why doesn't somebody do something?"

"Most of the local police are corrupt, and the machismo of the local men does not help. These young women, in their eyes, are abandoning the responsibilities of children and home and are taking jobs from the men."

"So it's okay to kill them?"

"They are seen as expendable."

"Why are you telling me this?"

He swallowed. "I do not think that you should get your hopes up that your daughter is alive."

I braced a hand against the seat and then shook my head. "He wouldn't kill her, at least not until he has me. She's the only guarantee he has."

"Have you spoken with her since she has been missing?"

"No." I stared at the bag of guns next to my boots. "We're headed south, toward the nature preserve?"

"Yes, but first we must visit a man, a friend who is more knowledgeable about the area where we are going than any of us. Now he is a doctor, a very good one, but in his youth, he was famous for his hunting skills and was a member of the CISEN. His name is Adan Martínez." The Seer grinned. "He is a *cabrón*—a bastard, but he is my friend."

"What's CISEN?"

"Our country's version of your Central Intelligence Agency."

"What did he hunt?"

"Jaguars."

I grunted. "Sounds treacherous."

"It is really his sister you must stay away from—the *Bruja de la Piel*."

Alonzo called over his shoulder for my benefit. "The Skin Witch—she is very dangerous."

We sat in silence as Alonzo drifted to the left. The dust broiled up behind us on a dirt road that seemed to stretch on till yesterday. I tilted my head back on the roomy seat and stared at the stars that didn't seem so much different from the ones back home.

I had powerful backup, but I wasn't so sure they would be able to find me where I was going. How would they follow my trail, or even have an idea of where I actually was? There are things I could've arranged better, but I knew I needed to get Cady back as fast as I could and the only way to do that was to first find her.

I pulled my hat over my eyes after a while, figuring at this point one part of the desert was pretty much like any other. I hadn't gotten much sleep lately and didn't figure I was going to be getting any in the near future, so I closed my eyes. In the darkness, I could only see the two giant rock towers that were pictured on the vintage linen postcard that I had received in Durant, Wyoming, with the postage mark from Juárez, Mexico.

Gemelos de Roca was the name given to the geologic formation on the card, with a dirt path tracing its way between the pinnacles, a few gnarled cactus, and a lone, sad-looking burro standing on the trail, evidently placed there for scale.

I had memorized every aspect of the postcard in my pocket, the faded crosshatches and the texture of the paper in the light blue skies, the vivid greens of the cactus, and the ominous towers of volcanic rock. *Gemelos de Roca, la formación en Chihuahua,* on one side and on the other a one-word message COME, with *Hecho en Mexico* at the bottom, the stamp an outline of the country with a golden eagle eating a snake in an almost purple ink.

The word was printed in the center, just to the left of a thin vertical line that separated it from my home address.

COME.

That word had haunted me for days and nights.

We had been in a battle with Tomás Bidarte for more than a year, and in that time he had hired the Dead Center Association to try to kill me, had murdered Cady's husband, and had forever damaged Vic. Then he had kidnapped my daughter, and we had gone from a removed, hit-and-run aggression to open warfare.

It was with that comforting thought that I must've drifted off to sleep.

I woke up with a start and rolled my head to the side, feeling my hat falling onto my lap. I wiped the drool from the side of my face and looked around, making out a two-story building with arched entryways to my right and what looked to be an abandoned mission to my left. There were a few small adobe structures and an old water tower with the words PUERTO SEGURO spray-painted on the side. Though picturesque and fragrant with the scent of a wood fire lingering in the air, the structures were in differing states of disrepair, and the entire village appeared abandoned.

There were mountains rising behind and in the stark moonlight, they looked like cardboard cutouts in some old serial-western studio back lot. There was a large, humped massif to the left shaped a little like Cloud Peak back home in the Bighorn Mountains, and there was a rough-looking road that split the tiny village and traveled up through the foothills before disappearing over a hill. There was a pass, a forbidding gateway that led higher into the black, charred lava rock that looked like scorched earth and that looked nothing like Absaroka County.

At the center of the village, there was a pole sticking up from the road. It was about six feet high and impaled on it was the head of a wild boar.

I pushed the seat on the passenger side of the Caddy forward and opened the door. Standing a little unsteadily, I took a deep breath and scrubbed the circulation back into my face, certain that if I hadn't slept long, I'd slept deep.

I gently closed the door on the Cadillac, and leaning on the ridiculous car, studied the nearest building. Made of adobe brick, the tan-colored structure looked as if it might've been a mansion or an old hotel. Either way it had seen better days, but there were multicolored lights on the second floor and I heard laughter and the soft murmur of Spanish voices.

A black cat with a white chest and four white paws came over and rubbed against my leg, and I reached down to give him a scratch when I noticed a gaping wound on the side of his head beside the jaw. I petted the top of his head, stood up straight, and nudged him away with my boot.

A set of stairs across the brick patio to my left led to an opening in the plaza. Mounting the steps, I passed a window and saw, through the parted curtains, a kitchen with two women, one of whom was cooking on an old, wood-burning stove.

I was about to continue the climb when I became aware of someone standing at the top. The backlit figure was female—very female. Holding a number of empty plates, she continued down toward me. "I told them to wait for all of you, but they are like *cerdos*." She stopped two steps above me, putting her at eye level, shifted the dishes into her left hand, and extended her right. "You are the sheriff?"

I shook it, and her fingers were strong. "Walt Longmire. I'm *a* sheriff."

"The one whose daughter was taken?"

I nodded.

She studied me, and from the trapezoid of light from the kitchen, I could see she was maybe fifty, remarkably beautiful with a thick coif of black hair waving to her shoulders, which were decorated with complex tattoos. She had unsettling eyes, a remarkable violet color—like a high plains sky before a lightning storm.

She paused for a moment more and then shouldered past me. "Go up, *a* sheriff. I will bring you some food."

"What's your name?"

She threw it over her shoulder. "Bianca."

I paused for a moment, trying to remember how the Seer and Alonzo had referred to her. "Nice to meet you, Bianca."

She turned at the bottom of the stairs and looked up at me. "Flour or corn?"

"Excuse me?"

"Tortillas, you like flour or corn?"

"I don't really know."

"You have never been to Taco Bell?"

I watched her go, turned, and topped the second floor. Looking to my right, I saw my party along with another man and woman seated on wooden chairs that surrounded a round table with a metal surface impaled by a large umbrella with a thatched cover, the Christmas lights strung around the periphery. There were a few remainders from dinner and a number of shot glasses and a bottle with a handwritten label.

"*Hola.*"

The Seer, without turning, motioned for me to approach. "Your Spanish is improving marvelously, no?"

I could see a large, old-fashioned flashlight, and all the handguns that had been in Guzmán's gym bag spread out on the table. "Those are mine."

The other man there, who I assumed was Adan Martínez, picked up a semiautomatic and casually aimed it at me. "What if I want this one?"

Already having it unholstered, I swung my own .45 around and pointed it at his head, centering on his right eye. "Then we'll have to see if the short-recoil operating and locking system that uses a diagonal cam at the rear of the barrel sliding against a diagonal receiver-mounted groove on that Obregón works better than the swinging link and pin of my Colt."

There was an uncomfortable silence.

The man exploded in laughter, hugging the woman beside him as the others joined in the merriment. "Not unlike the Austro-Hungarian Steyr M1912?"

I kept the 1911 pointed at him, noticing the sharpness of his features along with an abbreviated goatee and Dizzy Gillespie cookie duster under his lower lip. "Nope."

He raised the barrel of the Obregón toward the starry sky. "The conclusion that my country came to in the mid-thirties when they turned it down for military service, an opportunity they did not afford my grandfather."

I lowered my own sidearm. "It also helps if you put the magazine in it, which from my last inspection, appears to be missing—along with any .45 ACP ammunition."

He gestured toward my Colt. "You appear to have some, perhaps you will loan me?"

Stuffing the .45 back in my pancake holster, I glanced around the table. "Maybe later." Reaching over, I dragged another chair from the railing and sat as Martínez slid the bottle with the milky liquid toward me. "Mescal."

"No thanks."

"Made locally."

I glanced around from the perspective of the second story. "Doesn't particularly seem to be a bevy of going concerns around here."

He shrugged, glancing at the woman. "Ahh . . ." He looked toward the mountains. "It was a nice village once, before the locusts came."

"How is it you're allowed to remain?"

"We have an understanding, the cartels and I."

"And what's that?"

"If they come here, I will kill them."

"Have you had to kill many?"

"From time to time." He picked up the flashlight and turned it off and on twice in the direction of the water tower where someone flashed the same signal back at him. "Would it surprise you to know that you've had a .416 Rigby aimed between your shoulder blades since you arrived?"

"I would've been disappointed if there hadn't been something."

He smiled at the Seer for all the good it did, but maybe the blind man could hear smiles, too. "I like him."

The Seer sipped his own mescal along with Alonzo. "He does not rattle easily—no?"

"He will have other opportunities." Adan studied me. "Do you hunt?"

"I used to, when I was young."

"You are going to have to reinvigorate your sense of the hunt—in this part of the world you are either the hunter or the hunted." Martínez held out a hand. "Show me the postcard?"

I pulled it from my shirt and handed it to him.

He turned it in his hands like a relic, read the single word, and then handed it back to me. "I know this place."

"Is it far?"

"A lifetime away."

I glanced over my shoulder toward the mountains. "I need to get there."

"You cannot get there from here."

"I've heard that in Wyoming before."

He shook his head. "There used to be a bridge across the canyon on that road, but it caved in years ago, and the only way across now is a trail that leads to the old bridge and the river, neither of which are passable."

"Then how?"

"You will have to go south to Torero and then use the ridge

road that leads into the mountains, but Torero is a very dangerous town—the last semi-civilized place before you go into Estante del Diablo." He took the last sip of his drink. "It is south, but it is late and you must first eat and then get some sleep."

"I've been sleeping."

"Then you must eat." He smiled and hugged the unnamed woman at his side. "My sister has fixed food for you, but since the rest of us are going to bed, you may be more comfortable in the kitchen where she is waiting." He stood, indicating the party was over. "I suggest you get more rest after that—tomorrow will be a long day."

"*Rebocado*—it is a relatively simple dish."

I continued eating because it was delicious and because I'd rapidly discovered I was starving. Raising my eyes from my plate, I couldn't help but study her shoulders, where swirling floral images revealed skulls, religious symbols, angels, devils, and games of chance. "I learned a long time ago that anything that tastes this good is anything but simple."

"Slow-cooked stew of pork, chilies, and peppery purslane."

"I don't even know what purslane is."

"A weed." Bianca glanced toward the steamed-over window, and I noticed a number of smile lines creasing the corners of her mouth. "We have lots of weeds around here." Her eyes returned to mine. "Hogweed, they call it. It has a much more sour taste when you harvest it in the morning."

"Pork, huh?"

"Yes."

"I think I saw what was left of the Lord of the Flies on a stake in the middle of town." She looked at me questioningly. "The pig's head?"

She suddenly looked grim. "Adan's idea of a joke."

I pushed the bowl away on the rough surface of the orchard table and munched on a warm flour tortilla. "What's the joke?"

"His way of celebrating Día de los Muertos." She swept a lock of hair from her face and looked at me, her eyes darkening to purple. "A popular holiday with the narcos in the area— they've killed so many people, why not celebrate?" She nodded toward the empty bowl. "We would have had something more respectable for you to eat, but everyone is busy preparing sweets for the festivals and the altars of the honored dead."

"When is the festival?"

"Two days from now; tomorrow is Día de los Angelitos or the Day of the Little Angels or innocents, which pays honor to the deceased infants, followed by the Day of the Dead."

"Honoring adults?"

"Yes." She placed an elbow on the table and propped up her chin. "Are you religious?"

"Not particularly."

"You have a wife?"

"No, she passed." I smiled back at her, just to let her know I didn't mind. "You ask a lot of questions."

"I do. I can't help myself. I suppose it's because I'm the curious type." She waved a hand to scatter all the personal talk. "The festival was originally at the beginning of summer and was the time of Aztec celebrations, but when the country was colonized by the Spanish, it was moved. It was not very popular here in the north, but then the government made it a national holiday in an attempt to create a more centralized identity for the country."

I leaned back in the rickety wooden chair and felt the legs skip on the stone floor. "What happens during this festival?"

"The usual activities—religious ceremonies, a costume

parade, sacrifices of food and drink to the dead, dancing, drinking . . . lots of drinking in this region."

"Costumes?"

"The *Calaveras*, where men and women dress up in traditional wardrobe and paint their faces like those of skulls." She poured me another glass of water from a bottle with a fixed stopper. "So, you are the curious type, too?"

"Just attempting to pick up some culture as I go along."

She poured some water for herself into one of the thick glasses as a silence insinuated itself between us.

I stared at the worn, painted surface of the table, which I could see had been painted at least eight other vibrant colors in its history. "Will they be celebrating Día de los Muertos in Estante del Diablo?"

She studied the side of my face and then gathered the dishes, carrying them to the deep stone sink. She stayed there with her back to me. "You should go to bed."

I took a breath and then stood. "I'm sorry if I've upset you."

She dropped the dishes into the sink with a clattering crash and then turned to look at me. "You are going to die, and anyone you take with you will also be killed in that place."

In the face of such heat, I stood there for a moment. "I'm not taking anyone with me."

"The Seer, Alonzo, my simple-minded brother, and who else?"

I stood there for a moment and then slid my chair in. "I just need them to get me to the place where my daughter is being held."

She shook her head. "People are chattel there, they buy them, they sell them, and no one ever makes it back down. It is the largest cemetery in the sovereign state of Chihuahua." She took a breath. "There is a monastery, Monasterio del Corazón Ardiente, that no priest has gone to in more than forty years."

Taking my hat from the back of my chair, I placed it on my head. "Thank you for dinner."

She stared at me for a few more seconds and then turned back to the sink to gather up the broken remains of my meal. "My brother came here after having so many lives, a quiet place to retire. He could have been a great leader for our people, but he can be easily swayed."

"He didn't introduce me to the woman upstairs."

Bianca turned her head, offering me an exquisite profile. "Why bother, she won't be here tomorrow." Turning and folding her arms, she studied me. "I should hold my tongue." She sighed. "He was a doctor, a very good one, handsome and accomplished—the girls flocked to him, and I think he got used to it. He didn't have to try, so none of them held much value for him. Then he met a woman, a real woman, who bore his child, and he began working for the government. She got sick. He did everything he could, but she died. Ever since then I think he's been looking for a way to die." She shook her head. "Women, the narcos, and now you."

I ignored the remark concerning me. "So the cartels know him?"

"He knew them in a professional sense when he worked with the Intelligence Operation Center, but he is also the best doctor in the entire state, and in their business they sometimes have needed his skills. Lately they take care of their own with the twenty-cent cure." She pointed her finger at me like a pistol, pulling the trigger finger before dropping the imaginary weapon. "Now they simply fear him. If he no longer has the power of life, he and his Rural Defensas have the power of death. We have lost many, yes, but they too have paid a terrible price. That is what I have learned over the years—there is no safety, there is only retribution." She turned back to the sink. "And there is no end to that."

With deference for her words, I stood there a moment more and then walked toward the door, turning the knob and exiting into the long hallway that separated the rooms in the old hotel.

I looked out the archways as I walked toward my room and could see someone smoking, standing in the street. It was Adan, and I decided to have a word with him. "Tell the sniper not to shoot, it's only me."

"He knows that." I joined him, and he pulled another cigar from his vest pocket and offered it to me.

"I don't smoke." I took a few more steps forward, looking at the pig's head. "I'm afraid I've upset your sister."

"Bianca is easily upset."

"She seems to think I'm here to lure you into helping me."

He shrugged.

"I just want my daughter back."

He gestured toward the forbidding mountains. "And what do you suppose he wants?"

"Me."

"And are you willing to make that sacrifice?"

"Yes."

"You sound certain."

"I am."

He nodded and walked past me toward the macabre decoration at the center of the street. "They don't start out that way."

I glanced at the boar. "Dead?"

"Man-eaters." He stuffed a hand in the pocket of his trousers and exhaled a thick cloud into the street. "I began my medical career going after a jaguar that was killing the people of my village south of here."

"Your medical career started with hunting jaguars?"

"A man-eater is an animal that is compelled through stress of circumstance beyond its control to adopt a diet alien to it."

"We're talking about jaguars?"

"Among other things." He took another puff. "The jaguar in question was a female and relatively young, but she was unfortunate enough to have encountered a porcupine that cost her an eye and fifty or so subcutaneous wounds in her muzzle and forearm. To the best of my surmise, she was lying in the high grass attempting to remove the quills with her teeth when a village woman decided to choose that particular patch of grass to gather fodder for her cows. The woman reached the area right beside the jaguar and the great cat reached out and struck her, breaking her neck in one swipe."

"How could you tell?"

"Other than the blow to the head she was unmarked, still holding a sickle in one hand and a thicket of grass in the other." He walked toward the center of the abandoned village and motioned for me to follow as he strolled and smoked. "This jaguar limped away almost two miles before finding a hollow on the underside of a fallen tree. Two days later, a man was cutting firewood from this log when she attacked again and killed him. She struck him in the back, and this time since she was starving, she decided to at least taste him. Now, human beings are not the jaguar's normal diet, but she was able to sate her hunger. The next day she killed again, this time deliberately and without provocation, and went on to kill twenty more people—before I accounted for her."

"You said your medical career started with killing this jaguar?"

"I cut her open to see if I could find the source of the evil, but there was nothing there." He puffed on the cigar to keep it lit. "As I said, I was young, but I became an expert in killing killers, a difficult task in that the hunted are most usually hunters themselves and develop acute skills, which can make them formidable."

"And men?"

He turned and looked at me. "Are the worst, for they sometimes kill for no other reason than they can. I have never seen one like the one you are hunting. When the marijuana crops crashed, he made them make the white rocks from chemicals."

"Crack."

"It makes them crazier, if that's possible. Your enemy, he was bad when he arrived here but the competition to be the worst has overtaken him, and he has become a monster among monsters." Adan glanced around. "Sooner or later he will come for my home, simply because he wishes to take it, and that I cannot allow."

"What will you do?"

"Kill him, just as I have killed so many killers before." He held the cigar out, blowing away the ash, and then puffed life into the ember at the end of the cigar. "I have developed my own police force in the area, a group called the Rural Defensas, which enables me to hold these men in check."

"Your sister mentioned them."

"A militia, part-time, I arm and train them myself." He gestured toward the lonely road. "Our first action was to dynamite the remains of the old bridge between us and the mountains. They have nothing there we want, and we have nothing here we wish to give them."

"A Mexican standoff?"

He smiled. "If you will."

"Well, that would be your fight and not mine. I can't allow you to—"

"Allow me?"

I thought about many of the things his sister had said. "I don't mean any offense, but I wouldn't want you to confuse the issues and attempt to do my work for me."

He nodded and smoked some more as we stood there with the boar's head between us like he was a member of the party. "If this man Bidarte's death satisfies both of our issues, who is to say that we shouldn't work together?"

"I don't want to be responsible for anyone else."

He smiled, reaching out and touching the grisly prize. "This is not some movie, my friend. Bidarte has an army—a well-trained, well-armed battalion of killers who will do everything they can to stop you. If you face them alone, you will surely die or worse, and even though you are prepared for that, I doubt it will do your daughter any good."

"Nonetheless . . ."

His hand stayed on the head between us. "This boar, I captured and raised him from his infancy. He was fifteen years old and weighed almost seven hundred pounds. He used to follow me everywhere I went. He was like family, but last week I knew it was time for him to go and I had to kill him. It was like that with the jaguar too, and will be like that with Bidarte. I have the feeling that with your arrival, his time has come, and he must now go." He took one last puff on the cigar and then flicked it away a surprising distance, and I watched as it landed in the road where a small, red dot played over the thing before disappearing.

Martínez turned and looked at me and smiled. "One of my men—we play this game every night."

4

"I want to be a lawyer."

I paused with my fork halfway to my mouth. "Why?"

My teenage daughter glanced at my wife, seated at the dining room table of the tiny rented house where we lived on my meager deputy's salary. "I want to make a difference."

Martha studied me as I put the food in my mouth and chewed. They were ganging up on me, like they always did. "I thought you wanted to teach?"

"I've changed my mind."

"Why?"

"You." She smiled at my confusion. "You help people every day and that's what I want to do. I could teach, but I'm not much of a nurturer."

I rested my fork on the blue willow dinnerware that had belonged to Martha's mother. "Then what are you?"

She continued smiling. "I'm a fighter, and that's your fault."

I stared at the rough adobe interior and thought about how the Seer had said that I would probably hear things falling from the crack in the ceiling. He said there were two hundred and twenty-one species of scorpion in Mexico but only eight are poisonous enough to kill a man, but he wasn't sure which ones they were or whether they were native to the area.

Alonzo had suggested I sleep with my mouth shut.

I lay there and saw at least three of the critters fall from the ceiling, but they disappeared into the shadows at the corners of the room. I thought about getting up, but then what? Break open the mescal and maybe steal the Cadillac? I felt a smug sense of satisfaction in that I hadn't yet sunk to the point of drunken driving or grand theft auto.

I rolled over thinking about my daughter and entertaining the option of running across the desert toward the destroyed bridge in my underwear, swimming the river, climbing the cliffs, finding Tomás Bidarte, and strangling him to death with my bare hands.

Kicking off a scorpion that had fallen and hit the foot of my bed, I sat up when I heard voices outside. Creeping over to the French windows, I was careful not to make any noise, all the while attentive to what I was stepping on. I could see a group of men talking to Alonzo, all of them standing in the street near the ever-present boar head.

He gestured in my direction and when the other men turned, I could see they were armed, one of them cradling a flashy-looking Kalashnikov rifle. Standing there holding the flimsy red curtain just slightly aside, I wished I'd continued studying Spanish in college as they talked and I only caught every fifteenth word.

Alonzo pointed again, and the group began moving my way.

I let go of the curtain, quickly shook the sheet, and slipping my hand under my pillow around my 1911, crawled back into bed.

My cataract-ridden grandmother on my mother's side had slept with an 1847 Colt Walker .44 revolver under her pillow. Back in the dirty thirties, a drifter had shown up looking for work. She had him pull some weeds and had fed him and had even allowed him to sleep in the barn, but when he'd shown up later that night at the foot of her bed with a butcher knife in his hand, she'd blown a .454-inch-diameter hole through him at over a thousand feet per second. My father, one of the bravest men I've ever known, said he wouldn't go anywhere near their place after dark, even on a bet.

Punching the safety off, I closed my eyes just enough so that I could appear asleep but still see the shadow of the terrace doors that led onto the portico.

After a moment, one of the doors opened about a foot, and Alonzo looked in.

I didn't move, and he disappeared. I clutched the .45, ready to bring it out if need be, just as another individual poked his head in to look at me, then another, and finally the man with the Kalashnikov. I figured that if anybody was going to be doing the shooting it was going to be him, but the automatic rifle hung limp in his hand as he stood there and watched me sleep.

Another scorpion fell from the ceiling—it landed on its back on the mattress about four inches from my arm. Unmoving, I watched as it flipped itself over. I still didn't move and just lay there watching the man in the doorway watching me. After a moment, he gestured to his friends.

After a few moments, I assume the activity lost its compelling qualities and the door quietly shut behind them. With my fist still wrapped around the Colt, I expected them to kick the door in at any minute and open fire, but they never did and I just lay there, waiting for nothing.

The scorpion finally moved a quarter of an inch toward me. He was about two inches long, light brown, and held his wicked little tail at the ready.

Quickly moving my arm, I used the barrel of the Colt to brush my bedmate from the mattress and listened as he hit the stone floor and skittered away. I punched the safety back on the 1911, and hoping to keep my mouth closed, I must've half fallen asleep.

Eventually I gave up and yanked the sheets completely away, shook out my clothes and pulled up my jeans, shrugged on my shirt, and pulled on my socks, careful to empty out my boots as Martínez had instructed.

I jammed the .45 into the holster at my back and picked up my book. The early morning light brightened the tops of the hills in the east, and I was thankful for the leftover cool of the night that I knew wouldn't last.

Stepping into the street, I felt like there should've been an Ennio Morricone soundtrack playing. This was a strange land for me—I was used to high desert, but this was the real thing and strangely enough I liked it.

At least until the sun came up.

I walked west, toward the crumbling mission and the adobe buildings that dotted the immediate vicinity and tried to think of what kind of town this must've been. Mining, probably, back when there was a bridge leading to the mountains. Lord knows you couldn't grow much of anything around here with the exception of cactus.

I heard music coming from the ruins of the mission—it was tinny and most likely from a radio. Angling in that direction, I could see the entire back of the building had collapsed and the only thing left was a tiled section that must've been part of the church's interior.

There was a large cable spool on which was a vintage, battery-powered radio playing heart-felt music, spare with one guitar and a man's voice pleading *Madre Mía*. There were a few brightly painted folding chairs around the table and on one of them sat Bianca Martínez, smoking a cigarette and sipping coffee out of a mug she refilled from a carafe.

"*Hola.*"

She turned to glance at me. "Howdy."

Unsure of her response after last night, I stayed on my side of the broken wall. "This your morning spot?"

She nodded. "Me and Radio Cañón, XEROK radio, one of the border-blaster stations in Juárez. Back in the day they used to advertise Car Collins Crazy Water Crystals, and baby chicks by mail, and would try to get their listeners to send in five dollars for a free autographed picture of Jesus Christ with eyes that glowed in the dark."

"Sounds lively."

"I listen religiously." She stubbed out the cigarette on the corner of the table and then deposited the butt in an ashtray in the shape of a ceramic sombrero. "I like watching the sun hitting the top of the mountains. Besides, if I hang around the hotel everybody expects me to make them breakfast."

"I'd hide, too."

She gestured behind her. "The girls will be here in an hour or so, and they will be happy to make you something."

I looked toward the mountains where the rays were tickling the summits. "Not hungry."

She studied me and then nudged one of the other chairs with a sandaled foot. "Want some coffee?"

I moved toward the lower section of the wall and stepped across, pulling out the chair and sitting alongside her so that I could also take in the view; I put the book on the table. She shoved her mug toward me, lifted the ceramic carafe, and poured me a steaming cup. I took a sip of the burnt but delicious brew. "I want to apologize for last night."

"No, I want to apologize. It is a very noble thing you are doing, and I was being selfish."

"Look, just so you know, I don't have any intention of getting anyone hurt."

She took the mug back from me and shared a sip. "Besides yourself?"

"Oh, there are a few others I want hurt, but that has nothing to do with you and yours."

She handed me back the mug. "How did you sleep?"

"Not very well."

"Scorpions?"

I nodded and sipped the coffee.

"I don't know why they put you in one of the lower rooms—I must've killed a hundred of those things in there."

"There were other dangerous things that showed up, too." She turned to look at me. "Men with weapons; Alonzo was speaking with them."

She thought about it. "A lot of people pass through and most of them are armed. Were they in a vehicle?"

I continued to sip, thankful for the coffee. "I didn't see or hear one, and there were no tracks in the road this morning."

"I will ask Alonzo when he gets up." Her eyes landed on my book. "You are reading this?"

"Off and on."

She smiled, placing an elbow on the makeshift table. "I miss books—tell me about it."

I thumbed the spine. "It's a biography of a journalist and writer by the name of Ambrose Bierce. He wrote *The Devil's Dictionary* and a famous short story, 'An Occurrence at Owl Creek Bridge.'" I glanced around. "He traveled here in Mexico during the big revolution and disappeared—no one ever heard from him again."

I sipped the last of the coffee. "He was a soldier in the Union Army's Ninth Indiana Infantry in our Civil War, and he told about a battle at Brown's Ferry. The Confederate forces attempted a counterattack at a railroad depot in a small town. Things didn't go well for the Northern forces and they had to retreat, along with the Union teamsters who decided to abandon their wagon and their mule teams. Well, with all the cannon fire and explosions, the mules became terrified and stampeded through the Confederate lines. It was dark, and the Southerners, figuring they were being charged by a large number of enemy cavalry, broke and ran." Unable to help myself, I began chuckling. "I guess Bierce wrote a report to Washington that recommended the heroic mules be promoted to horses—which might have signaled the end of his military career."

She laughed along with me, and then her eyes went back to the mountains and mine followed. The peaks carried a golden light that crept down on the ridges above the canyons like the wax from a melting candle, and it was hard to believe the place was a harbinger of evil.

She reached over, taking her coffee mug from me and half-folding her arms. "You are crying."

"Sorry." I laughed some more, wiping the single tear from my face, sitting there silent, afraid to speak. "It's the normalcy of just sitting here with you and talking and drinking coffee—all this violence, chaos, and just plain madness." I took a breath and slowly let it out. "I miss normalcy."

It was a large bag full of small blue-and-white replica footballs.

"What am I supposed to do with these?"

Alonzo continued eating his breakfast on the other side of the small table in the hotel portico and smiled through rice, beans, and tortillas. "Sign them 'Bob Lilly.'"

"So the guys last night were not Bidarte's?"

"La Línea, Los Aztecas, scouts for Sinaloa, or maybe just independents, but they heard about you being here in Mexico and brought these footballs to have them signed." He continued eating and glanced at his uncle. "This dodge might be the best ever—I'm not sure why we haven't done this before."

The Seer, a little hungover, sat on the wooden pew where his nephew had placed him, a piece of furniture that looked as though it might've been purloined from the destroyed mission. "One reason might be because we never had anybody who looked like they might have played American football."

Pulling out my ubiquitous blue Sharpie, I found a smooth spot on the pebbled texture of each one and began signing. "When do we leave?"

"As soon as you finish signing footballs."

"South, to Torero?"

"Sí, but not ending in Torero, eventually a small ranch to the west, the ORFANATO, where we lose the car and take burros."

I wondered what Bob Lilly's signature really looked like. "The only way up there?"

The Seer pulled his porkpie hat down over his eyes as he slouched in the corner of the pew. "There is a ridge road that takes four-wheel-drive vehicles, but it is heavily patrolled by Bidarte's men who would kill us before we ever got to the village where they must be holding your daughter."

"Must be?"

Alonzo finished his breakfast and slid the plate toward one of the women from the kitchen, who retrieved it and disappeared without a word. "The postcard of the rock formation is on the

trail we are taking, the old road. If she is there, we will find her."
He shrugged. "You must remember, no one has seen her."

"You've asked?"

Before he could answer, a voice rang from above. "Casually,
so as to not solicit interest from unwelcomed quarters." Adan
Martínez descended the steps with a leather rucksack thrown
over one shoulder, his roach-killer boots clattering on the sun-
warped wood planks. "She is there." The doctor rested his
hands on Alonzo's shoulders. "This is my country; it is my business to know these things."

I stopped signing. "Someone has seen Cady?"

"Yes." He grinned a toothsome smile. "How was your breakfast?"

I tossed the last of the tiny footballs back into the bag. "She's
alive?"

"Yes."

I put the cap on the pen. "What condition is she in?"

"That, I do not know." His hands slipped from Alonzo's
shoulders. "I have told you everything I can."

I put the pen in my shirt pocket. "But not everything you
know."

"Fortunately, in my time with the government, I learned to
not extrapolate on the facts." He paused for a moment and then
started toward the kitchen door. "We should be loading up the
car so we can get going before the sun rises and it gets too hot."

I stood and cut him off. "You need to tell me what you know."

Casually stepping around me, he attempted to continue into
the kitchen. "No, I don't." I reached out and took his shoulder,
but he shrugged away and leveled a finger at me. "Don't ever
touch me again—I have killed men for less than that."

We stood there for a moment more, and then he continued
into the kitchen.

I thought about going after him but figured there was plenty of time on the trip south to get our house in order, so I turned and picked up the bag of footballs and handed them to Alonzo. "Anything else?"

He glanced in the kitchen doorway. "I have the feeling the two of you are going to have a dealing."

"Maybe so."

He stood, sliding the straps of the shopping bag onto his shoulder. "I want to check the oil in the godforsaken, goat-fornicating, flat-beer-tasting Caddy and see if Adan has any petrol."

"I'll get my bag." We crossed, each of us going in opposite directions, and I paused to speak with the Seer. "Are you all right?"

He pulled the hat from his face, his opaque eyes searching for mine. "Yes, but I suppose I am tired." He shrugged. "Getting old."

"This kind of work can make anyone feel old. Can I get you anything?"

"When you come back, my chair—it is in the hallway inside. Alonzo has already put my bags in the car."

"Have any scorpions in your room last night?"

He shook his head. "No, why?"

"Just curious." I patted his shoulder and went to my room. I picked up the Dallas Cowboys gym bag, stuffed my book and Henry's knife inside, and watched a small scorpion scramble under the bed.

There was some noise a little farther down to my right where a dining room connected to the kitchen from the hallway, and I could hear raised voices in Spanish. Again, I could only understand one in fifteen words and figuring it wasn't any of my business anyway, I circled the Seer's wheelchair and started back to the patio, almost running over Bianca who was hurrying down the hallway, her hand covering the side of her face, her eyes full of tears. I reached out, but she brushed by and continued on as Adan rushed out of the dining room.

She saw him and went in the other direction, and I can't help but think he was a little surprised when I extended an elbow and bounced him off the opposite wall.

He looked after her and then at me.

"You want to kill me now or later?" He started past again, but I blocked him with an arm, leaning over and completely blocking the narrow passage. "My daughter?"

He looked up at me and for a moment, I really thought we were going to do it. "I do not have time for this right now." He sighed. "The men who Alonzo spoke with last night, I know one of them, and he leaves me messages about the goings on at Monasterio del Corazón Ardiente. He says your daughter is there, but that was all he said."

"Why didn't you just say so?"

"Because he is my man, and I do not wish to compromise him, you understand?"

"With whom, the Seer, Alonzo?"

"Anyone." Glancing around, he leaned in. "You are new to this country, and you do not understand—trust is like a broken mirror, you may still see yourself, but you can never dismiss the crack." Ducking under my arm, he continued after his sister, and I stood there holding a wheelchair, well out of my depth.

After setting the Dallas Cowboys bag in the backseat, I opened the trunk of the Cadillac, placing everybody else's bags inside along with the Seer's chair, as Alonzo busied himself under the hood. I circled around and joined him. "Trouble?"

Looking at the big V-8 engine, he shrugged. "This misbegotten motherless son of a whore . . . always." He gestured toward the firewall. "The heating core is leaking, and I'm out of anti-freeze."

"Why don't we just close the system off by looping the hose?" I glanced up at the climbing sun. "I doubt we're going to need the heat today."

We set about pinching the hoses and undoing the clamps and reattaching them as Bianca came out of the kitchen. Straightening, I noticed that the red mark on the side of her face had faded a little and watched as she came over to where we stood, holding a large carpetbag out to me. "Do you have room for my bag?"

Adan joined us, looking none too happy about the situation, standing on the stoop with his own bag and making an announcement. "I have decided that my sister will come with us to provide a sense of cover by posing as your wife."

"What?"

She looked at me, the picture of defiance. "It is decided."

I glanced at all of them in turn and then settled on Bianca. "Not by me, it's not. Just last night you said I was putting your family in danger—"

"You will be safer with me along."

I stared at her. "Safer?"

"*Sí*, I will only be accompanying you till we get to Torero."

"What, like the people there aren't going to know who you are?"

She walked past Adan, opened the passenger side door, and nudging the Seer, she forced him to move over so she could climb in the back. "I've never been there."

I glanced at Adan. "All it takes is for one person to know who she is."

"We will only be going into Torero for supplies, then we will go to the ranch where they have the burros—no one will know that we are there." He threw up a hand in surrender and trudged toward the back where he deposited his own bag and turned to look at us. "Anything else to go back here?"

Adan closed the trunk and climbed in the seat beside the Seer, and Alonzo climbed in and hit the starter, then hit the starter again. The convertible shuddered and then lumbered to loping life.

"My wife? Have you people lost your minds?"

"She might be handy."

Alonzo glanced back at her in the rearview mirror. "She's a witch, maybe she can cast some spells or something."

Shaking my head, I swung around and hoisted myself over the pink flanks of the monster car and settled into the spacious backseat. Bianca had slipped on an oversized pair of sunglasses and refused to make eye contact with me.

After a moment, Adan put on his own sunglasses and gestured forward. *"Avance!"*

Alonzo swung around, and we headed south on a road with crumbling asphalt and potholes that could've swallowed a fifteen-inch, bias-ply shod wheel with no trouble. In a few minutes he turned on the radio and mariachi music.

I couldn't understand the conversation that was taking place in the front of the car and after a while found myself watching the mountains, the ridges bare and forbidding looking although the valleys looked lush.

I adjusted the gym bag and had started to lean back into the corner when I noticed Bianca studying me. She had been resting the nail of a forefinger between her teeth, but removed it to speak. "So, tell me about your family."

I readjusted in the enormous seat. "It's not very large, my family."

She scooted forward. "You said your wife had passed?"

"Yes. We had only one child, Cady, the one who was kidnapped." I sighed. "She was a lawyer in Philadelphia, but then she took a job with the attorney general's office in Wyoming."

"You are telling me about her job—tell me about her."

"She has my eyes."

She leaned farther forward, studying me with a frankness that was a little unnerving. "Gris."

"Nickel-plated is what Cady calls them."

She shook her head. "Not that cold, more like an autumn sky or like the ocean—clouded and deep."

I thought about it. "She's smart, really smart, and she can read me like a book."

She digested what I'd said. "Your wife, she has been gone long?"

"It's been a while now." The silence returned, and I altered the subject. "Her daughter has different eyes . . ."

"Your granddaughter?" She slipped off the sunglasses and smiled. "And her husband, the father of your grandchild, what is he like?"

"He's dead. He was a police officer in Philadelphia, in Pennsylvania, and I have reason to believe that Bidarte is responsible for his death." We drove on, only the engine and the wind and the music making any sound. "How about you?" Glancing at her fingers, I reaffirmed the lack of a ring. "You're single?"

She shrugged. "I was married, for a time."

"What happened?"

"He was killed. He was also a doctor, but he had political leanings and they killed him." She looked at the road or maybe the back of her brother's head as her voice rose. "He was a radical—he had these crazy ideas that people should be able to live their lives without fear."

"I'm kind of radical about that, too." I waited a moment and then asked, "Any children?"

She shook her head. "No, we were only married for a few months."

I nodded, realizing that she wanted to talk about her dead husband about as much as I wanted to talk about my dead wife. "Can I ask you a question?"

"Sure."

"When we first met, on the stairs?"

"Yes."

"You referred to me in the plural, and now that I've gotten to know you I can see that it wasn't a simple slip of tense, your English is too good. So what did you mean?"

She glanced toward the front and then studied my face. "You know what they call me."

I thought about what Alonzo and the Seer had said before we'd arrived. "A skin witch?"

"A *bruja de la piel*, yes." She raised a hand and touched her shoulder. "This, this is what I used to do."

"Tattoos?"

She nodded. "I started as an apprentice in a shop in Juárez but then had an opportunity to work with a man in Los Angeles, a legend, Sebastian Ramírez. You have heard of him?"

"No, but I don't know anything about tattoos."

"You have none?"

"No, and I'm a Marine."

She took my arm in her two hands and ran one over the inside of my forearm and I had to admit that it felt good. "First you have to shave the skin, even if the hair is fine, and then clean the surface with antiseptic. Then you apply a thin layer of deodorant to help the stencil image stick. The stencil image is taken from a drawing sandwiched into a ditto master and thermofax machine, which produces a thin paper with a gummy side you lay on the skin." She allowed her fingers to pause there on some of my scars, and her voice became breathless. "Next you peel the paper away and tear open a packet of autoclave tubing, you know, like lab or hospital tubing?"

"That I've had experience with."

She glanced at the ragged teardrop in my skin, but asked no questions, lost in touch. "Then you dip the needle into a tiny cup of ink and stretch the skin, which gives just a little before allowing the needle to penetrate. Dip, press, pierce a thousand times a minute." Her hand stroked my arm. "The skin begins to rise and tiny blood bubbles appear with angry welts like flagellation." Her fingers and eyes stayed on my arm for a moment more. "There is no art without sacrifice from the artist, no?"

"Or the subject, evidently."

She leaned back and released my arm. "It doesn't matter. Anyway, I learned the trade from him. When I began doing my own designs, strange things began happening."

"I don't understand."

"I had to quit."

"Why?"

She clutched a handful of wayward hair, pulling it back from her face. She looked at the road, steering the large, black sunglasses onto her face again and looking like some Italian movie star from the sixties.

"I began seeing things in them as I see things in you."

"Meaning?"

"The dead, they hover near."

5

We drove into town under a white homemade banner with handwritten blue lettering that read, Bienvenido Bob Lilly Campeón de los Cowboys!

"In and out, huh?"

Adan turned to look at me.

"No one will know we are here, huh?"

It was a small village, but you wouldn't have guessed from the amount of people who filled the narrow streets. *"Mira qué cabrón . . . "*

Cars and trucks were parked along both sides of the road in the late afternoon sun, and people in Cowboys jerseys and T-shirts waved blue and white flags, all the time honking their horns and yelling.

Alonzo turned and smiled but still looked worried. "You seem to have a lot of fans here."

"Boy howdy." Now people were now rushing up with pens and things to be signed. "What do we do?"

"We roll with the punches, my friend."

Alonzo slowed the car as we approached the center of town where a broken fountain sat in the middle of a tiny square. Four two-story buildings that made up the majority of the town flanked the crossroads, and there were lights strung over the street where small white tents had been set up. There was a platform beside the fountain festooned in blue and white crepe paper and my greatest fear, a podium.

When we stopped, a number of men in shabby suits, one of them wearing a Dallas Cowboys ball cap, approached the front of the Cadillac and began smiling and talking with both Adan and the Seer.

Bianca leaned over in the seat and spoke in a low voice. "Don't be too impressed—I think they were preparing for the Día de los Inocentes tomorrow and must've decided to integrate you into the festivities."

I glanced around. "This is really embarrassing."

"Wait, it will probably get worse."

Alonzo had turned in the seat and was listening to the dignitaries, smiling at what they were saying. "They have prepared a dinner. They are very apologetic, but they had little time to get ready."

People were forcing their way to both sides of the car in an attempt to hand me scraps of paper and more toy footballs. "This has gone on far enough, you have to tell these people that I'm not . . ."

He leaned back over the seat and spoke to me in a ferocious whisper. "Do you want to save your daughter?"

"Yes."

He smiled at the people around us, while speaking through the side of his mouth. "Then keep quiet and enjoy the party."

I glanced around, still unsure. "Look, somebody's going to know."

"You're a big white guy." He made a face. "You all look alike to us."

I glanced at Bianca, who was smiling at my discomfort and

shaking her head. She looked at Alonzo, and he shrugged apologetically. "They have a sports team, here in the village."

I took the treasured blue Sharpie from my pocket and began signing things for people. "So."

"A soccer team, our *fútbol*, the Torero Matadors, and they would like to have an exhibition game this evening in your honor."

"Okay, but I don't know how to play soccer."

"No, they want you to make a speech."

I glanced at the podium again. "Oh, hell."

Her smile broadened. "I will help you."

When I looked toward the front, the dignitaries appeared to be smiling at me, kind of like I would at a porterhouse steak. "What am I expected to talk about?"

She dismissed the subject with a wave of her hand. "Something about sport building character . . . I don't know, foolishness like that."

Adan pushed open the passenger-side door, stood before the group, and, taking on an air of diplomacy, urged them back, all the while talking a kilometer a minute. A few people started helping with the luggage, but I held the gym bag close if for no other reason than it was full of guns.

As I stepped from the Caddy there was an uproar, which I ignored by turning and assisting Bianca from the car; only then did I look around at the hundreds of people, still trying to disguise the fact that I felt like a complete idiot.

"They have a room for you and your wife in the bank building right over here." Adan had gotten the Seer situated in his wheelchair, and our entire group moved toward the building to our left.

"The bank?"

"Not in use anymore, but the mayor says it was robbed by

some of the finest *bandidos* in history, including your John Dillinger."

"He got around, huh?" I snorted. "What about you guys?"

"We are staying at the local hotel; believe me, you got the better of the deal."

It appeared that the mayor was the man in the ball cap, and he accompanied us, along with the other members of what I assumed were the city council, as we entered the wreckage of what had once been a bank with tall ceilings and marble floors. In a fit of hospitality, they had decorated the place as best they could and had set candles on all the steps leading to the second floor.

The dignitaries stopped at the stairs but bid us to continue as Adan took Bianca's bag and a couple of the masks that the townsfolk had given him and led the way to a mezzanine, which in better times had probably housed offices. He opened the door to the farthest room, and you could see that the poor villagers had done the best they could to fix something akin to a bridal suite.

There was a large poster bed with gauzy material draped all around and more candles, and as beautiful as it was, all I could think was that the place was a fire trap.

Adan set the bag on the bed along with the masks. "You two will stay here."

I glanced around as Bianca moved toward the window overlooking the square where music was playing and you could still hear the crowd. "There's only one bed."

"Personally, I don't care if you sleep on the floor, but for appearance purposes the two of you sleep in here." He turned to his sister. "The speech will be in an hour, after a banquet and before the soccer demonstration. We'll do all of this as a courtesy to the village, but then we will leave very early in the morning."

I set the gym bag on the bed with the other things. "What about supplies?"

"Alonzo will be covering that tonight."

I nodded. "Any chance of Bidarte's men being down here?"

"Practically none—they will be preparing for their own celebration on the mountain."

I picked up one of the masks. The skull on it was ornately designed with cutouts and colorful appliqués and even sheet music applied to it. I tried to read the notes and finally came up with the piece. I had played Mozart's Requiem in D Minor, the one he left unfinished at the time of his death.

Appropriate.

I held it up to my face, but it was a little small. "Practically none?"

"You never know." He cocked an eyebrow. "Some of the young people from this village, they go up there for the celebration."

I lowered the mask and tossed it back on the bed, folded my arms and stepped toward him. "In God's name, after what you've told me, why would anybody voluntarily go up there?"

"Food, drink, liquor, drugs, sex—what more can you want, eh?" He glanced toward the window and listened to the noise from the crowd before extending a finger toward me. "Be careful what you say and who you say it in front of in this place, every ear is guaranteed to have a running mouth."

"That was the worst speech I've ever heard, let alone translated."

It was a little unsettling to have a skull-faced woman reviewing my performance, as I gestured toward the crowd and turned in the folding chair next to her. "They liked it."

She adjusted her mask and the large red flower in her hair, which complemented the lovely flamenco dress she'd produced from her suitcase and was now wearing. "They liked it because you told them that the Torero Matadors were known across America as the greatest soccer team of all time."

"A slight exaggeration." I shrugged and signed the last scrap of paper that a little girl held out to me, feeling only slightly guilty as I placed it in her hand and then watched as she raced away.

"A sheriff is a politician, yes?"

The band had started up again at the other side of the fountain, and I tossed the blue marker onto the table and shook my hand in an attempt to get some blood back in it. "Yep, but I'm pretty lousy at that part of the job, to be honest."

"What part are you good at?"

"I'm still working on that."

Adan appeared through the crowd, glad-handing as he came with his own mask pushed up on his head. "That was the worst speech I've ever heard."

"That seems to be the consensus, so the next presentation we have to do, one of you can do it." I reached over and opened a soda from the table and stood, leaning on the broken portion of the fountain and having a sip as I glanced around at a street party that looked nothing like it was winding down. "Is this going to go on all night?"

"Probably."

"When will some of these misguided pilgrims begin their journey to the mountain?"

"Sometime tomorrow during the day."

"Why don't we just go up with them and use the crowd for cover?"

Bianca moved past us, glancing at the throng as another

individual approached with one of the tiny footballs; she shook her head and turned the man away. "Because you stand out like a polar bear."

There was some noise from the other side of the fountain, beyond the band and the people dancing—probably a fight. "So, we leave early?"

"*Sí*, at sunup." Adan fanned some fingers at the municipal building where we were staying. "We will pull into the alley behind you and leave at five-thirty."

There was more noise at the fringes of the crowd, and I was about to mention it when I heard the unmistakable sound of a quick burst from an automatic weapon. People screamed, and the crowd seemed to shift en masse, but there was no more shooting. "What the hell?"

Adan leapt up on the fountain. "There are some men approaching, and they are heavily armed."

Just as he'd finished speaking, Alonzo appeared in the crowd, waving and pushing people aside to get to us. "It's men, Bidarte's men."

Adan stepped down. "We will just continue with the illusion we have created."

"How many of them?"

"A half dozen, at least."

Peering through the crowd, I could catch glimpses of a group of men, some of them carrying bottles of what I assumed was liquor. Leaning to the side I could see the strikingly handsome man who appeared to be the leader, an individual who was out of place with blond hair poking out from under his ball cap.

David Culpepper.

This was the man I was certain had killed Ricardo, my daughter's housekeeper's nephew, and possibly the one who had actually kidnapped Alexia and Cady. I'd only met him once, but he would most certainly know me on sight.

I reached over and took Adan's mask, removed my hat, and slipped the disguise over my face. "The white guy in the front, his name is Culpepper and we've met—he'll know who I am."

Turning, I slipped my arm around Bianca and pulled her close as the group of men broke through the crowd and Culpepper pointed toward us with what looked to be an M16. He staggered a little and took a swig from a mescal bottle in his other hand; great—drunk, psychotic sociopaths with automatic weapons.

He stopped about twelve feet away and extended his arms, threw his head back, and screamed, "How 'bout them Cowboys!"

A few of the men behind him, who were also carrying AK-47s, fired a few rounds in the air as punctuation.

He grinned a crazy smile with a lot of teeth, and it was all I could do to keep from leaping over the table and taking him by the throat.

"Bob Lilly!" He turned to the group behind him. "Number seventy-four!" His face swiveled back to me. "Mister Fucking Cowboy!"

I released Bianca and stood straighter.

He staggered forward a little closer, finally clutching the edge of the table for support. "My uncle used to tell me stories about you."

I nodded but didn't say anything.

"Twenty-nine-yard sack of Bob Griese in Super Bowl Vee-Eye—a fucking NFL record!"

I adopted a gravelly voice and gently placed a hand on Bianca's shoulder. "Excuse me, but my wife . . ."

He studied me for a second, his wobbling eyes finally focusing. "Oh fuck, I mean . . ." He set the bottle on the table and stepped back and actually swept the hat from his head and placed the rifle across his chest, bowing just a bit. "I am dreadfully sorry, ma'am. You'll have to forgive me, but I've been down here in this godforsaken country in this den of killers and thieves so long that I've forgotten my manners."

Bianca inclined her masked face at him.

"I was brought up better, I can promise you." He turned back to me. "David Culpepper, sir. A proud son of Texas, Throckmorton to be exact, and I bet that rings some bells with you, now don't it?"

Actually, it didn't. "Absolutely."

"Where you played your senior year." He raised a palm. "Greyhounds!"

We struck hands, and I nodded. "Greyhounds."

He looked at me questioningly. "Something wrong with your voice?"

I gestured toward my throat, but Adan quickly stepped beside me. "Mr. Lilly gave a wonderful speech and has been talking with fans all evening, and I'm sure his voice has reached its limits."

Culpepper nudged the mescal bottle toward us. "Well hell, give him some of this—that'll cure him." He turned to Bianca. "Excuse my French, ma'am."

"Mr. Lilly doesn't drink."

"Really?" After a second he turned back to Adan. "You're a little far south, aren't you Doc?"

Adan squared off with the armed man, and I had to respect his nerve. "We are escorting Mr. Lilly and thought it best that he have some native speakers with him—in case you haven't noticed, there are unsavory characters in the vicinity."

Culpepper picked up the bottle again and took another swig. "That so?" His eyes swiveled to me again. "Well, just don't let this son of a bitch work on you, Mr. Lilly. This witch doctor's worked on a couple of ours, and they didn't make it, and I'm still not sure if it might've been intentional."

"I would've thought you were preparing for the festival in Las Bandejas."

His eyes went back to Martínez. "Yeah, well . . . The boss don't know it, but we decided to come down here and see Mister Cowboy for ourselves, you know?"

"Well, now that you have seen him . . ."

"Hey, there's no reason to be like that, Doc." He swung the M16 toward Adan. "You keep actin' like that, and we're gonna get the feeling you don't want us around." He pressed the muzzle of the automatic against Adan's chest. "That's not the case, is it, Doc?"

Unfortunately, I've found myself in a lot of situations like this, in wartime and not. I don't take a particular pride in knowing when a man is going to pull the trigger, but I knew that David Culpepper was preparing to do just that.

With one quick move I snatched the weapon away from the drunken man as the group behind him leveled their guns on me, the sound of chambering rounds the only noise.

Undeterred, I flipped the rifle over and with the power of rote muscle memory punched the button and dropped the magazine onto the table. Cocking and releasing the safety, I squeezed the trigger, then cocked it again and set the safety. Quickly pressing the button, I removed a screw, freeing the lower receiver assembly. Removing the charging handle, I slipped out the bolt carrier, the firing pin, retaining pin, removed the bolt cam pin, and plucked out the bolt, lining the parts up on the white tablecloth like a display.

The entire action took about nineteen seconds.

Semper Fi.

"Damn." Culpepper stared at his disassembled rifle and waved for the others to lower theirs. "You weren't in the military, were you?"

I shrugged.

"Damn." He took the last swig from the bottle of mescal. "You got a bag? I'm too fucking drunk to put it back together." He stuck out a hand. "I just wanna shake, Mr. Lilly."

I paused for a second and then gave it to him.

He squeezed for a moment and then looked through the holes in my mask. "You sure are in good shape to be as old as you are."

"I still work out, a little." I stepped toward Bianca and slipped an arm around her waist in an attempt to indicate that the evening was over.

He continued to smile at me. "Well, maybe we can have breakfast tomorrow or something."

Figuring we'd be gone long before he was up, I agreed. "I don't see why not—we'll be around."

"Good." He raised a fist. "Go Greyhounds!"

I returned the cheer. "Go Greyhounds."

He nodded and then half-turned away, motioning to one of his underlings as he pitched the bottle into the fountain where it shattered. He gestured toward his disassembled rifle. "Pick that damn thing up and let's go find something more to drink."

We watched as they did as he said, and then they all disappeared into the crowd. Adan leaned into me and grinned, breathing through his teeth. "Let's go watch a soccer game, Mr. Lilly."

I closed the door behind us and slid the mask off my face, happy to be rid of the thing. "How did I do?"

Bianca slipped off her own mask and looked up at me. "Much better than the speech."

Not knowing much about soccer, I'd stood and cheered whenever everybody else did and seemed to have made it through the game without committing any terrible errors in sport etiquette. I hadn't seen Culpepper or any of his men at the event and figured they'd either drunk themselves into oblivion or had found some other way to entertain the baser instincts of their natures.

Fatigue was seeping into every part of my body, and I felt like I was wading in water as I turned and sat on the foot of the bed. I looked at my boots and wondered what the hell I was doing.

"You must be exhausted."

Raising my face, I looked up to find her standing over me. "I am."

"That was very brave, what you did to save my brother. It was also very foolish." She stepped in closer and rested a hand on my shoulder. "But thank you."

"That's kind of my trademark, the foolish thing."

She leaned in and placed my head on her breast, and all I could think about was the sound of her voice and how good she smelled. "You should come to bed."

It took a few seconds to summon the strength and the will, but I pulled free and stood straight. "I've been thinking about that, and I think maybe I should go into one of the other rooms and sleep."

She placed a hand on my chest and looked up into my eyes. "I promise I won't take advantage of you."

"Yep, well, I don't know if I can make that same promise."

Her head kicked sideways, and she stepped in, draping a hand around my neck and pulling my face down to her lips where she kissed me very softly and then turned the side of her face and rested it on my chest. "That would be even better."

Taking her shoulders, I gently stood her back up and looked at her. "It's not that I don't find you painfully attractive . . ."

"I guess I'm not much of a *bruja*, am I?"

"Oh, yes you are."

Her eyes dropped. "There is someone else?"

I thought about Vic. "There is, at least I think there is—someone else."

"If you think, then it must be so."

Feeling even more like an idiot, I patted her shoulders and stepped back. I'm not sure why I picked up the gym bag from the bed, but I did and then stepped around to get a pillow and a cover I could use.

Reading my mind, she started pulling the light cotton blanket from the foot of the bed. "Take this, the night is warm enough that I only need the sheet."

"There's another image I can carry through the night." Gathering it from her, I stood there for a few seconds. "I'll see you in the morning."

Taking the mask from the bed, she reached up and took off my hat and slipped the thing over my face again. "Your disguise."

Looking through the eyeholes, I took in the curves at her hips. "Right."

"And if you change your mind . . ." She turned and began unzipping the flamenco dancer dress she was wearing; I took advantage of the moment to bolt for the door.

It was dark in the hallway, only a few of the candles on the stairs remaining lit. I stood there in the flickering, amber light and felt like a stranger in a strange land. My job had some relatively strict parameters, and even though I sometimes stretched them a bit, I was pretty much off the map now.

There was a buzzing in my head that I couldn't seem to shake, a feeling that I was doing something wrong. Maybe I shouldn't even be here. Maybe I was endangering my daughter's life with all this cowboying. Maybe I should've stayed in El Paso for the backup that was probably desperately attempting to find me, but I knew the clock was running and whatever it took, I was going to see this through.

I turned to find the door to the other room and stared into the barrel of a 5.7x28mm Five-seveN pistol held in the slightly unsteady hand of David Culpepper.

"Bob Lilly didn't do his senior year with the Greyhounds. There was a drought, and his family moved from Texas to Portland, Oregon."

I took a breath. "You know, I always thought I should've paid more attention to high school football in Texas."

"Friday night lights, motherfucker." He gestured toward the doorway of the next room.

I raised my hands slightly, still holding the gym bag, and sidestepped out of the hallway, my boots crunching glass from the tall, broken windows where a slight breeze from the desert blew the torn and sun-faded curtains inward.

Still holding the pistol on me, he gestured again. "Take off that stupid mask."

I took my hat off and transferred it to the bag hand and pushed the mask up. "I thought you were drunk."

He shrugged as he glanced both ways in the hallway before following me in. "Well, there's drunk, and then there's drunk." Once again with the pistol, he gestured for me to back up some more. "Now, if it was up to me, I'd just shoot your big ass right now, but the boss wants you alive, so I guess we gotta figure things out. You got any handcuffs with you?"

The way he was looking around, I was pretty sure that he was alone, maybe because he wanted the credit, or maybe because the others really were drunk. "No."

"A lawman without handcuffs?"

"I told you no."

"You wouldn't lie to me, would you?" I didn't say anything. "What's in the bag?"

"My jock—you want to sniff it?"

"Funny." He raised the semiautomatic and aimed it at my head and then motioned with it toward the bag. "Drop it in front of you."

I did as he said, and from the clunk it made on the tile floor, it was easy to discern that it wasn't sports equipment.

He smiled and slowly kneeled down to check it out for himself. "The boss didn't have much doubt that you'd be coming."

"Where's my daughter?"

"She's up at the monastery."

"She better be safe."

He glanced at the gun, palmed in his hand. "Or what?"

"Did you kill Ricardo?"

"Who?"

"Alexia's nephew."

He actually thought about it. "The housekeeper?"

I lowered my arms just a bit, but he didn't seem to notice. "What, you kill so many you can't keep track?"

"You know, I do." He nudged his ball cap back on his head with the barrel of the gun and grinned up at me. "He was pretty easy, but I gotta tell you, herdin' that monster of an aunt of his was a real pain in the ass."

"She's not a part of all this?"

He barked a laugh and bumped the sights of the FN on his

teeth. "Nope, the boss took her to look after your daughter. He figured it'd be a lot easier if she had somebody she trusted with her, but in the end I'll end up doing her, too."

"You gonna *do* me?"

"Naw, I told you, the boss has special plans for you." He reached forward with his free hand to unzip the duffel. "But hey, is that hotshot second-in-command of yours on her way down? The boss wants her skinned and on a wall, but I'd like to entertain her a bit before he does it." He continued grinning. "White meat's kinda hard to come by around these parts."

He had the gun, but I knew he'd be in trouble if he shot me without Bidarte's consent. I guess he figured I was old or that I was tired and he was right, but I was also highly motivated to kick his teeth in—which I did.

He clamped his jaw, saving the ivories, but I kept moving forward, half stepping and falling on him as he fell backward. I tried to get a knee on his gun arm, but he was young and probably a lot better trained in hand-to-hand than I was, so I settled for the front of his shirt. He swung like a spider monkey and wrapped an arm around my neck.

I threw myself backward, somehow still blocking his gun arm. The wall shuddered and splintered, the plaster and lath exploding in the air, but he'd clamped his legs around me and was beating his head against the back of mine.

I spun and made for the other wall but tripped over the gym bag and fell, luckily landing on his shoulder. I had the satisfaction of hearing the pop as it dislocated and he screamed, but somehow still held the gun.

I put more pressure on that arm and rolled onto my back on top of him. I began slamming my head back, feeling the crunch of his nose and wondered just how much it was going to take to get him off me.

I'd just raised my head for another slam when he managed to snatch his gun hand away so that I had to roll in that direction just to keep him on the floor. That proved to be a mistake because it left his legs free, and he braced both of them against my chest and with a surprising amount of strength was able to push me away.

I was near enough to grab his leg again, so I pulled him toward me, happy that I wasn't looking down the barrel of the 5.7x28mm again; when I looked up, I could see the FN was lying amid the broken glass by the open doorway.

I kept pulling him toward me and away from the gun, but he got a desert boot free and cropped me a good one on the chin. I reached up and caught the waistband of his pants, but they gave way and he continued slithering bottomless toward the doorway and the gun. He paused in the effort just long enough to smile a bloody grin at me.

I scrambled onto all fours after him, but it was a foregone conclusion that he was going to get the semiautomatic. I'd pretty much figured that I had done enough damage to him that he was unlikely to forgive and forget even though Bidarte had told him that he personally wanted to kill me. It was strange though, because when I reached forward and touched his legs again, they weren't moving.

Slowly, I raised my face and saw Culpepper's naked ass in the moonlight, and above that, the even more impressive sight of a naked Bianca kneeling in the doorway with the FN pistol in her hands, smiling as she pressed the barrel against his forehead.

"*Hijo de puta*, how 'bout them Cowboys?"

6

As fast as I went I couldn't seem to catch up with myself. I was unmoored and disconnected with the feeling that I wasn't in control anymore.

"You look like shit, *amigo*."

I had given Adan the oil lamp I had carried and had raised the brim of my hat so he could get a clear view. "Yep, well, you should see the other guy."

"I have actually." He followed me into the bedroom where Culpepper was tied to one of the metal office chairs with a bunch of wire hangers I'd found in the closet. "I think you are cutting off the circulation to his hands."

"He's lucky I don't wrap one around his neck." Dressed in jeans and a white blouse, Bianca stood off to the side along with Alonzo. I took a breath. "You okay?"

"Yes. Where were you?"

"I had to go check something." I turned to Alonzo. "We're out of here in an hour?"

He looked nervous but nodded. "Or less, if we can manage."

I gestured toward Culpepper. "That's up to him." I leaned forward with my hands on my knees and looked at him. "How you doin' there, Tex?"

He raised his bloody face, some of the glass shards from the floor still stuck in his flesh. "Fuck you."

"Rip-roaring and ready for love, right?"

Culpepper spat and grinned, flipping the strands of hair with dried blood from his face. "You better let me go."

I took a deep breath, still winded from the fight and then the stairs. "Of all the things that are going to happen, I don't believe that's one of them."

"I'm telling you that if you know what's good for you . . ."

"Look, we can do this the easy way, or we can do it the hard way." I straightened and looked down at him, picking a few more glass chips from my hands. "I'm going to ask you a few questions."

"Save your breath."

I paused for a few seconds. "I promise I'll keep them short so you can answer with one or two syllables."

He strained against the wire as he enunciated each word. "Fuck. You."

I stared at him a moment more and then stepped around, turning the chair and dragging him out of the room backward. "I guess we're doing it the hard way." I glanced at Bianca and Alonzo. "You two stay here." The back legs of the metal office chair scraped on the tile surface as I pulled him toward the stairs. "C'mon Adan, I need someone to carry the lamp."

Culpepper thrashed a bit, but I'd wired him in good. "Where the hell are you taking me?"

"What do you care?" I think he was a little worried I was going to pitch him off the balcony but didn't breathe any easier as I started dragging him down the stairs, the metal chair with him in it sounding like the *1812 Overture* as we crashed our way down. Adan dutifully followed as I made a right and ventured farther into the building, past some counters that had been broken up and a few more vacant offices cluttered with debris.

There was another set of stairs to my right, and I followed the same procedure as we descended into the depths of the building, Adan's lamp the only light. I'm pretty sure I'd loosened a few more of Culpepper's fillings by the time we got to the bottom.

"Where the hell are we going?"

I dragged him past a short hallway lined with empty shelves to our final destination. Propping the chair back up, I turned him so that he could see the large, steel door of the vault.

The doctor entered and stood to the side, still unsure of my intentions but holding the lamp high so that we could all look around.

I toed some debris as I pulled Guzmán's brass knuckles from my back pocket. "When felons were induced to talk, they first were shown the instruments of their torture."

"What is that supposed to mean?"

I slipped the brass onto my hand, glinting menacingly in the lamplight. "The difficulty we're having here is that right now you're more afraid of Bidarte than you are of me, and I'm going to have to convince you that you need to be more afraid of me without damaging you so much that you can't tell me what it is that I need to know."

"Fuck. You."

I punched the corner of the wall, pieces of concrete flying and filling the air with dust. On the other side of the doorway, Adan coughed and quickly pulled his shirt over his mouth. "Primitive, but damned capable these things. I think it was the Sikhs in the eighteenth century that came up with the basic design of the Sher Panja, but they really came into their own in our country during the Civil War. There wasn't hardly a self-respecting soldier who didn't have a set of these made out of brass or cast iron or even if they had to carve them out of wood or cast them out of lead bullets molded in dirt."

"Fuck. You."

I stepped toward him. "Now, you're going to tell me all the things I need to know, like where exactly my daughter is, Bidarte's plans, the basic layout at Monasterio del Corazón Ardiente, his manpower and armaments, and anything else I can come up with."

He smiled. "I don't believe you will use those."

I stood there, not moving.

His head dropped, and he laughed. "One of the things I'm good at is knowing how far people will go, and you, Sheriff, aren't capable of following through on this threat, even with a piece of shit like me."

I could feel the muscles bunching in my right arm, calculating the distance between the two of us and the trajectory and amount of force it would take to loosen his jaw without shattering it.

There was part of me, that vengeful, wrathful monster who was goading me forward, that wanted to beat him to a pulp and maybe to death—but in the end, I knew he was right. I pulled the knuckles off and stuck them back in my pocket.

"That's what a clear conscience gets you, Sheriff, nothing." The grin broadened. "Now you're talking sense. Get me out of this chair, and let's get going. I can't promise it's going to be a good trip for you, but maybe we can just let your friends go home."

"Nope."

The smile faded a bit. "Nope, what?"

"You're not leaving."

Culpepper glanced around and sounded a little less sure of himself. "What the fuck is that supposed to mean?"

I leaned against the wall and folded my arms just to give them something to do. "In the seventies, when I got back from Vietnam, we had a rash of bank robberies in Wyoming. Nothing too sophisticated, just the usual smash-and-grab kind of thing. Anyway, the security at a lot of the banks was out of date, so they had this big show in Casper about all the new varieties of equipment and vaults." I walked to one of the walls and patted it. "I'm thinking this was built around the same time." I turned to look at him. "Torero was probably a thriving little town before your kind got here."

"Fuck this town and fuck you. Look, if you want to get those knucks back out and beat on me, big man, you go ahead and do it, but I've been beat on before and I didn't say anything then and I'm sure as hell not going to say anything now."

I studied him a bit more and then patted the wall again. "Reinforced concrete about five feet thick, backed by about six inches of steel." I ran a hand toward the doorway. "Vault door with an iron face and another inch and a half of cast steel, another twelve inches of burn-resistant steel, and another inch of open hearth steel. This particular vault door has twenty bolts, each an inch in diameter that holds the door into a sixteen-inch steel jam set in sixteen inches of concrete." I tapped the steel. "Now the door is precision made so you can't pour anything into the seam." I glanced around. "Even ol' Dillinger would sure as heck have had trouble with this one."

He licked his lips, and I could see the panic growing in him like a virus. "Look, if your plan is to bore me to death . . ."

I took the lamp from Adan. "Doesn't look as though there's been any money in here for quite some time." I came over and set the lamp at Culpepper's feet. "When it was in operation, I bet this place was kind of hard to get into." I brought my face up to look at him. "However, what you should be specifically concerned about is getting out."

He was perfectly still now and not so talkative.

I glanced back at Adan. "How long do you think this lamp will last?"

He shrugged. "A half gallon of oil, it will probably burn for 150 hours, give or take."

"Six days." I turned back to Culpepper. "You'll be long dead before that."

He stared at me.

I nodded. "People are always worried about starving to death, but it's really dehydration they should worry about—it usually takes a week, but with your lack of body fat and recent alcohol intake, I'd say you're probably already on your way." I glanced back at Adan. "What do you say, Doc?"

"Five days at the most."

"Do you stay hungry and thirsty all the way to the end?"

He stepped forward, his voice surprisingly conversational. "No, the body is an amazingly adaptive mechanism—it will cry out for food and drink for the first day or two but then realizes that it isn't getting any more and adjusts."

"How?"

"It begins devouring the fat cells within itself, fat cells being full of water. It is how camels survive in the desert, by living off the fat cells in their humps." He took another step toward Culpepper. "But you, my friend, have no hump."

"Side effects?"

"His bowels and kidneys will continue to evacuate until they are empty, and there will be a great drying of the lips and mouth, but other than that, not much."

I stood. "Is it painful?"

"After the period of hunger and thirst, no, I think not. In the research that has been done in voluntary suicide by dehydration, I have heard that it's actually quite peaceful."

I shook my head. "That's too bad."

His eyes flicked between Adan and me. "So what are you going to do, walk out of here and lock me in?"

I pulled a piece of paper from my shirt pocket. "I found the combination chalked on the vault, pretty smart actually. I copied it down and then rubbed it off the door. Now there might be a few old-timers around here who remember the combination, but I don't think it's going to matter, because when I close that door, there isn't going to be a living soul who knows you're down here besides Adan and me." I turned to the Doc. "I'm not going to tell anybody, are you?"

"No."

I walked over and patted Culpepper on the shoulder. "So you get to sit here and shit and piss yourself until your tongue turns to boot leather."

He snorted, waiting for me to say more, but I didn't. "You haven't got the guts to do this."

"You have my daughter. You watch me."

"You're sworn to serve and protect."

"Not you—the last time I looked you weren't a resident of Absaroka County." I walked over to Adan. "In a sense you're right, I mean I don't think I could stand here and beat a bound man into talking without hating myself, but this way I'm just walking out, closing the door, and letting nature take its course."

His eyes were a little wider now. "I'll scream and yell and—"

"Weren't you listening? These walls are five feet thick—nobody is going to hear you." I turned to Adan, and we made for the door. "I don't know if I'd want that lamp or not, but then I'm not afraid of the dark and I've got . . . What is it you called it? A clear conscience?" Ushering the Doc through the door, I turned back. "See you around, Culpepper."

He raised his voice. "You're going to regret this."

I nodded. "Yep, I probably will, but I'll get over it."

"That's not what I mean, asshole. He's got an army up there."

I held the door, now about two-thirds closed. "Tell me about it."

He spat the words, the bloody saliva still dripping from his mouth. "Fuck you."

"I guess you won't be needing this after all." Picking up the lamp, I began pushing the steel door, the lamplight squeezing on the floor as if I were mashing it. *"Adiós."*

Urging the heavy thing forward, I was within an inch of it closing when he screamed, "Wait!"

I opened the door a bit and looked in at one of those pale blue eyes that was still visible in the thin strand of light that pierced the vault. His expression hadn't changed—if anything, he looked more vengeful, the strings of saliva dripping from his mouth with the words, "I'll tell you whatever you want to know because it doesn't make any motherfucking difference because you're gonna be dead in a matter of days—and that I can guarantee you."

"How did you get him to talk?"

I placed Bianca's bag in the trunk of the Caddy with everyone else's and gestured toward her brother. "We plied the better angels of his nature."

She looked at me doubtfully. "Did you kill him?"

I sighed. "No, I'm not a killer—at least not when I don't have to be. I've learned over the years that killing people is just lazy—better to use your imagination." I closed the trunk of the Caddy. "More fun, too."

"I'm beginning to think you're psychotic."

I rapped the side of the dusty convertible and offered her a hand as she climbed in on the driver's side, the Seer already in the front. "You might be right."

I followed her and pulled the seat back so Adan could get in. "The lock of the vault doesn't work?"

"Broken, but he didn't know that."

Alonzo climbed into the driver's seat after we were situated in the back. "Do you have somebody you can call to go down and let him out in a few days?"

Adan nodded. "The mayor."

As Alonzo started the car and slipped it into gear, the Seer finally spoke. "You should have killed him."

I glanced at Bianca and gestured toward the blind man. "There's your killer."

He shook his head at me. "We have an old saying in Mexico, *bondad a un asesino construye ataúdes.*" I waited as he stared back at me, the dead eyes completely hidden by the heavy sunglasses. "Kindness to a killer builds coffins."

We took the road north, back the way we'd come, and then Alonzo took a left and we bumped along on another dirt road that angled toward the mountains. The sun was just beginning to ease up our spines when he circled a funky-looking old blue bus, and a broken-down corral with a lone cow standing in front of an ancient Aermotor windmill, and a large stone building that looked to be holding a lot of loosely bound hay. The lights were on in a small cottage about half the size of the barn where a bunch of people were standing on the porch in the quarter light of dawn. Alonzo cut the engine, got out of the car, and flipped the seat far enough forward for us to get out. "The Orfanato, an unofficial title."

I helped Bianca out of the Caddy. "How many children are there?"

She placed her hands at the small of her back and stretched. "Who knows? It varies. The old woman here, she takes in the unwanted children."

I went to the back and got the Seer's wheelchair.

The cow bawled at us, and Bianca walked across the dusty turnaround to rub the creature's nose. "What's her problem, do you think?"

Adan and Alonzo approached the house as I set up the Seer's chair. He expertly flipped himself out of the car and into it, and I started to push him toward the small stone building. "I'd say she needs milking."

We opened a small gate, which led to the porch where a gnomelike woman was gesturing emphatically. Wheeling the blind man in closer, I listened to the conversation although not understanding much of it as a good half dozen children of different ages hung to the posts or leaned against the wall.

A young girl with large eyes who clutched one of the wooden poles like it was a lifesaver stared at me.

I looked back at her and smiled. *"Hola."*

She hid behind the post.

I waited a few minutes listening to the cow bawl and the adults argue and decided I might be more useful in the corral.

I left the Seer with Bianca, swiped a metal pail, and then started back toward the cow.

Climbing over and using one of the lower poles as a seat, I began milking her and she immediately calmed. She wasn't very big and a little on the lean side, but she was putting out, and after a bit the bucket was half full.

"You look like you've done that before."

I turned on the stool and looked at her, backlit by the very first rays of the sun. "I grew up on a ranch, a cattle ranch I grant you, but I've been around a dairy cow or two." Patting Bossie's side, I nodded toward the porch. "What's going on?"

"The burros and mules have not been gathered and are scattered all over the place, so it will take time to bring them in."

"She didn't know we were coming?"

Bianca laid her arms on the top rail and peered at me over them. "It's Mexico."

"Who's going to wrangle?"

"Adan and Alonzo, I suppose."

"I'll pay money to see that."

"Me, too."

"So how does she take care of all those kids?"

"She says she is a strong tree with branches for many birds."

I rose and carefully handed Bianca the bucket. "Here, give that to the strong tree and see if it improves her mood."

Watching Bianca walk back toward the house, I couldn't help but admire the view, and she must've known because she slipped a glance at me from over her shoulder as she passed her brother, who was coming my way.

Adan got to the corral and assumed the same position in the same spot as his sister had. "We may have to walk, the stock are scattered all over the desert."

"So I heard." I nodded. "Does she feed them?"

"I don't know."

"Find out, and then how she does it."

He nodded and started away but then stopped. "How do you wish to proceed?"

"What do you mean?"

He shook his head and sighed with a sense of resignation. "My sister and the Seer, they wish to come with us."

"On the burros?"

He laughed. "There are supposedly four mules, but they may be in Guadalajara for all we know." He smiled. "Alonzo I am not so sure about."

"Adan, I think it's time we leveled with each other." I walked over to him and tipped my hat back. "As feeble as it is, this has all the makings of a military ops and people are going to die— and the more people we have to worry about, the more likely it'll be us."

"Agreed."

"No to the Seer and no to your sister." I shrugged. "Alonzo can make up his own mind and for that matter so can you. I don't expect you to do this either, Adan, but from what I understand you've been trained and have a knack for this kind of thing."

"I was originally with the Dirección Federal de Seguridad, but when they started to protect the Nicaraguan Contras and the assassinations and torture became too disturbing, I objected. For this I was given a forced disappearance, as they call it." He looked at his shoes and then at me. "I am assuming you have friends and coworkers back in the US who would have assisted you?"

"Yes."

"Why aren't they here?"

I reached into my shirt pocket and held up the postcard I'd shown him before. "Because this says 'Come.'" And I assumed now. I stuffed it back in my pocket. "I know that Bidarte has a habit of popping up and also of disappearing, and I can't risk that he might do that with my daughter." I glanced north. "Anyway, I outran my friends."

"What you are attempting to do to *us* now." He pulled out a cigar and lighter. "Did you keep Culpepper's gun?"

"I did."

"I wish we had more weapons."

I thought about the fact that we pretty much just had the Colt at my back, the FN, and the collection of antique weaponry in the gym bag. "Me, too."

He lit the cigar and pocketed the lighter. "You know he is going to kill you."

"I know it's a possibility."

He took a deep puff, savoring the tobacco, and then slowly exhaled. "I'd say it's a probability."

The name of the girl with big eyes was Alicia, and she watched me as I shook the bucket with the cracked corn rattling like a maraca. The mule looked at me but didn't move. "Look, we can do this the easy way or we can do it the hard way."

My grandfather had had mules, a team of them actually, and I didn't remember them being difficult or recalcitrant, but I did remember him saying that a good mule is ten times better than a horse but that a bad one was a hundred times worse.

I glanced at the little girl and shook the bucket some more, and the mule readjusted her forefeet in a try.

With the help of the children, we'd captured three donkeys and three other mules rather quickly with the bucket, but this larger one had been a little more standoffish. Taking a step closer, I held the lead rope behind my back in hopes I wouldn't spook her, but my patience was running thin, and if she didn't take the food in the bucket before long, I was going to be walking to Bidarte's village as none of the other animals looked large enough to be able to carry someone my size.

I ached to get going but knew it was futile without assistance. I shook the bucket some more and angled it toward her. "C'mon, you're not going to find any corn out here other than this."

She was dappled gray and most likely had had an Appaloosa mother. She had expressive eyes and a lot of scars; the old woman had said her name was *La Rucia*, which means gray in Spanish, because that's what color she was.

"*La Rucia*, you know she's not the first to have that name." Alicia studied me.

"Sancho Panza's mount was *El Rucio*." I shook the bucket some more and was just about to give up when she took a step my way and tilted her head at me, the long, sensitive ear twitching.

"Read much Cervantes, Rucia?"

She eyed me but did extend her nose.

"We're going to go tilt some windmills, you wanna go?" She nudged the bucket but then backed away. "Granted, they're highly armed, psychotic windmills."

Alicia reached into the bucket and scooped out a miniature handful and took a step toward the mule. She held it out to her, and Rucia lowered her head to nibble a little from the flat of the girl's palm.

"Of course, that story ends with Don Quixote on his deathbed threatening to disinherit his niece if she marries a man who reads books about chivalry." Sliding the lead rope from my shoulder, I handed Alicia the loop and watched as she gently draped it over Rucia's nose and then on tiptoe tried to reach it over her crown, whereupon I reached out and slipped the loop around the mule's head and over her long ears. "Not quite as whimsically literary as the first part, which Cervantes had written ten years previously, but the old guy was dying and needed to get a book out."

The mule started, and I dropped the bucket but held the rope, and we stood there, the three of us looking at one another. "I'm not so sure the old Don should've ever recovered his senses."

Alicia held her hands out, and I lifted her onto my shoulders, picked up the bucket, and led Rucia reluctantly through the cactus and volcanic rock back toward the little ranch. "Sometimes, when there aren't any other options, you should just stay crazy."

We talked the whole way back to the dry ranch, none of us understanding the other but all of us enjoying the conversation. The sun was all of a sudden hot, and as I rounded the corral, I could see the full complement of our party engaged in a passionate argument on the porch as the three burros and three mules that were tied to the rail looked on.

I handed the little girl to Bianca, who was waiting at the edge of the porch. "You are ditching us?"

I tied the mule up with the other three and the three burros that I was thinking were too small to be of use. "To be honest, there are people who are going to be killed, most likely many people who will be killed, and I don't want to have to worry about anybody while I'm up there."

She held Alicia on one hip. "Worry about us? What, the woman and the blind man?"

"Everybody."

She stepped off the porch and looked up at me. "Funny, because if I hadn't been there in the bank you would probably be dead."

"I'm not saying you weren't a help."

She sat Alicia down on the porch and then turned to thrust her chin out at me. "I will be again."

"I can't risk it."

"*You* can't."

"My party, so I send out invitations." It was harsh, I knew, but I couldn't see me taking the entire ragtag team up the mountain to certain death. "I don't know what Adan's plans are, but if you want to help you'll wait for us here." I glanced toward the mountains. "If we make it . . . If we make it, I've got an idea we'll be headed back this way at a high rate of speed and we'll need somebody with the motor running."

"You are so lacking in imagination."

I nodded. "You wouldn't be the first woman to tell me that."

I collected my mule and took the leads on the three others, taking them all to the corral before she could say anything more. Alonzo had collected the gear and piled it on the railings along with a packsaddle and some large canvas bags.

The short stocky mule took the pad and packsaddle easily, and I had the suspicion it wasn't the first time he'd had it on his back. "Are there any riding saddles?"

Alonzo stared at me. "I don't know."

I nodded and glanced toward the barn but figured first we needed to get a few things straight. "Are you coming? The only reason I'm asking is that if you are, I'm going to have to do something different with the mules."

He glanced back at the house. "You really think we're going to die?"

"Probably."

"How can you be so calm about it?"

I thought about the running monologue I'd engaged in with the little girl in the desert and how I doubted she'd understood a word but was also glad that I'd had something to do other than stand out there and scream. "My daughter."

He studied me, his face a question mark. "Because you love her?"

"Because I'll do anything to get her back." After tightening the cinch, I lifted the bags onto the cradle and balanced the load. "I've been in this business almost my whole life, and I can tell you that who's the biggest, meanest, toughest, smartest doesn't mean a damn thing. It's who is willing to go further than anybody else, and to save my daughter, I'll go as far as hell and back and never blink an eye." I looked at him from over the packsaddle. "I don't expect anybody else to do that—I couldn't. So if you want to sit this one out, Alonzo, nobody's going to hold it against you. Honest."

I turned and walked toward the barn, entering it through the stalls beside a crumpled stone wall and found the tack area where a few old McClellan saddles were propped up along with some desiccated leather halters; I didn't see any bridles so figured the halters must be what was used. When I moved them away from the wall, I uncovered some writing that read ZAPATA ESTABA AQUÍ!

"Somehow I doubt that."

There was a noise to my left, and I saw Alicia standing by the rock wall. "Hi, you."

She didn't move, so I pulled down the halters and found a rag to wipe off the dust and cobwebs. I figured if there was any oil in the leather I might coax it out by rubbing the surface, so I stretched the things on the rough countertop that covered a manger and began rubbing the life back into them, and before long a slight shine began showing. "You don't talk much, do you?"

She still didn't say anything but sidled along the wall to stand near me.

"I was pretty much the same way—you can learn a lot by being quiet, people forget you're there."

She watched me polishing the tack and rested a hand on the edge of the counter.

"This job would be a lot easier if there was some oil around here—you don't happen to know where some might be, do you?"

She stared at me.

Running through my high school Spanish, I searched for the

word, finally coming up with one for the wrong type of oil but hoped it might get the meaning across. *"Petróleo?"*

Looking up at me, she pushed on the lid of the manger just a little, and I could see that it was hinged in the back.

"Gracias."

I readjusted a few things and lifted the heavy top, revealing a compartment with more rags and a cleaning kit with small hammer and sickle emblems pressed into the tin, along with two AK-47 type III assault rifles.

"Well, maybe Zapata was here after all."

7

I let Adan lead with the assumption that he knew where he was going, which might've been an exercise in hopeful thinking. "Are we lost?"

He paused on the trail leading up from the rustic bridge at the river, just long enough to push his perfectly white hat back on his head and glance at me. "There is only one trail—why?"

"You didn't look certain."

"I'm on a mule, that alone makes me uncertain."

The river was below us, the trail no more than two feet wide, and I watched as the mules carefully picked their way, sometimes crossing their hooves to stay on the narrow path. "And this is the good way, huh?"

He shrugged. "The best way to not get shot."

Alonzo had elected discretion over valor and had decided to stay at the Orfanato with the others. "But the fastest way down is where the missing bridge is, near your place north of here?"

"Yes, but as you say, there is no bridge—at least not one you would want to cross."

"Can you ford the stream up there?"

"It is dangerous this time of year."

"But it can be done?"

He turned in the saddle to look at me. "Why do you ask?"

"Well, if things go as badly as I'm anticipating then we're going to be looking for the fastest way out of there, and I just want to know if that's it."

"It is, but it's dangerous." We climbed up the steep trail to a switchback. "Can I ask you something, Sheriff?"

"Sure."

"Why did it take you so long to load the mules?"

I thought about whether I wanted to tell him, whether I wanted to tell anyone, but figured that since he was the only one risking his life by coming along with me on this harebrained scheme, he had a right. "I'll show you when we get to the rim of the canyon."

It took another forty minutes, but we finally made the top, and I reined up the two mules beside him on the hard-packed dirt, then draping the lead over a dying white pine, I dismounted.

I moved to the pack mule, folded the canvas cloth aside, pulled one of the AKs out, and showed it to him. "Romanian MD-65 with the underfolder stock and thirty-round mags—there are two of them."

He took one, holding it up and examining it. "*Cuerno de Chivo*, Horn of the Goat, that's what the narcos call these things. It refers to the curve of the magazine." He shook his head. "Now, what is she doing with something like this?"

"I thought maybe you might know."

"Why would you think that?"

"Proximity."

He shook his head. "I've never met her before."

"Your sister referred to it as the Orfanato, the orphanage?"

He nodded. "The place is well known as a depository for unwanted children and has been since long before I was born."

"Maybe the old woman doesn't know these things were there. Who else do you know that has access to that place?"

"Difficult to say. Traffickers roam this area, as you saw." He handed the assault rifle back to me. "They could belong to anyone."

"You don't think this is how she makes her money then?"

"No, I don't think so, but these days who knows?"

I placed the weapon back in the pack bag, careful to cover it up. "There were also Spam cans of ammo, 122-grain, full metal jacket, 20 rounds a box/32 boxes/640 rounds per can—1,920 rounds."

"You brought all of them?"

"He did." I patted the pack mule, stroking his rump. "Do you know how to operate an AK?"

"Yes, do you?" He smiled as I resecured the pack with a few knots. "Then this is a windfall."

"I suppose." I looked at him. "When I was heading down here, a friend gave me some advice. He said to not trust anybody—the police, military, anybody."

Adan swung a leg up on the horn and turned completely toward me. "Good advice."

I studied him long enough to enforce the question. "So I'm going to ask you once, just once . . . Can I trust you?"

A smile crept onto his lips, and he waited before answering. "Let me ask you a question in return. You saw the way the man Culpepper was looking at me in Torero when you distracted him by disassembling his weapon?" He leaned forward, still smiling. "If you hadn't done that, do you think he would have killed me?"

I gave it actual thought. "Yep, I do."

"When he attacked you later, do you think he would have killed you if my sister had not intervened?"

"Yep, I do."

He turned back in the saddle and started off. "Then you have your answer."

I supposed I did.

I climbed back on my mule, gigged her, and we were off. The terrain wasn't getting any easier, and I was pretty glad to have the mules. We appeared to be above the tree line where only a few scrub pines and cactus pushed their way through the rocky rubble that rose in a straight incline toward the dark mountains on the horizon, chest-high creosote bushes stretching in front of us like a stunted and dead forest.

The sky was clear and the temperature hot as the sun rose above us, and I slipped my Ray-Bans over my eyes and settled in for the ride, thinking about what Culpepper had told us and about how I wanted to use that information.

Adan had listened as I'd questioned the man but had said nothing. I'd gotten a good idea of the place and even drawn up diagrams on a few sheets of thick paper from of all things, a Big Chief notebook. I thought about my friend Henry Standing Bear, and more than anything wished that he were here. This operation was his cup of tactical tea, the kind of thing he'd trained to do with the recon groups he'd worked with in Special Operations in Vietnam. But at the moment he was back on the Northern Cheyenne Reservation standing guard over Lola.

I contemplated dragging the notebook out, but until we got there and I saw the lay of the land myself, I didn't see any reason to commit to a plan of action. It was frustrating, but if Culpepper was lying through his loosened teeth, then we were back to square one.

As Adan had said, the Kalashnikovs were a windfall, but I didn't trust luck, good or bad—as the old Marine saying goes, luck can't replace preparation and a good strategy.

All I wanted was Cady back.

The trail straightened up the shelf leading through a pass

that looked like a blocked-in area, surrounded on three sides by mountain steeps, the perfect place for a monastery or a fortress. There was a fork, the first I'd seen, when we'd topped the chasm where the river flowed. "Where's that go?"

It had been more than three hours since either of us had spoken, so it was only natural that Adan was slow turning in the saddle, finally cocking an elbow on his cantle. "Excuse me?"

I pointed to the right. "That trail there, where does it go?"

He turned the other way to look. "To my ranch, eventually."

Glancing around, I wasn't assured by the options. "If we beat a hasty retreat, there isn't going to be much of an opportunity to cover our tracks."

He laughed mirthlessly. "I wouldn't worry about it. If we come back this way they will assume we've taken the trail back to the Orfanato we took to get here."

I studied the road less traveled. "Why?"

"Because only a madman would go that way. I told you, we blew up the bridge, and the one that remains is barely passable and then you have to cross the desert."

"If we return the way we came, and they're following us— what will happen to the old woman and the children at the Orfanato?"

He reined in his mule and studied the ground as I pulled up beside him. "They will kill them all, which is why it is important to cut the head off the snake so that it can no longer bite."

"Bidarte."

"Yes." His eyes came up to mine. "You may be here for your daughter, but I am here to kill a man before he kills my land. There used to be an unwritten law that if you were not part of the drug trade you were safe, but that is no longer the case." He glanced around. "Sooner or later his people will come for me and mine, and that is something I cannot allow. With a man like this you have two options—you either leave him to do as he wishes, or you kill him."

"Why are you telling me this again?"

"Because the Seer is right, you should have killed Culpepper— why didn't you?"

"It's difficult to explain. I mean if it had been during the fight I would've if I'd had to, but with him incapacitated it just didn't seem right. I've spent most of my life making judgments and living a moral code as much as I am able. I won't kill anybody I don't have to."

"Like me, you were a soldier."

"That's different."

He studied me some more. "You may have to learn."

"Your sister hasn't. She had the opportunity to shoot Culpepper in the face, but she didn't."

"He was valuable at that point, and she knew it." He turned his mule and started off. "If you think my sister will not kill outright, you are a very foolish man."

I sat there for a moment more and then started after him. The trail rounded a hill to the right where I could see the mountain village about a quarter of a mile below.

There was a single, round stone building a little closer, then a hillside leading down to a cluster of red roof-tiled buildings and a plaza where the main road ended. There was a larger building at the rear, its back pressed hard against the cliffs, that I assumed was Monasterio del Corazón Ardiente. As I'd figured, Estante del Diablo was a dead end, surrounded by rock precipices that dove two thousand feet—one way in, one way out.

I could see that metal towers had been erected in the town with work lights attached and even speakers. "The place has electricity?"

Adan shook his head. "Generators."

I reached in my pocket and pulled out the diagrams I'd made from the information we'd gleaned from Culpepper, studied the outline, and compared it to the scene below.

Adan climbed off his mule. "We should move back and find a place to stake the animals."

I moved my own mule from the edge toward an open area and nudged her next to a rock outcropping that looked familiar. I pulled the postcard from my shirt pocket and held it up. "Gemelos de Roca—must be the place."

He nodded.

"Do you think they have patrols?"

He followed me and as I climbed off, sorted through one of the pack bags and pulled out an impressive pair of M19 Bell & Howell binoculars. "No, the one thing we can rely on is their arrogance."

While I unloaded the mules, he crept back to the edge overlooking Estante del Diablo. I glanced around, but this being the only area with any grass, I figured the mules wouldn't wander far. I stacked the saddles near the rocks and began unpacking the large canvas bags, putting the contents into smaller piles.

When I finished, I brought a canteen over and joined Adan at the drop-off. "What's going on?"

"Nothing. I see almost no movement. Things will pick up this evening when the festival begins." He lowered the Vietnam-era binoculars and handed them to me. "That will be the time when we can approach, when there is cover."

I could see a few people moving about but not many. "The building to the right is a sale barn?"

"Yes, the monastery used to be famous for their goats that produced milk and cheeses. Buyers used to come from all over the provinces."

"I wonder what they use it for now?"

"I don't know." He studied the layout. "But I am sure your daughter will be in the monastery at the back."

"Yep. It looks like the only way there would be to go behind the sale barn and along the cliffs at the rear."

"There are walls."

"Some, but that's better than the main road and the plaza where we're bound to get spotted before we can get in there." I lowered the binoculars. "When will people be arriving for the festival?"

"All through the afternoon, I would imagine."

I handed him the M19s and after one last glance at the mules, who were loitering and munching the strawlike grass, I lay back and pulled my hat over my face. "Let me know when things start hopping."

"Does that look like a patrol to you?" I was pretty much awake before, but I was fully awake now that Adan had spoken.

"Where?" I snatched the hat from my face, rolled over, and looked in the direction he indicated; there were three armed men who had rounded the sale barn and then had stopped in an opening by the wall to smoke. The light was just beginning to fade, and there was a great deal more activity in the village, where vehicles of all stripes lined the sides of the approach road.

There was an older man in a cowboy hat and two younger men, practically teenagers, who were following what most certainly was the trail that led to the right and up the hillside toward us.

I glanced around at the lack of cover and realized that the precipice where we'd made the climb was at least a half mile away. "Well, hell."

Adan followed my eyes. "Where can we go?"

"You can just continue on toward the monastery, but I'm going to be hard to explain." I glanced at our pack animals. "And if there's shooting, those mules are going to scatter like magpies."

Adan followed me as I began gathering up the animals and pulling them in a line toward the trail about twenty yards from the rock outcropping. "What are you doing?"

"I'm going to hobble them and then half cover myself over by those rocks with my hat over my face. When they get up here, you tell them that I started celebrating a little early and that you're just waiting for me to sober up enough so that we can keep going."

"What about the guns on the pack mule?"

"I'll hide them behind the rocks."

He glanced back down the trail where they would be coming. "And if they find them?"

I pulled Henry's Bowie from the small of my back.

He nodded and began unloading the AKs from the inside canvas packs as I drew out a cotton blanket from the other side and draped it over my shoulders. "I'm thinking if they figure out I'm Anglo, they're probably not going to go for the Bob Lilly thing up here, so don't even try it."

He nodded, carefully placing the rifles nearby in a small opening behind the rocks where they wouldn't be seen. "I won't, but what do we do if you have to shoot them?"

I settled in and took a seat amid the rocks in what shade there was, pulled the blanket up around my face and settled my hat, the big knife held loosely. "We'll cross that bridge after we burn it." As an afterthought, I leaned forward and stuck a few fingers down my throat, heaving, but bringing nothing up.

Adan stood over me. "What are you doing?" Repeating the procedure, I brought up the breakfast the old woman had made for us, and the Doc jumped back.

Clearing my throat, I spat on the ground beside me. "One thing I've learned in almost a half century in law enforcement—drunks puke, and it disinclines closer inspection."

"Are you going to piss your pants next?"

I nodded, pulling my hat back over my face. "If need be."

I listened as he joined the mules, pulled some personal items from the packs, and laid them on the ground with his own blanket.

We waited longer than I would've thought to hear their voices on the trail. Arguing as they approached, it was pretty obvious that stealth wasn't part of their program, until they saw Adan and the mules and became silent.

"*Hola.*" Adan sounded annoyed, and I figured that was a good play. He commented on the weather as near as I could tell and asked them about their day. The older one did the talking, and he didn't seem too suspicious until one of the younger men pointed at me.

Adan let loose with a stream of curses and then began complaining about his drunken companion, and even though I didn't understand that much of it, I could tell the performance was at an Academy Award level.

The younger men stepped in closer and commented on the puke, whereupon Adan cursed again and the two began laughing.

The older one barked at them and then went back to asking Adan questions, which the Doc passed off pretty easily until one exchange that sounded a little sharp.

I tightened my grip on the stag-handled knife.

One of the teenagers had drifted over toward me and said something, and even with my limited vocabulary, I could tell he wanted to wake me up so he could watch me suffer. The older man approached, and it seemed as though the three of them were no more than ten feet away.

Adan said something again, but the response was dismissive. There was a brief conversation about hats among the three, and I saw the muzzle of an AK dip under the brim of mine.

Slowly lifting the knife under the blanket, I was getting ready to move just as a burst of automatic fire ripped the air like a thick sheet of satin being torn. Brushing my hat aside, I looked up as two of them fell, the third scrambling backward and tripping over me as I brought the butt of the Bowie against the back of his head.

I relieved him of his rifle and glanced at the two dead men on either side of me. The mules were crow-hopping, scared but still restrained by the hobbles, and Adan was holding one of the Kalashnikovs, the muzzle still smoking.

"They would have killed you."

We dragged the bodies and lodged them against the rocks in an upright position and then gripped the one I'd knocked in the head. The mules had settled, and Adan had begun reloading the packsaddles with the armament, keeping the AK for himself. "We have to move quickly—they will have heard the gunfire from the monastery."

"Will they send another patrol, do you think?"

"Who knows? With these people weapons are like firecrackers, and with the celebration of the dead there is a lot of shooting."

I gestured toward the bodies. "But these three will come up missing."

"At one point, yes."

I rolled the second teenager over and nudged the American soccer team ball cap from his head and examined the goose egg just behind his ear. "What do you want to do with this one?"

"Cut his throat."

I looked at the kid. He was maybe fifteen. "I can't do that."

Adan aimed the AK. "Then I'll shoot him."

"No."

"Ah, right—better not make more noise." He looked toward the precipice that we had just climbed. "We can throw him off the cliff—less noise."

"No." He stared at me as I gestured toward the unconscious young man. "He's a kid."

"And he's the one who would've likely shot you first."

"Maybe." I studied the teenager. "Back in my county he'd be bird-dogging chicks and saving up to buy a car."

"And in my country, he is selling poison and killing people and then skinning their faces and sewing them on soccer balls."

I stared at him. "They do that?"

"Yes."

Still holding the knife, I stepped between them. "Well, I can't let you kill him. It would be the same as doing it myself."

"A sin of omission?"

"Something like that."

Adan shook his head and continued loading the weaponry onto the mules. I kneeled and slapped the kid's face a few times before his hand came up to brush mine away. He groaned, his eyelids fluttering, and then his eyes settled on me.

"Howdy."

He started to move but stopped when I scratched the side of my neck with the point of the Bowie knife. *"Habla usted inglés?"*

"Um, yeah."

"What's your name?"

He accented the second syllable. "Iván."

"Iván, we've got a problem here, but I'm thinking you and I want the same thing."

He glanced around, getting the lay of the land, his eyes staying on his two dead companions. "What's that?"

"I'd like to keep you alive. . . . Do we agree on that?"

His eyes came back to mine. "Um, yeah."

I pointed at Adan. "He wants you dead, and he's made a pretty convincing argument."

The kid was silent.

"You know who I am?"

He nodded. "The gringo, the Ranger from *el norte*."

"Sheriff." I cleared my throat. "You know why I'm here?"

He paused. "No."

"You lie to me again, and I'll kill you myself."

He nodded. "They have your daughter."

"You've seen her?"

"No, they keep her in the *monasterio*, upstairs, guarded in the central room on the second floor. Two at the doors of the plaza, two at the stairs, and two at the door where they are keeping her. One of them fell asleep two days ago, and they killed him."

Figuring I'd check some of the information I'd gotten from Culpepper, I questioned him a bit more. "How many men?"

"I don't know, I only started working with these guys three days ago."

I nodded. "When does the party start?"

He shrugged. "There is no time, it will just build and happen and then go on through tomorrow."

I met his eyes and stayed there. "Your English is very good, Iván."

He smiled for the first time. "I have an aunt who lives in Tucson, and I spent two summers in your country doing landscaping."

I reached out and took hold of his chin, turning his face toward his two companions. "You should've stuck with the landscaping." I released him, and he slowly turned back to me. "I want you to think about something that's going to be hard for you to understand. These guys are dead, dead and not coming back. There's no reset, no do-over, there's nothing, they are gone." I gestured toward the bodies. "And if they could talk, they would tell you only one thing, that it's better to be alive—you got me?"

"Um, yeah."

"Really?"

"Yes."

I stared into his eyes, looking for a comprehension that wasn't there. "No, you don't, you think you are invincible." I shook my head and gestured for Adan to come closer. "Doc, the face-skinning thing, how do they do it?"

Leading one of the mules, he knelt down next to me, tracing a finger under the kid's jaw and taking the Bowie from my hand. "It truly is an art form. You start by making an incision at the top of the head where you punch through tissue but hit the bone of the skull rather quickly. When you meet the bone you cut down to the neck, which makes a horrible scraping noise but you get used to it." He reached around behind the young man and touched the base of his skull with the knife. "Then you jam your thumbs under the skin and begin unwrapping."

Iván tried to move back, but there was nowhere to go.

"Then you peel the skin over the forehead and begin dispatching the eyelids, which is something of a gooey mess, but nothing compared to the nose, because you have to take some of the cartilage to keep the shape." The knife blade came up, tracing the kid's face. "The mouth is tricky because it's hard to retain the shape there too, you know?"

The kid heaved, just a bit.

"Then you have to decide how much of the scalp you want, but that depends on the soccer ball. . . ."

The kid gagged.

Adan nodded. "For most faces a full-size soccer ball is too big, so they tend to use the balls they make for juniors."

I examined Iván's head. "Do you do it before or after they're dead?"

"Depends. You can do it with them alive, but you need a couple of men to hold them down." He gestured with the big knife. "I can show you if you would like."

"We'll wait." I took the Bowie and turned back to the kid. "The way I figure it, we can let you go down the trail we just came up, never to come back here, and you move on to a better life, or you can have some random kids in some nameless village scoring goals with your face."

He stared at me.

"Which is it going to be?"

He took a moment to speak, and his voice was a little shaky. "I will go down the trail."

"Smart choice, but remember, don't turn back." I stood along with Adan, and we looked down at him. "There are men in the village you just came from who are going to die in the next twenty-four hours, and you don't have to be one of them."

He wanted to stand, and I let him. He was careful not to step on his comrades. "Okay."

I hid the stag-handled knife. "One more thing, Iván."

"Yes?"

"Throw your buddies off the cliff."

———————

"Do you believe he had the nerve to ask for one of the mules?"

We shared the last of the canteen water and watched as the kid disappeared down the trail we had come up. "You don't think we should've given him water?"

Adan shook his head and hung the canteen over his shoulder. "There's a river—I don't think he can miss it."

"You can lead a teenager to water . . ." Letting the words trail off as I gathered my mule and walked her back toward the outcropping, I looked up at the sun and saw the image of two women, one of them all dressed up for her senior prom being twirled at arm's length by her mother in our tiny rented house— the moment so brilliant I was sure that like looking at the sun, I would most certainly go blind.

"Are you all right?"

I turned to look at Adan. "What time would you say it is?"

He glanced at his wristwatch. "Two."

"How long before they send out another patrol to look for this one?"

Adan got his own mule as I rounded up the two pack animals, preparing to pony them behind me. "Who knows?"

"Think we can work our way down the trail they came up and get behind the wall that leads to the monastery before dark?"

"Not without being seen, but with the amount of people arriving it is possible we can approach without appearing too suspicious."

We walked to the precipice and looked down where more vehicles were parked and the streets showed a little more activity. Adan pointed to the round building. "There's some activity there also, but if we can get past those two spots, it could be done." He looked again. "We can't get the mules over the wall, so they will have to stay near the sale barn, but they are mules, so no one should question their presence."

I climbed on my ride and patted her withers. "I'm beginning to like my gal."

Adan climbed aboard his mule and swung around to look at me. "Hopefully you will see her again tonight when we are making a quiet and leisurely escape with your daughter." He looked past me, and I turned, hoping I wouldn't see that the teenager was stupid enough to be coming back, but the trail was empty.

"Today is the Día de los Inocentes, so you have done your part."

"Feels good, doesn't it?"

The look he gave me told me he was not so sure. "But tomorrow is the Día de los Muertos—it would be nice if we did not have to join their ranks."

Gigging my mule, I road past him toward the village below. "Can I ask you a question?"

"Sure."

"How come you know so much about skinning the faces off of human skulls?"

He studied me for a good long time. "Well, from first-year medical school basic anatomy class." He smiled. "The rest I made up."

8

The mules wouldn't go near the walls with the signs plastered on them that read NO FUMAR, and when I climbed up one of the buttresses, I could see why. I lowered myself and stepped back from the crumbling edifice and stood there just trying to breathe.

"Are you all right?" Adan, holding the skittish mules, stood a little away. "What is it?"

I shook my head and looked over the hill. "We'll tie them off to that hitching post behind the sale barn. I doubt anybody will mess with them all the way back there."

Adan took the mules over. "Then we go over the wall and make our way to the monastery?"

Tying off Rucia and the pack animals, I took another breath.

It was then that a young couple came around the barn, kissing on each other and probably looking for a secluded spot. Adan froze but then reached for the canvas packs.

"Get the hell out of here!"

They stood there.

"Did you hear me?" I moved, advancing toward them. "I said to get the hell out of here now!"

Adan yelled, *"Váyanse!"*

The young couple tripped over themselves and disappeared.

Shaking with anger, I turned and looked at Adan. "What do they think this place is, Disneyland?"

He finished tying off the mules. "What is wrong with you?"

"What is wrong with this country, with these people?" I gestured toward the tiny village. "These people are monsters, murderers—you don't associate yourself with these kinds of animals."

He waited a moment, petting the rump of one of the mules before responding. "I think you are being unfair to the animals."

"You're damn right I am."

He nodded toward the wall. "What did you see?"

"Men, women, children . . ." I shook my head. "Bodies, dozens of them tied up and piled in the space between the wall and the cliffs. They're just lying there, some of them hacked up like a charnel house sliding off the edge."

He glanced at the wall. "Why can we not smell them?"

"Residual sulfur from the mines, and they threw lime on them as well, which means that some of them were butchered recently." He stared at me. "Arms, legs, torsos, heads . . ."

"Was . . . ?"

"Not that I could see." I reached out and stroked the sweat off the back of the mule. "Why do they do that, cut them up?"

"Each dismemberment stands for a different punishment in the narco culture. The hands are for thieves, the legs for attempting to escape, the heads for betrayal or territorial influence."

I laid an arm over the back of the mule.

He nodded and then looked at the wall. "I can disguise myself enough to get to the monastery on this side, but I'm afraid the only way you can get there is to go over the wall, my friend."

I accepted the inevitable. "Do we have to worry about that couple?"

"No, they'll be too scared to remark on their interaction with us—afraid of who we are and that they might be killed."

I nodded. "I just work my way to the left and then what?"

"The walls are staggered so when you get to the monastery you can climb over—but be careful, I'm not sure what's on the other side. If there are too many people, simply wait for me to find you."

I nodded, pulling the canvas bags from the packsaddle. "You want a weapon?"

He patted the small of his back. "I have one."

"I'll take the rest."

"Are you sure you don't want to stash them somewhere?"

Slipping the straps of the canvas bags onto my shoulders, I studied the distance to the monastery. "No, I want them with me in case anything happens."

"We won't be able to find out much until this evening, but I can roam around a bit and explore the area; maybe talk to some people and see if I can get more information on exactly where she is."

I started toward the graveyard. "Be careful."

I put a foot on the buttress and pushed the canvas bags on the top of the wall. Bellying up, I swung a leg over and glanced around, but the only other person I saw was Adan as he climbed the small hill and disappeared around the stone building.

Concentrating on the work at hand, I leaned down and lowered the two bags to the ground where there was a clear space and then rolled off the top, landing heavily but avoiding the macabre footing.

As I looked more closely, I could see that the body parts were not simply dumped in this small canyon but that they stretched around the bulge ahead, lining the way as far as I could see.

The smell of decay was strong on this side of the escarpment, and I pulled the bandana from my jean pocket and tied it around my face. I started off with the bags and stumbled along the uneven ground and the rocks, trying to avoid stepping on anything human and keeping my eyes to the left where I wouldn't have to look at the bodies.

I'd done pretty well until I slipped on something. I fell against the wall but was able to catch myself. I just stood there. Under my boot was a hand, the skin desiccated and the bones broken.

Breathing shallowly, I started off again.

"I killed the son of a bitch."

I scooted my chair closer to the hospital bed in hopes that she wouldn't raise her voice any more. "You shot him, yes . . ."

"Fourteen times." She raised a hand to run fingers through her raven hair, the IV trailing along with her arm as one tarnished golden eye focused on me. "No sign of him at all?"

"Nothing." We'd searched every exit way in the canyon in an attempt to find some sign of Tomás Bidarte but had found nothing, not even a drop of blood. "Henry checked everywhere, and he doesn't miss anything."

"I hit him, I know I did." She dropped her hand and winced, then lifting it again grazed the spot where the stiletto knife Bidarte had thrown had entered her body, depriving her of the ability to ever have a child and killing the child who had been there. "You know?"

"I do."

After a while, I could hear people talking. I wasn't sure how far off they were, but it sounded like more and more of them were gathering on the other side of the wall. I'd passed through the killing field and sat in the shade of the rough stone.

The back side of the monastery was sheer rock with only a few windows overlooking a crevasse. It had been a few hours into my sojourn, and I'd taken off my hat. Swiping the sweat from my forehead with a shirtsleeve, I watched as a large woman started stringing some laundry on a line hanging from one of the windows. She'd been unable to see me, considering the vantage point, and once again it made me feel better seeing somebody doing something normal amid all the abnormality I'd witnessed in the last few days.

I'd watched until she'd ducked back inside and then slipped my hat back on before realizing it was Alexia Mendez.

I immediately stood and looked at the laundry line, which was tied to a sturdy young pine holding on to life and a rocky purchase at the base of the cliff. Yanking the binoculars from the bag, I focused the M19s on the window, but I was too late.

To get to the tree where the pulley was attached, I'd have to get frighteningly near the drop-off and would be in plain sight of the half dozen or so windows. I hadn't seen any activity other than my daughter's housekeeper, but that didn't mean there wasn't somebody in them, looking out.

I also didn't really know if I could trust her—she could have been kidnapped along with Cady or it was possible she was in league with Bidarte even with Culpepper's opinion that she was not. Given that Culpepper had killed her nephew, I decided to give her the benefit of the doubt.

I glanced at the windows and figured I could cut the line free and then return to the base of the building and climb my way up—it was also possible that I could sprout wings and just fly up there.

One thing at a time.

Making sure my .45 was tucked in tight and the binoculars were around my neck, I scrambled over the rocks toward the base of the tree, careful to keep my footing and not fall into the crevasse, which led who knew where.

I stepped behind the trunk and stood there for a moment before glancing around and then looking back at the monastery windows. About half of them were shuttered closed, and there was no glass in the three that were open, off-white curtains drifting in the slight breeze. The one where the laundry line was hooked was toward the middle and the highest up, of course, about sixty feet if it was an inch.

I pulled myself onto one of the lower limbs and climbed up the back side so as to not be seen, settling into a notch and finally reaching the sand-cast metal pulley, threaded into the end of a piece of hand-forged iron, a heavy hook that was hanging around one of the branches.

The line was a weathered hemp rope, and I was amazed it even held the dozen or so pieces of laundry—so much for that idea. Frustrated, I pulled on the rope and watched the clothes sway and tried to think of a way to let Alexia and Cady know that I was there. I had nothing with me that I could use to write a note.

I had a thought, and I began pulling the line toward me, immediately recognizing the blue blouse my daughter had been wearing when I saw her last in Cheyenne. I reached out and took hold of it and could smell her on it, even through the laundry soap. Tears filled my eyes as I reached into my shirt pocket and slipped out my wallet, pulling my badge and pinning it to the light blue fabric, the six-point star shining like a vow of vengeance.

Running the line through my hands, I began working it

back the other way when I froze, seeing someone in one of the other windows, a dark-haired man in sunglasses, who luckily only seemed to be interested in the sky.

Edging behind the trunk of the tree, I stayed there, waiting until he yawned and disappeared. I waited a minute more and then began moving the line at a slower pace, pulling the first piece of clothing up against the stone wall, something I hoped Alexia might find strange.

I looked through the lenses of the M19s and searched the windows, starting with the one where I'd seen her, but all I could make out were the gauze curtains. I must've kept the lenses on the window for ten minutes, but nothing showed, so I began working over the others, finally settling on the one in the lower right where a shadow played off an opposing wall.

I had just pushed my hat back to wipe the sweat away from my eyes when I noticed movement on the clothesline and turned to look up in time to see the blue blouse disappear.

I waited until Alexia appeared in the window again after about ten minutes. She re-pinned the blouse to the line and began threading it back toward me. The badge was gone, and in its place was a folded envelope, attached to the line with a clothespin.

DADDY!

Oh, my God what are you doing? Alexia says that you're outside. Where's Lola? Is she safe? Who do you have with you? Henry, Vic, the FBI, CIA, the Marines? I can't believe you found me. I'm okay, but this place is a madhouse. Please be careful, these people are insane. I'm locked up in one of the second floor rooms, but

Alexia got this envelope and a pencil to me. Thank
goodness she's here or I think I would've lost my mind.
What do you need us to do?
    I LOVE YOU!

                        Cady

Reveling in the fact that it had been in her hands only moments ago, I watched my hands shaking as I reread the note. A stubby pencil that she must have used to write the note was in the envelope, so I pulled it out and began composing a response. There was no plan, so I stuck to the things I wanted to tell her.

Punk,

Lola is safe back home with Henry. I've got people with
me and more on the way, so sit tight and just be ready
because no matter what, we are coming.
    I love you, too.

                        Dad

I reattached the envelope to the blouse with the clothespin and waited until it slowly began bobbing back toward the window. I waited a few more minutes and gave the sky a look, the sun now angling over the precipice behind the monastery. There was a sudden coolness and before long it would be dark. I looked west but couldn't see any hoped-for clouds, just the clear but faded blue over the Chihuahuan desert.

I had carefully climbed down the tree and made my way back up the scrabble and rocks to the base of the wall. I sat there, thinking about what I wanted to do with this new information, the location of the room not collating with what I'd gotten from Culpepper or Iván. Anyway, it appeared we were going to have to make a more frontal assault.

People were cheering and chanting along with the cacophony of the music, and I was losing my patience and about ready to just climb over the wall to see what was going on for myself when something bobbed against the brim of my hat. Tilting my head back, I could see that it was a pony bottle of Pacifico beer hanging from a piece of twine. Looking further, I could see Adan holding the other end.

He glanced around as if admiring the countryside as I untied the bottle and then slowly wrapped the twine around a few fingers, palming a beat on the top of the wall mimicking the drums that were now thrumming in the square with trumpets sounding in counterpoint.

I continued to watch him, but after a moment he turned and greeted someone. I listened to him and another man, talking and laughing as their voices faded off into the fiesta, or whatever it was called.

Looking at the condensate rolling off the small bottle of beer, I thought about whether a negligible amount of alcohol was allowable. I decided that it was preferable to dying of thirst and took a swig, and it was the best beer I'd ever tasted. When I lowered the bottle, I noticed that I'd drunk half the thing with one swallow.

I took off my hat and sat there thinking about what I had planned; I wasn't really sure if it was going to work. If we were able to overpower the first team, we might have a chance of working up the ladder, but that was going to take a lot of skill and a lot of luck—neither of which we had in abundance.

I looked back up at the wall and gauged the distance from

there to any of the windows. The first set, which included the open one, was about twenty feet up, but then I studied the shuttered windows and thought that maybe if they led to uninhabited rooms, they might provide a better route inside, making up for that lack of skill and luck.

I needed rope and a grappling hook.

I looked at the tree from which I had just recently climbed down, where the makeshift clothesline was attached to the pulley on the hook. The hemp rope might not hold me, but the hook would.

Rope, where in the hell was I going to find twenty or so feet of rope that would hold my weight?

The bodies.

The bodies back where we'd left the mules—some of them had been tied.

I hoisted myself up with the weight of a man returning to hell and started off from whence I'd come.

None of the pieces of rope were long enough in themselves, but I was able to collect enough pieces so that I could fashion a line almost twenty feet long, and I figured the knots were going to be handy in the ascent.

Adan would be a lot better at climbing than I would, but he wasn't around, and I didn't want him losing his position. The other trick was letting him know what the heck I was doing so that we could coordinate our actions.

Waiting there with the rope and hook, I kept looking up and down the wall, but he didn't show, and neither did anybody else as the noise from the crowd, the drums, and the horns continued to escalate.

I walked back to the monastery, looked up at the laundry line hanging limp, and wished Alexia would reappear.

I chose one of the assault rifles from the pack bags, loaded the magazine, and yanked the action before setting the safety. I also grabbed a brick of ammo, placed it in the Dallas Cowboys bag, and slipped the straps of both over my shoulder.

The one partially open window on the first floor on the far right was inviting as a target and really my only choice as I was pretty sure I wasn't going to be able to hook on to a shutter of one of the closed windows without a great deal of noise, and I was also pretty sure that the rotten wood would pull right off the wall.

Hoping I wasn't throwing the grappling hook into a poker game of armed men, I relied on my calf-roping skills and began twirling the heavy hook; with every turn I thought about what a harebrained idea this was.

I glanced back at the wall where Adan had been, but there was still nobody there. I twirled the thing a few more times and then let it fly, which it did, entering the opening and making what would have been a loud thump if there hadn't been all the racket from the town's party. Pulling the rope, I felt a little resistance, then a touch more before it clanged off the rocks and landed at my feet.

This kind of thing never happened to Errol Flynn or Will Rogers.

Picking up the hook, I tried to calculate the angle of the point in hopes that it might catch on something if I got enough English on it, twirled, and threw again. The same sound was covered by the same noise, but I was a little more careful when I pulled the contraption back and it caught on something. I breathed a sigh. Tugging with one hand, I felt the hook set and just hoped it was in something that would carry my weight.

I checked it with both hands and felt it sink deeper.

I jumped for the nearest knot and pulled, immediately regretting every part of this plan. Struggling to get a hand up to the next knot and then the next, I climbed the best I could and figured I had reached about halfway.

I hung there for a moment and then reached up without the benefit of another knot, slipping a bit as I brought my boots up against the wall. I grabbed for the next knot and one fist over the other made good progress, ending up only about three feet from the ledge of the window.

Grabbing the last hitch, I lifted myself again and finally throwing a hand over the sill, I clambered up, chucking a leg over and tumbling inside, making a terrible racket when I hit the floor. I scrambled back toward the window, pulled the AK around in front of me, and switched off the safety.

Breathing heavily, I sat there letting my eyes acclimate to the darkness, the only light coming from the moon, which had risen large and orange in the eastern sky. There was no movement, and as my breathing slowed, I stood, pulled the rope up and out of the way, and moved next to the wall so as not to be any more of a target. With rows of boxes piled up to the ceiling, I was pretty sure the room was being used as storage.

I nudged one of the top boxes with the barrel of the AK, caught it before it hit the floor and flipped the stapled flap back, revealing stacks of taped packets about the size of a ten-pound bag of ice. It didn't take much imagination to figure out what the stuff was. There were smaller boxes by the door, so I quietly stepped across the room and kneeled down to pull one open, finding plastic-wrapped bundles of US currency hundred-dollar bills. Judging from the ample amount of small boxes, I estimated there were millions.

I studied the door, heavy and wooden with hand-forged hinges, handle, and lock. Moving to one side, I brought the AK up again and tried the handle, which did not move.

"Well, hell." I'd scaled the wall of the place just to be locked in a twelve-by-twelve room.

I kneeled and spotted the hole where the key would have been inserted. I went back to the box of drugs that I had opened and noticed that there were a couple of large staples that had held the top closed. I crept over and pulled one out of the cardboard.

I'd monkeyed around with these kinds of locks before on the basement door of our office back in Durant and had found them not so difficult to pick. I straightened one side of the staple and left an angle on the other for a little leverage as I inserted the straight end and began threading it around. Finally feeling a little tension, I jammed it to the right.

The door jumped just a touch and then pulled loose from the jamb about an inch.

Frozen, I stayed there without moving, pretty sure that if anybody was in the hallway outside they would've had to have heard the noise or seen the movement. I placed my ear to the opening but didn't hear any footsteps coming toward me.

Easing to a standing position, I leaned against the wall and nudged the muzzle of the automatic weapon through the opening and peered out with one eye. As near as I could tell, I was at the end of an empty hallway. Figuring that if there was anybody in the corridor I'd at least have the thickness of the door between me and them, I pushed it open a bit farther.

The arched hallway shot off to my right, narrow, with just a few small alcoves where lit candles dripped onto the stone floor. There was a blue light coming from a partially opened doorway at the far end of the hall, like one from a TV, but the only sound I could hear was the noise coming from out front.

Easing through, I led with the AK and followed with the Dallas Cowboy bag.

I closed the door behind me, careful not to close it completely in case I needed to beat a hasty retreat, and then took a few steps forward, studying each door as I passed it, each one closed like the others with no light from inside.

I got within sight of the last door. The bluish light that spilled out changed and fluctuated, and I was pretty sure that it was indeed a television, but there was no music or dialogue, just a strange, reoccurring plastic sound that was almost like Ruby typing back at the office.

Edging a bit farther along, I could see metal shelves, racks of electronic equipment like computer servers, and other communication devices with lights going on and off in sequence. Leaning in, I could see the edge of a large, flatscreen television and the back of somebody's head with a ball cap on backward and a set of headphones covering his ears.

There was a stunning amount of muffled noise coming from the headphones, and as I stepped sideways again I could see that it was some kind of video game with a person aiming a sighted rifle and a squad of individuals fighting their war across a dystopian, urban landscape, all the while impressively blowing things up and shooting everything in sight.

I stood there in the doorway looking at the individual in the room, his back to me, humming as he operated the game with the keyboard in his lap, completely unaware that I was there.

He had long, blond dreadlocks and was wearing a white San Diego Padres T-shirt, jeans, and a pair of leather sandals with flowers between the toes.

I thought about shooting the TV for effect but figured that would just bring the whole monastery down on me, so I waited a moment and then reached out and tapped his shoulder.

He didn't respond, so I nudged him again.

"Go away, I'm Arma-Battlefield four—"

I poked at him this time.

"I told you, man, beat it."

Bumping him one last time, I placed the barrel of the AK plainly in his line of sight, mimicking the weapon on the screen, and leaning around to look at the other side of his face. "Howdy, Peter."

"All I do is run the computers, man, honest."

I sat on the table in front of him, the AK resting easily in my hands and uneasily against his skinny chest. "You did surveillance on my family."

"No, I—"

I tapped him with the muzzle, thirty 7.62x39mm rounds ready to fly through the space where his heart was at 2,350 feet per second.

His hands strained against the zip-ties that I had used to attach them to the arms of the gaming chair. "Okay, yeah, I did. Your family, they're sweet . . . I mean your daughter is a knockout. Hell, I'd date her."

"Chances of that are slim." I leaned in. "Look, Peter, or whatever your name really is, I'm here to get my daughter and then get the hell out by killing the smallest number of people possible, and right now you are ruining my plan."

He looked at me. "You're here by yourself?"

I ignored his question. "Where is Cady?"

"I don't know."

I poked him again.

"She's on one of the upper floors, but I don't know where. Nobody is allowed up there. I mean, you go up there and they kill you in strange and sickening ways."

"Bidarte?"

"Who else?" He paused for a moment and then volunteered, "They have a camera in her room."

"You can see her?"

"Yeah."

"Show me." He did as I asked, his fingers tapping the keyboard as the image switched to a bird's-eye view of a room with a stone floor and a few carpets. The screen was huge, and I watched as Cady came into view. She walked past the camera with something in her hand.

"Can I talk to her?"

"No, it's just a camera, man."

Reaching out, I touched the screen as she stopped and looked up at us, unmoving. "How do I get there?"

"There are steps, but there are dudes, armed dudes, man."

I nudged him with the Kalashnikov again, reminding him I was an armed dude, too. "Nobody ever goes up there bringing food, laundry, nothing?"

"Well, yeah. I mean the housekeeper they brought, she goes back and forth, but nobody else."

"My daughter's housekeeper, Alexia?"

"Yeah, she tried to scratch Bidarte's eyes out, but he promised her that if she didn't do what he said, he'd kill your daughter, or worse." He bit a lip and then looked up at me. "Hey, man? I am so totally ready to get the fuck out of here." I stared at him, and the next words came out in a rush. "This is too much, I mean the guy is loco, you know what I mean?"

"Yep."

He shrugged a shoulder, lacking the means to gesture. "I might as well be a prisoner around here myself—and there doesn't seem to be any kind of retirement program in the outfit, if you know what I mean?"

"I do."

His eyes suddenly became more intense. "Get me the fuck out of here, and I'll do anything you want."

I thought about it. "Is this the communications center?" I glanced around at the banks of equipment. "All this?"

"Yeah."

"Is there a phone, one that'll reach the US?"

He smiled. "You mean like one you drop a quarter into? No . . ."

"Well, that's disappointing."

"Dude, I've got satellite, ultra-high-speed internet, six-G, high-def. . . ." He nodded toward the wide-screen TV behind me. "I can personal interface you with anybody in the world in seconds." He laughed. "All I need is a phone number, email address, anything! Who do you want to talk to?"

Pulling out my wallet, I extracted FBI Special Agent-in-Charge Mike McGroder's card and started to hand it to him. "I'm assuming you can do this with one hand?"

He sighed. "Slowly."

"Right or left?"

"Left."

"Figures." I pulled the Case knife from my back pocket, flicked it open, and slid it through the nylon tie, releasing his hand as I stood and moved to the side, pushing him back to the table with my hip and placing the Fed's card on the desk in front of him. "Make magic."

His fingers swept across the keyboard before reaching out and pulling the headphone plug free. Immediately I heard a ringing, but the TV remained black.

After a few more rings, the screen suddenly leapt to life, and we were treated to the foreshortened image of McGroder's face in what I assumed was his office in El Paso. "Whoever this is, you better have a damn good reason for bothering me when . . ."

Peter Lowery looked up at me as I leaned in over his shoulder. "Do you want them to see us?"

"Sure."

He hit another key and there was a blip as McGroder stared at the screen, silent and unmoving.

I glanced at the electronics expert. "Did it work?"

My answer came from the FBI man. "Holy Mary Mother of God."

I grinned my most becoming smile and tipped my hat. "Howdy."

His eyes darted above the screen and around his room as people began crowding him, along with a dark-haired woman with gorgeous, tarnished gold eyes. "Where in the wide world of fuck are you?!"

9

"It was that maniac Guzmán." McGroder buried his face in his hands. "I never should've put the two of you together."

I lowered my head so that I could be seen, even though I had no idea where the camera was. "Mike, there's no way you would've let me do what I needed to do when I needed to do it, and he was very helpful . . . along with a number of other people."

He peered at me through his fingers. "What other people?"

"Other people, on a purely unofficial basis." I gestured toward the blond Rastafarian. "Peter Lowery for one, who has agreed to help me so long as we don't pursue further prosecution against him."

"What? Who? What?"

"Try and stay with me here, Mike."

"Is the Seer with you?"

"At this juncture, no. I deemed it irresponsible to have a blind, legless soothsayer along at this stage."

"Irresponsible? Irresponsible? I'm glad to hear at this stage that there's anything you deem irresponsible!"

Vic pushed the FBI man aside. "I repeat—where in the wide-world-of-fuck are you?"

I tried to remember exactly what Adan had said to me. "Far-ther south than Médanos de Samalayuca Nature Preserve in a place called Estante del Diablo, a monastery—Monasterio del Corazón Ardiente—near a town by the name of Torero." I glanced at Lowery, still attached to the chair, rather proud of myself. "How was my pronunciation?"

"I couldn't understand a word you were saying, man."

I gestured toward the computer. "Can you give them the coordinates of this place?"

He reached across and began typing. "I can give them the coordinates of this room."

I glanced at the screen as Vic crowded in again. "What's the current situation?"

"Difficult to say." I glanced at Lowery. "I've just arrived, and I'm inside." I lifted the AK. "Heavily armed, and I'm getting ready to do a little reconnoitering to try and find out exactly where they're keeping Cady."

"Stop." McGroder stuck a finger out at the screen. "Whatever you're doing is going to get you killed and possibly create an international incident. Now that we know where you are we can come to you."

"When?"

He hesitated. "Well, we have to negotiate things with the Mexican authorities . . ."

I shook my head. "Can't wait that long."

"It's a foreign country, Walt, we have to go through channels."

"Mike, it's Cady. I need to get to her now."

"Just give me a few hours . . ."

"I gotta go."

"Can we contact you through this number?" His eyes played across the screen. "What is this number?"

I glanced at Lowery again, who shrugged. "It's a private server and IP address, but I can unblock it."

Vic interrupted. "How are you?"

"I'm okay, but the fun's about to begin, and I wish you guys could be here with me with a team of Navy SEALs, a squad of Army Green Berets, or a patrol of MARSOC Marines."

She glanced at McGroder and then gave me a curt nod. "We're on our way to you now."

I felt better with that thought. "Be careful, these guys are kind of ruthless."

Vic leaned in, her dark hair swinging forward like a curtain on the third act. "So, these motherfuckers are soon to learn, are we."

I watched as Lowery typed some more and then when he hit one final key, the civilized world disappeared. Taking a deep breath, I stood. "Okay, which way is up?"

He was about to speak when there was a heavy knock on the door behind me. I raised the AK and flipped off the safety lever, but Peter lifted his hand and motioned for me to step back toward the wall behind the door. I did as he directed but kept the rifle aimed at whoever was on the other side.

Lowery hit a few more keys, and the video game materialized back on the screen, frozen in mid–submachine gun blast. "Yeah?"

The door opened about halfway, and a man with a thick Mexican accent grunted. "You okay, *soldado*?"

I watched as Peter gestured toward the screen. "Yeah, just catching up on my mad game skills, *Jefe*."

"Right. You gonna show me those tricks to get me to Arma-Battlefield two?"

"Yeah, yeah, I'm just a little busy right now."

"You coming to the party? It's getting wild out there—lots of *puta*-poontang."

"Maybe later."

There was a long pause.

"*Amigo*, why is your hand tied to the chair?"

There was an even longer pause.

"Because I'm right-handed, and sometimes I immobilize it and force myself to play with my left so that I can get better with it."

"I thought you were left-handed?"

". . . No, right."

The man leaned against the doorjamb. "I sometimes do that when I beat off."

Yet an even longer pause.

". . . Cool."

"Hombre Cabeza is making an announcement later, make sure you don't miss it."

"Not on my life."

"Don't joke about that."

"Yeah."

The door closed, and we both listened to his footsteps fade, and I sighed, stepped away from the wall, and whispered, "That was very well done."

"Yeah, and more information than I really wanted."

Taking Henry's knife from the small of my back, I slipped it through the nylon zip-tie, freeing his other hand. "There isn't any back way to the second floor, I suppose."

"Um, no." He thought about it. "I mean, there's a stairway outside in the plaza by the front door along with the one on the inside, but there are armed dudes there, at the base of the inside stairs, and there's supposed to be two more at the door upstairs." He looked at me. "Why don't you just wait, like they said?"

"Not in my nature." I returned the stag-handled Bowie to the waistband at my back and glanced at the door. "Is there anything that would get those guys to move?"

"Not really, there was a guy that fell asleep—"

"Yep, I've heard the story." Going to the door, I looked back at him. "What about food or a changing of the guard—and how many guards are there and do they know each other?"

"I don't know, man—I know there's a turnover because Bidarte keeps killing them. That's the head of security's deal—Culpepper. You meet him yet? He can be a real pain in the ass, but you know I haven't seen him around lately. Shit, maybe Bidarte killed him."

"Maybe." I threw a thumb toward the corridor. "Are there any rooms across the hallway that face the plaza, so I can get a look-see? I mean ones that aren't full of armed, umm, dudes?"

"The rooms at the end of the hallway are used for storage, but they're mostly unlocked."

"Nice security you've got here."

He smiled and shook his head. "Nobody steals from Hombre Cabeza, man. You know how he got that name, Head Man?"

"Because he's the boss?"

"No, because he skins the faces off of—"

"I've heard that one, too."

He looked at me questioningly. "About the soccer balls?"

"Yep."

He shrugged. "You don't scare easy, do you?"

"Nope."

"Yeah, there's nobody in this wing but me and storage."

I cracked the door, and the sound of the drums, horns, and crowd resonated through the building. "How long does this party last?"

"Tonight and tomorrow—or as long as the crack, marijuana, cocaine, heroin, alcohol, and overly active libidos hold out. Then they have the auction."

"The what?"

"The auction will be tomorrow night, after everybody is good and wasted and ready to spend some money."

"What do they auction?"

He looked at me like I was the last passenger on the last bus from Dumbassville. "You don't want to know, man."

I'd moved a number of the boxes that were covering the windows from one of the rooms in the corridor so that I could see part of the plaza and to give me cover in case anybody happened to come in. There were shutters, but I adjusted the louvers so that I could also see the stretch of the wall where Adan had lowered me the beer.

I was thinking about the auctions, and the bodies on the other side of the wall behind the barn—the unfortunates who I guess hadn't been lucky enough to have found a buyer.

Evidently, it was the way Bidarte got rid of unwanted employees or people who had fallen into his hands whom he had no use for. Lowery said the sale was usually held once a month, but that this one was a big one. I could only think of my daughter upstairs and what he had in mind for her.

Watching the young people through the shutter, I shook my head and wondered if they knew what kind of game they were playing. Maybe that's the way it was here, that life had little meaning and the span not so great, so you might as well have a good time while you can.

The tiny portion of the Day of the Dead torchlight fiesta that I could see was in full swing with everyone either with garishly painted faces or wearing skull masks. They were drinking and dancing and pawing each other, and I was wondering what I could do to get Adan's attention if I saw him.

I had kept the empty pony bottle, because even in this hell-hole of trash and death, I hated to litter, so thinking of how he'd gotten my attention, I reached into the gym bag at my boots and pulled out the bottle and some twine that had unraveled from the hemp rope I'd thrown together to climb the building. There was enough of the stuff to tie around the bottle and slip it under the bottom of the shutters. I tied it off on a loose nail head and waited, hoping that if he walked by, he would notice it.

The drums and the horns continued playing what sounded like the same song over and over, and I rested my head against the stone wall, which was cool and felt good. I looped the string around my finger and had closed my eyes for what I thought was just a moment; then I felt something pulling at the bottle.

Adan wore a skull mask and top hat. He was carrying a torch and was looking around, refusing offers from quite a few women and quite a few men.

There was an old oak barrel in front of the wall and he grabbed it, tipped it, and rolled it in front of the window. Standing on it, he pretended to watch the festivities from a higher vantage point.

He turned his head, speaking from under the papier-mâché mask. "How do I look?"

"Like a dead Fred Astaire."

"What are you doing in there?"

"I found a way in, and we've got someone on our side."

"Who?"

I hunkered near the window. "What does it matter, we can use all the help we can get."

"Just remember what your friend said about not trusting anyone."

"Well, he let me get a call in to the FBI, and they're on their way."

"When?"

"Well, they weren't exactly clear on that."

He leaned back. "With what?"

"We didn't get to that part either."

He sighed and looked around, still selling the idea that he was watching the festivities. "We will stick with the original plan in hopes that we can get out of here with your daughter and our lives. Have you found where she is?"

"As near as I can tell, it's like Culpepper told us, she's on the second floor but heavily guarded every step of the way."

"Ideas?"

"I've got one, but it's not the best."

He turned his head once more. "So it's a bad plan?"

"Better than no plan at all."

"Not necessarily."

"Do you think you can get inside the building?"

"Maybe."

"Can you get a few more masks?"

"Probably."

"There's just one more thing. . . . We need another guy."

"This is a bad plan, man."

"Just put your mask on while we figure out where to put all your damned hair." I stuffed the dreadlocks into the top hat and pushed it down on his head. "There, your own mother wouldn't know you."

The skull mask rattled as he spoke. "I never knew my mother."

"Well . . . There you have it." I turned to glance at Adan,

who looked much more convincing than Lowery. "You're sure you can't find somebody who is really Mexican out there?"

He glanced around the communications room. "In this group? That we can trust? No."

"So what all did you find out?"

"Not a lot. Bidarte is supposed to be making a celebratory speech later this evening, but the party goes through tomorrow and tomorrow night there's the auction."

"I heard about that and saw the aftermath on the other side of that wall behind the sale barn."

He turned to look at me. "We should probably get your daughter out of here before then."

"Agreed." I opened the gym bag and took the magazine from the AK and began pushing the rounds out, emptying it entirely; after reattaching the magazine, I handed it back to Lowery.

"I get the rifle but no bullets?"

I gestured toward the computer screen. "I've seen you shoot—you're lucky I let you carry one at all." I turned back to Adan. "You still have your pistol?"

He pulled it from his trousers. "Yes."

I nodded and began sliding zip-ties onto my wrists until there were about a half dozen on each arm. "There, that should work unless they get really curious." I looked up at them. "Okay, here's the deal. We use the inside stairwell, because there will be less spectators, but the trick is getting these guys down without alerting the ones upstairs—so no shooting. If they hear us, it's all over."

Lowery slanted his head to one side. "So what do we use, our scary masks?"

"You don't do anything—my friend here will take one and I'll take the other." I turned back to the Doc. "Look, I know there are two men downstairs and two upstairs, but there might be more than that, so if you want to back out of this, now's the time."

Adan shrugged.

Lowery glanced at him and then back at me. "Fuckin'-A, I want out."

"You don't get to choose."

He gestured toward Adan. "Why the hell not, he does."

"I'm not paying him."

"What are you paying me?"

I nudged him toward the door. "Your life."

"Lotta good that's going to do us spilling out here on the floor riddled with bullets."

I opened the door, peeking around but not seeing anything. "C'mon."

They followed, but I stalled out and turned to Lowery. "You lead, but let Adan do the talking." He slipped by, plastering himself against the wall and swiveling his head, looking all the world like a bad TV cop. "What are you doing?"

"Clearing the hallway; clear and sweep, man."

"We're supposed to be acting like we belong here."

"Oh."

I nodded toward Adan to take the lead—he didn't know the layout of the building, but at least he wouldn't get us killed. We followed as I nudged Lowery to the rear. "Keep the AK trained on me at all times, got it?"

He nodded, some of the hair creeping from under his hat. "Got it."

Adan followed the hallway that led us to a larger opening that looked like it would lead outside, so he went through another smaller archway to our right. There were lights every ten feet or so, electric ones now that we approached the center of the building, which cast a golden glow on the uneven walls. If not for current circumstance, it was a beautiful place.

Adan suddenly pulled up short and held up two fingers.

Showtime.

I reached behind me, finding the muzzle of Lowery's AK, and pulled it into my back. "C'mon."

As we rounded a corner, I could see that there was a stairwell leading to the right and a landing where the stairs changed direction and continued up. The two guards were looking at us as we approached, and I held my hands together and my head down.

A rough-looking one glanced past Adan at me. *"Qué está sucediendo?"*

"Tenemos él que el jefe estaba buscando."

He stooped a little to look under the brim of my hat. *"Quién?"*

"El sheriff."

"Ah . . ."

As he finished the statement, Adan hit the man on the back of his head with the pistol with enough force to practically kill him, and he dropped like a poleaxed steer.

I threw myself at the other one, slamming him into the wall and knocking out his air. Grabbing the Kalishnikov from a stunned Lowery, I popped the guard on the side of the head with its butt. Unbelievably, both men started to stir. Adan pushed me aside and using a syringe, injected something into their necks.

"What the heck is that?"

"You have your weapons, and I have mine. It's a concoction of my own making, and they will have wonderful dreams for the next three to four hours."

Handing the rifle back to Peter, I glanced up the stairs to make sure the activity hadn't brought out any spectators.

Pulling a small bottle from his shirt pocket, Adan reloaded the syringe. "Let's go. I thought we were in a hurry."

Adan crept up the stairs, paused, and again held up two fingers. We caught up, and I assumed the same demeanor I had before, wishing I'd wiped a little blood from the men below onto my face to make the entire scenario a little more believable.

When I made the landing, Adan took me by the elbow and pulled me along as Lowery brought up the rear. *"Qué está pasando?"*

The two men stepped from the wall by a door about halfway down the hall, the smaller one the first to speak.

Adan yanked me along, and I felt like we were getting pretty good at this. *"El hombre buscado."*

"Vamos a ver cuánto él esté buscado." The man laughed.

The other man looked past us at the ludicrous figure of Lowery. *"Qué estás haciendo con él?"* We were getting close now, and he gave the impression that he thought something was wrong and began raising his weapon. *"Te conocemos?"*

Slamming my arm down, I knocked the rifle from his hands and then brought an elbow into his gut and he collapsed.

By the time I got turned, Adan had the other man against the wall and was attempting to hammer the side of his skull with his pistol, but the angle was bad, so I reached out with both hands and simply slammed his head into the rock wall.

As he dropped, Adan took out the syringe and stuck this one as I turned and kneeled down to the one I'd hit, who was still trying to catch his breath. Rolling him over, I kneeled on his back and held him there till Adan injected him as well.

He shuddered once and then lay still.

As the Doc checked his pulse, I stood and tried the handle on the door, feeling the clasp give as I pressured it with my thumb. Turning to look at the other two, I could see Adan was ready, but Lowery was standing a little down the hall looking like he might run.

Whispering, I motioned for him to move his ass. "Get over here."

He did as I said, and the two of them joined me at the door.

The Doc looked up at me. "Are you sure you want to go in first?"

Pulling the Colt from the small of my back, I pushed the latch the rest of the way and swung the door open enough for the butt of an M16 to get slammed into my face with all the force of an angry mule.

I clawed at the door facing to try to catch myself and was rewarded with another slug in the face and a dozen or so automatic weapons locking into place from all around us.

The world was spinning and things started to go black, but I was aware of somebody raising my head and screaming, "Howdy, Sheriff!"

10

My face hurt.

My head hurt.

Pretty much everything hurt.

I tried to raise my head, but my neck muscles weren't cooperating; besides, it was dark, and my left eye was pretty well swollen shut, the skin scraped off down to the end of my nose, which was clogged with congealed blood.

I lifted my left hand, but there were heavy chains attached to it, and it was almost more effort than I could summon to get a finger to my nostril to do a farmer's blow, which I immediately regretted. I cleared half my nose, but it felt as if I might have lost a quarter of my brain along with it.

I waited till the throbbing faded and tried raising my head again, this time getting a little farther so that I could see my boots at the end of my legs. A foot was dangling off to one side, and I thought it might be broken, but I moved my leg and it straightened out.

My right hand was not so lucky and as I stared at it resting on my thigh, I could see the forefinger was bent at an extreme angle—no way that wasn't dislocated.

So I guess they had my gun.

I started reaching for the wayward finger with my left hand but a wave of nausea welled up, and I decided to wait a minute.

I looked around. To my surprise, it was not a suite at the Brown Palace Hotel in Denver, Colorado; instead it was a stone floor, stone walls, and a heavy door with a tiny window covered with bars which was the only source of light.

I took a deep breath. The room was even smaller than the others we had been in, with a thick coating of dust and cobwebs. I guess this particular cartel didn't go to great pains to incarcerate their prisoners—just took them out back and shot them.

I was honored.

I cleared my throat, not particularly because I wanted to say something, but because there was something in it. A few seconds later someone's head, backlit by the hall light, appeared in the door's small window and then disappeared just as quickly.

I could hear some people talking in the distance and waited but didn't hear anything more.

Deciding to while away the time by getting my finger back in its socket, I reached across and took hold of the tip, feeling a familiar albeit excruciating pain. I'd dislocated a finger or two in my time, and sometimes it wasn't convenient to get medical assistance. I had learned the technique from Coach Cagle Curtis back in my offensive lineman years as a Durant Dogie.

Folding the digit in a hyperextension, I pulled and it popped back in place, just as I was about to puke or pass out. I took a big breath and just sat there letting the waves of pain travel up my arm and into my head, which, already overloaded with pain, refused delivery. "Ouch."

I looked over my shoulder and could see that the manacles were attached to each other with a heavy chain that ran through an iron ring in back of me. Turning a little, I yanked on the chain, but the whole apparatus showed no sign of moving.

There was noise in the hallway, closer this time, and I could hear someone inserting a key and unlocking the door. The massive wooden slab swung open, and I saw a familiar silhouette.

"Hey, there's a new sheriff in town." I said nothing as he stepped inside and crouched down with the same rifle in his hands. "Damn, you look like hell."

He didn't look so good himself, courtesy of the beating I'd given him in the abandoned bank building. "Back in my day, the stock on that M16 would've broken like a Mattel toy."

"Yeah, they're making them a lot better these days." He gestured with the space-age weapon. "I just can't bring myself to carry one of those Russian pieces of shit."

I grunted. "A patriot."

"Something like that." He leaned in. "How's your head?"

"It hurts."

He snorted. "Yeah, I'm in trouble for that—I wasn't supposed to mess you up, but I explained to the boss that you were a little hard to bring down. Hell, at least I didn't shoot ya."

"Thanks."

He flapped a hand, tucked the rifle in the crook of his arm, and pulling the fixings from his shirt pocket, began rolling himself a cigarette. "Don't mention it."

"So how much of it was a setup?"

"The whole thing . . . I mean not getting my ass kicked back in Torero, but everything since you got up here."

"The patrol?"

He lit the cigarette and inhaled. "Think of it as collateral damage, one old man and a couple of kids—I'm assuming you killed them?"

"Two out of three."

"You let one live?" He shook his head. "You gotta get with

the program, Sheriff. Hell, if you'd killed me, you wouldn't be in the mess you are now."

He extended the cigarette toward me, but I shook my head. "How did you get out of the bank vault?"

"One of my guys went looking for me."

"Lowery was in on it?"

"Yeah, right about now your friends with the FBI are looking for you at the Taco Garage Restaurante in Mexico City, the bright spot being the food ain't bad and the margaritas there are incredible."

"I'm sure they'll appreciate that." I looked at him with my one eye. "Be sure to tell Lowery that the next time I see him I'll make an exception and kill him."

He took a few puffs and then broke the silence. "Will do, but I'm not sure how much of an opportunity you're gonna get."

"Where's Adan?"

"The Doc? He's not my problem—I'm in charge of you." He smiled. "Now, we can do this the easy way or we can do it the hard way. . . . Does that sound familiar?"

I didn't say anything.

"I have to get you cleaned up, but I can't take the chance that you're going to do something stupid, so I'm getting someone who you won't harm and who is dying to see you."

"My daughter?"

"No, too soon for that." He stood, stubbing the cigarette out on the wall and then flipping it at me. "We want you in good shape, kind of like a prize steer." He smiled the grating grin. "You want some water, food, a shot of tequila?"

"No thanks."

"Well, if you change your mind, you let her know." He stepped back to the doorway and ushered Alexia in, holding a medical bag and a basin and towel. "Ta-dah!"

She backed against the wall, her hand over her mouth.

"Aw, c'mon, he doesn't look that bad." He turned and studied me a little more closely. "Actually, I guess he does." He nudged her the rest of the way in. "You two have fun, and I'll be back in a bit." Then he closed the door behind him.

I smiled up at my daughter's housekeeper. "Hi, Big Al."

"Oh, Sheriff . . ." She shook her head and began crying. "I am so sorry."

I continued to smile, at least I think it was smiling—with all the bruises and cuts it was hard to tell from my side. "How's Cady?"

She immediately kneeled beside me and set the medical supplies on the floor. "She is fine, Sheriff."

"Walt, please."

She dipped the washcloth in the hot water and began dabbing at my face. "They have not hurt her. She is under the strict protection of Mr. Bidarte. One man said an inappropriate thing to her, and they cut his throat."

"Not a lot of job security around this place, huh?"

She continued working on me, wringing out the towel and dipping it in the bowl for fresh water. "This is a terrible, terrible place."

"Have you seen the man I arrived with, Adan Martínez?"

"No."

I thought about her loss. "I'm sorry about your nephew."

She nodded but kept working, now applying ointment to my face. "He was a good boy, but he has gone on to a better place."

"Well, that wouldn't take much." I glanced around. "Do you have any idea what it is they have planned?"

"No." She placed a few bandages on my face and then leaned back to look at her handiwork. "Oh, Sheriff."

"Walt." I tried to smile. "That's all right, the worse I look the more trouble I can cause between Culpepper and Bidarte." Even in the depths of the building, you could still hear the drums and horn blasts from the square. "The party is still going on?"

She scooted in closer. "I have something for you." She reached into the pocket of her dress and produced my star. "Miss Cady, do you want me to tell her?"

I took the hardware. "No, and give this back to her, if you would. Tell her I'm fine, and that help is on the way."

"This is true?"

"No, but tell her anyway."

The thick door creaked open enough for Culpepper to stick his head in. "All right *Mamacita*, let's get out of here and let him rest—he's going to need his energy." He studied my bandaged face. "Jesus, you still look like you got hit by a train."

"What do I need my energy for?"

"The headman says you're going to be part of some public presentation tonight, so you better get some rest."

I yanked on the chains. "I'm supposed to rest like this?"

He stood there looking at me. "You need to go to the bathroom or anything?"

"No."

He slammed the door. "Good, 'cause you weren't going to get to anyway."

Lucian Connally, the previous sheriff of Absaroka County, lifted his dark eyes from the chessboard to mine. "Kill him."

I skipped my bishop to the side, avoiding his knight, and then looked up at the old sheriff, my mentor. "I don't even know where he is."

"Then find out—it ain't like you're without resources."

I studied him as he studied the board. "Have you ever heard the phrase 'sleeping dogs'?"

"Yes, I have, but I also know that if the bastard goes for your throat a couple of times you make damn sure that he sleeps for good." His dark eyes came up to mine and stayed there as he leaned back in the hair-on wingback. "In case it has escaped your attention, you are in a war." His eyebrow arched over the mahogany eye. "You remember war, where the sons-a-bitches are tryin' to kill you?"

"I seem to recall."

"Well, welcome back." He reached out and took the tumbler of Pappy Van Winkle's Family Reserve 23 Year Old, doming the glass with his fingers and shaking the remaining cubes. "There ain't no law to this. He killed your son-in-law, most likely your child, neutered your woman, made threats against your daughter and granddaughter, and tried to kill you a couple of times." Holding the tumbler up, he spoke again before sipping. "Hell, I'da killed him for any one of those things."

We sat there in silence for a while. "Maybe he's done."

Lucian lowered his drink, setting it on the table, adjacent to the board. "The hell he is, he ain't gonna be done till he takes everything of importance to you and then he's going to take the only thing you got left, your life."

It wasn't real sleep, just that quasi-sleep where you waver between the two planes not really gathering much from either. I was slumped against the wall when I heard somebody unlock the door.

I couldn't see who it might be, so after a few seconds I gave up and slouched into a sitting position. "Who are you, and what the hell do you want?"

"It's good to see you."

I started in spite of myself and then sat up, allowing my eye to adjust. "Having trouble sleeping?"

He smoothed his thick mustache and studied me. "Sometimes."

"I would, if I were you."

"I'm glad you have come."

"I had a choice?"

Another individual carried in a chair and set it beside the door. Bidarte lowered himself onto it with a little difficulty and carefully held out a plastic cup to me. "Life is choices, some good, some bad."

I took the cup and smelled; it was water. I took a sip and then rested the cup on my leg. "You don't look like you're moving very easily."

He laughed sourly and then adjusted his white hat. "Thanks to your deputy, Miss Moretti."

"She wants to know why you aren't dead."

"I sometimes wonder that myself."

I slumped back against the wall. "Are you responsible for the death of her brother, Michael?" He stared at me, saying nothing. "My son-in-law?"

"You are keeping score?"

"Always."

"I gave up keeping score a long time ago, I'm afraid." He motioned for me to sip the water. "My mother is dead. You were kind to her, and I wanted you to know. The medical facilities here are not as good as in the US, and there were complications with her diabetes."

"I'm sorry for your loss, but that doesn't change the situation. Let my daughter go."

He waited before responding. "We will discuss that later."

"Let her go. Now. She has nothing to do with any of this."

"Have you ever been to the bullfights, Sheriff?"

"No."

"A pity, it is the truest form of sport." He paused. "When I was young, between beatings, my father took me to the arenas. It is the only art form in which the artist is in danger of death and in which the degree of brilliance in the performance is left to the fighter's honor."

"I'd likely root for the bull."

"Anything capable of arousing passion in its favor will surely raise as much passion against it."

"Did you just come in here to quote me Hemingway?"

He slowly smiled and then changed the subject. "How much money do you have, Sheriff?"

It took me a moment to put together what he was asking. "Excuse me?"

"In liquid assets, how much do you have?"

"I don't know."

"Four million, two hundred and eighty-two thousand, four hundred American dollars and sixty-two cents." He turned his head to look at me. "Inherited mostly from your grandfather I would assume, a little from your parents, which is mostly tied up in a ranch where you do not live, and then your meager savings from a lifetime of public service."

I took another sip of water. "More than I thought, but I'm sure you're right."

"How much would you give to buy your daughter's freedom?"

"All."

"All of it?" He cocked his head. "Perhaps you will soon have the chance." He slowly stood, sighing deeply. "I have learned one thing in my lifetime, Sheriff. Power is everything, anything else is simply a means to power." He stopped and looked around the room. "From this perspective you might not agree, but this is the true land of opportunity. At first, I simply came here to hide out, but the prospects that presented themselves were more than I could resist." He looked down at me. "Have you never wanted to reinvent yourself, Sheriff—to start anew?"

"Not like this."

"With great opportunities come great risks."

"So you've moved up from the protection racket to management." My turn to look around. "I'm not impressed, and it's not the risks that bother me, it's the immorality."

"What about the immorality of what you do? Are you not in the protection racket, as you call it, yourself? You protect the assets of the people of your county, their money, their homes, and their families. Do you see that as being so different from what you perceive that I do?"

"I don't sell poison, and I don't kill people to do it."

"But you do, you have, and for so very little. The difference is that I get paid a great deal more, Sheriff."

"What I do, I do for the common good."

"Call me a privateer then." He took a step toward the door. "You must be lonely, down here by yourself."

He started to go, but I stopped him. "One more thing."

He paused. "Certainly."

"Why?"

He looked momentarily confused. "Why?"

I gestured around, the manacles a clanking emphasis to the question. "You could've killed me, hired someone to kill me . . ." I pulled the postcard from my shirt pocket, the one he had sent. "But instead you did all this—why?"

He leaned against the door and sighed. "I have led a varied life and have found myself pitted against many men, bad men, greedy men, hard men, shrewd men. . . . You are one of the very few truly good men whom I have ever encountered."

"Let my daughter go."

"You will be making that decision yourself." He glanced around once more. "I do worry about you spending your time here alone, so I have made arrangements for your company." Stepping through the doorway, he picked up something draped in a plastic shopping bag and placed it on the chair.

He pulled the bag away to reveal a soccer ball smeared with blood and with Adan Martínez's skinned face stitched to it, the empty eye sockets dark, his mouth an open gash.

I stared at Adan's face through most of the night.

Thinking about the man I had called a friend, I tried to remember every detail of him that I knew. Henry Standing Bear says that the greatest thing you can do to respect the dead is to remember them, to keep them in your mind so that they do not slip away into that cold, dark infinity that awaits all of us.

The risks he had taken to accompany me weighed heavy on my heart. I owed Adan Martínez a debt I could never pay, and the only thing I could do was make his sacrifice worthwhile.

I flexed my fingers and could still feel the stiffness in the index finger of my right hand. Then I reached up and pulled the bandages from my eye—the worse I looked, the better. I had ugly work to do, and the clearer they saw me, the fairer it would be. I wondered strategically whether they had found the weapons cache I'd covered with rocks on the other side of the wall.

Bidarte's men came and got me relatively early, taking Adan's face away first, and then quickly returning to unlock me from the wall, one of them on each side and another standing in the hallway through the open door with an AK pointed at my stomach.

Marching me through the hall in handcuffs, they took me up the stairs and into the plaza, my eyes blinking in the unaccustomed light. I stood there for a moment squinting in the morning sun, before the one with the gun nudged me forward toward a fountain at the center of the stone-paved plaza.

The place was trashed with beer and liquor bottles, napkins, articles of clothing, and confetti scattered everywhere. Even a few crepe paper floats had been thrown in the walkways of the monastery, the giant marionettes looking like oversized skeletons sleeping off the night's revelries.

As they poked me forward, I could see someone holding a rifle and smoking a cigarette standing at the other end of the plaza beside some sort of wooden structure.

Stumbling across the stones, I pulled up and stopped, looking between a few buildings and down the main road that curved out of sight, choked with vehicles and more trash.

Culpepper turned to look at me. "Sleep well?"

"Well enough."

"I heard you had company."

I stared at him for a good long while. "You know, I didn't think it was possible for me to regret not killing you more than I already had."

He smirked.

"Before this is all over, I may be making a stronger effort on your behalf."

He moved his free hand like a puppet. "Bark, bark, big dog— we're about to put a collar on you." He gestured at the heavy wood structure he leaned against. "This thing was here when we set up operations—can you believe that? I guess if the monks got out of hand they threw them in these and calmed 'em down. What do they call these things?"

"Stocks. They were used in medieval times and even in

colonial America—the earliest reference, though, is in the Book of Acts in the Bible; Paul and Silas were arrested and put in them."

"Well, you're following good company then, huh?" He patted the worn-smooth grain of the ironwood. "The last guy that we stuck out here for three days, he croaked, but then nobody brought him water or food."

I stared at him.

He flipped a few clasps and pulled away a locking rod. "Just sit your big ass on that stone and stick your legs through the holes, if you would."

"And if I don't?"

He rested the butt of the M16 on his hip and puffed his cigarette. "I'll blow your fucking brains out."

"I don't think Bidarte would like that."

He sighed. "Well, I can at least smash the rest of your face in until you do what I say." He looked bored. "Get in the thing, will you?"

The gunsel with the Kalishnikov nudged me in the back, and I'm pretty sure he wasn't expecting what happened next, as I slipped sideways, bringing my left elbow into the side of his head and snatching the automatic rifle as he fell, catching himself on his hands and knees. Bringing the stock down on the back of his skull, I watched as he dropped face-first and didn't move.

I turned back and carefully tossed the AK to one of the stunned men standing a step away. "Consider that an object lesson." Luckily, he caught it, and I stared at Culpepper. "Shoot and save your life."

"I'm tempted." He smiled, one blue eye peering at me from over the gun sight as he motioned with the muzzle toward the stocks. "Do us all a favor and get in."

I did as he said, sitting on a large block of stone about the size of a mini-refrigerator, and rested my legs into the holes as he and the other two men lowered the top and locked me in with padlocks that looked old enough to have held Ambrose Bierce.

"Just so you know, things get a little crazy out here leading up to the party tonight, and it's not unusual for people to throw garbage, spit, or do other horrible things to whoever happens to be in here."

I leaned back, locking my elbows for support.

He plucked my hat from my head and placed it on his own where it wobbled like a clapper in too large of a bell and kicked the still unconscious man lying on the stones, finally flipping his cigarette at him. "You still didn't kill him, so I'm not all that impressed."

I ate the beans, rice, eggs, and tortillas; Alexia rested my metal cup on the thick slab of wood that held my legs. Watching as she poured me more coffee from the beat-up percolator, I studied the square, where the few people who were moving studiously ignored us. "Is everyone sleeping in?"

She set the pot down. "They are sleeping in preparation for later today and tonight."

"Have you spoken with Cady?"

She nodded. "Just long enough to bring her the breakfast." Alexia leaned in close. "And give her back the star." She glanced around, but we were alone. "She wants to know if you have lost the mind."

"I figured that would be the response."

"She is very angry with you, but she says to tell you that she loves you very much."

I couldn't help but smile and nodded. "Okay."

"I lie to her and tell her help is on way."

"Good."

"No one is on way?"

"No. Well . . . Eventually, but they've got to find us, and it's the federal government so they've got satellites, global positioning and all that . . ."

"They not find us."

"No, probably not." I sipped more coffee, trying to avoid the cuts in my mouth and my broken nose, and practiced focusing my sore eye. "I'm still trying to figure it out. I mean, Lowery allowed me to contact the States, the FBI for goodness sake, and for the life of me I can't figure why they would take a chance like that."

"Mr. Lowery is nice man."

I rattled my legs to remind her. "He ratted us out." She looked at me blankly. "Told on us."

She shrugged. "Mr. Culpepper, he is the one responsible for the death of my nephew—I would like to see him dead, along with Mr. Bidarte."

"Well, I think we can all agree on that."

"They kill your friend?"

"Yes."

"I am so sorry."

Anxious to change the subject, I cleared my throat. "How are you?"

She shrugged, sitting on the short stone wall that surrounded the plaza. "This evil place, it is *bruto*, crazy, they kill the people for breathing." She watched as I reached out and flipped the padlock that held me, a bulky and corroded beast that had no pity. "But they have not harmed Miss Cady in any way."

I wondered for how much longer. "That's good."

Someone yelled in Spanish, and we both turned to see a man

standing near the monastery, waving for Alexia to come, at least I assumed it was her in that I was temporarily indisposed.

She stood with the pot, and I handed her the empty plate while palming the fork and keeping the tin cup just in case my plan with the fork didn't work out. She glanced around, looking for the fork, so I showed it to her; she nodded and turned without another word and walked toward the monastery.

If she wasn't used to the game, she was picking it up quick.

It was a cheap fork and bent readily. I twisted the tines back and forth until they finally succumbed to metal fatigue, and I was left with a roughly fashioned lock-picking tool. I tried the lock and discovered the tool was too thick to fit in the hole, so I reached down and began scraping the metal against the stone on which I sat.

As I ground the thing down, I watched the people starting to populate the square as if I were in some park back home. There was an old man who appeared with a wooden push broom and began driving the detritus toward the fountain at the center of the square, finally plucking a garbage bag from his pocket and slowly filling it.

A few others crossed the plaza in a hurry to go someplace else, and a few more wandered out into the open, obviously still inebriated from the previous night. Some congregated in the shade of the monastery and glanced my way, but they didn't come close.

I checked my pick but could see it was still too thick and began grinding it again.

After about forty minutes, the drummers and a couple of trombone players showed up in full mariachi garb and started to set up right behind me. "Oh no, get the hell out of here."

They stared at me.

"Look, sticking me in this damn thing is bad enough—I'm

not going to have you guys pounding in my head all day and night." Gesturing, I used one of the words from my limited vocabulary again. *"Vámanos!"*

They laughed, I guess thinking I was joking or else they thought there was little I could do about it, but their minds changed when I picked up the tin of coffee.

Either concerned with what I might do to their elaborate costumes or whether I'd bounce the heavy tin cup off one of their heads, they moved away, grumbling and making gestures toward me.

I turned back and began grinding the pick again, sipping my now cold coffee and watching them set up near the fountain. The sun was getting high, and I was beginning to regret not having my hat as time passed and more people poured into the plaza.

The drummers began beating away in the same rhythm I'd heard yesterday and most of the night, and the elongated trombones and trumpets began emphasizing the beat; before long even more people began showing up for party day two. The majority still had on the masks, makeup, and period costumes from the night before, some looking a little worse for wear. There were also a few new celebrants, dressed to the *nueve*, swaying to what passed for music.

Half-cut barrels were rolled out from the archways of the monastery, filled with ice and bottles of beer and wine, while whole barrels were set up in a couple of locations with planks laid across as a makeshift bar, crates of hard liquor underneath.

Reaching down, I fit the tine into the lock and felt around for the tumblers. I pushed a bit but could feel the tine bending.

"What did you do?"

I turned to see one of the revelers looking at me questioningly through the eye holes of his papier-mâché mask, reminding me for all the world of Adan's skinned face. My head slouched on my shoulders. "I killed somebody who kept asking me questions."

His own head kicked sideways and the top hat almost fell from his crown. "You should be nice, the last guy they had in there? Everybody brought him drinks, so much so that he died."

I picked up my cup again. "Scram, before I bounce this off your head."

He took another sip of his beer, gave me the finger, and moved back toward the group. "Stay thirsty, my friend."

Watching him go, my eyes dropped to the cup in my hands, the watery coffee barely covering the bottom. Setting it down, I wiped the sweat from my face with a shirtsleeve and wished I'd asked the most interesting man in the world for his hat.

Working a different angle with the fork, I got frustrated and jammed the thing in in an attempt to get some kind of response from the lock and was rewarded with a slight metallic sound and watched as the faux pick slipped from the mechanism and fell onto the stone street with a diminutive *tink*.

The party was in full swing with a few gunshots going off at the far end of the square, but the only thing I cared about was that the sun had dropped behind the monastery, the long shadows stretching across the plaza having finally found me, the darker shadows of the tail end of the volcanic massifs leading into the desert like the final scene of a bad dream. A faded ochre- and umber-colored plain seemed to stretch forever into the distance, past the manmade mess below with open doorways caped in shower curtains where doors should've been. I was struck by the thought that the world might well be better off without people.

The square was full of dancers and drunks, the demarcation not so easy to discern as the crowd moved in one throbbing mass. There was still a little space between me and the mob, but I figured it was only a question of time before things would get out of control. A few celebrants had shot me hard glances and a few articles of trash had been thrown in my direction, or maybe at the drunk who lay on the steps behind me.

I turned and looked at the man, half on the steps and half on the ground. He'd been wearing a sombrero that had fallen off and now lay between us. Stretching a bit, I was able to get the tips of my fingers on the brim and edged it toward me. I picked it up and placed it on my head, and to my fortune the guy had a big one and it almost fit. I crossed my arms and rested my chin on my chest. I tried to doze a bit, but the position was uncomfortable and the noise was too much.

It was when I lifted my face that I saw the woman at the periphery of the crowd.

There were a number of men attempting to dance with her, but she would twirl and twist from them when they got too close, casting longing glances and showing dance moves that stated flatly that she was not a casual operator but rather a professional.

Every once in a while, she would glance over at me, the whites of her eyes and teeth flashing ever more apparent through the black-and-white makeup that transformed her face into an animated skull. She wore a tight black flamenco dress cascading with lace, fringe, and a boa of roses, a deep crimson.

Staking out an area about twenty feet from me, she stamped the stones with her high heels, and all I could figure was that if I was going to die, this wasn't the worst image to go out with.

Some of the men reached for her, and even a few women, but she pulled away, strutting into the no-man's-land that surrounded me and flicking the boa in a wide swish that fell over her shoulder, twitching at the end like an agitated cat's tail.

So this was how wolves circled.

Swaying to the music, she leaned in and shimmied before continuing the inevitable approach like I was a captive field mouse. The others on this end of the crowd began to hoot and holler as she made it clear that I was her prey.

I thought that maybe she was simply attempting to tantalize me and remain out of reach, but her progress brought her closer and closer until she was no more than arm's length away.

Turning from me, she undulated her backside just beyond my boots, shooting her arms out to the sides and then caressing herself along with the rhythm of the drums, her long black satin gloves running up and down the length of her body.

I watched as she turned, going so far as to climb onto the wooden slabs that held me, the split at the front of her terraced dress revealing stockings with lace tops and the black straps of a garter belt.

She was close enough that I could make out the details of her makeup, a field of bone white with a red rose at her forehead surrounded by cobwebs and turquoise leaves and a black ace-of-spades at the tip of her nose, another rose at her chin, and faux stitches around her lips.

It was her eyes that held my attention, though, with black sockets and irises a remarkable violet color—like a high plains sky before a lightning storm.

She pursed her lips in a provocative way, only inches from mine, and then extended her tongue, snakelike from her beautifully symmetrical skull—and there at the end of the pink was a skeleton key.

11

Pulling back from a deep kiss, she released me. *"Bruja de la Piel."*

And without another word, Bianca Martínez climbed off my lap with a smile and twirled toward the crowd again to uproarious cheers.

I tipped my hat to a few hecklers, palmed the key, and rested a hand on the slab of wood, slipping the other one to the side and reaching for the lock that held me. I'd dealt with old padlocks my whole life and knew that if this one was anything at all like those, the key would work. Turning the loop handle I listened for the loud click and then watched as the latch dropped like a slackened jaw.

I looked up again just to see if anybody had noticed and saw Bianca flash a smile and then disappear into the throng, dancing her way toward the fountain.

Careful to keep my hands low, I slid the rod aside and then rested it on the upright next to me. I was free from the stocks, but what good was that going to do if I just got apprehended the moment I stood up?

I could wait until Culpepper came to get me, but he wasn't likely to come alone. I looked around, and my eyes lit on the drunk.

It was his sombrero anyway.

I would have to wait until the majority of attention was drawn away from the square toward the monastery, which proved not to be too much of a problem now that Bianca was in the midst of a flamenco, but I would have to move fast and with confidence. I checked the area just to be sure that there weren't any guards around, or anybody else that might actually know me.

There was a loud noise from the monastery and it sounded as if somebody might be celebrating by shooting one of the Kalashnikovs. Figuring that now was the time, I flipped the top plank up and stepped out like I'd been planning to do it all along.

There was only one individual looking my way, so I waved at him and turned around to hoist the drunk onto the stocks. Placing his legs in the holes, I lowered the top plank and then arranged him, his legs extended, and placed his hat back on his head.

I glanced around again, but the one witness had joined the other revelers. I patted the drunk's shoulder and could've locked him in, but he didn't seem to be in the mood to wander, so I started off in the direction of the sale barn to get to my cache of weapons. I circled around on a cobblestone street where I plucked a cotton blanket and a ball cap with, of all things, an AK-47 embroidered on it from a low wall where two teenagers were making out.

There were a few people walking in the twilight, but every time I met a group I'd either go down another street or turn away and act as if I were going to throw up. Nobody bothered me, and I'd almost made it to the sale barn when I saw an armed contingent and ducked around a corner in time to see Culpepper and a few of his men who appeared to be headed to the sale barn as well. I waited until they were gone and then peered around the bend where one of their own stood by the double doors, originally designed for the entry and exit of livestock.

I was trying to figure out what to do next when I spotted Bianca coming up the pathway. I waved. She saw me, glanced around, and danced her way to the building where I was standing, pressed hard against the wall. Clutching her skirt, she advanced and slipped to my side. "If anybody sees us, they'll just think we're kissing, like everyone else in this wretched place."

I wrapped an arm around her. "How did you get here?" Her violet eyes flared up at me. "Not that I'm complaining."

"We drove."

"We?"

"The Seer is in negotiations with the government, so it is Alonzo and me."

"In the Cadillac?"

"What else? And we are not alone—there are a number of expensive automobiles parked below, and it is strange, but people who are not of my country are entering the monastery."

"Are you armed?"

"*Sí*, one of Adan's pistols."

"Let me have it."

She reached under her skirt and pulled a snub-nosed .38 from who knew where. "Here." She handed it to me and looked around again. "Where is Adan?"

I didn't say anything, because I was unsure as to what to say—my eyes met hers and it was already said. "I'm so sorry."

Her face grew still, and then her eyes dropped. She brought a finger up to wipe the tears. "How did they kill him?"

"You don't want to know."

The eyes came back to mine. "Which one?"

"I don't know." I flipped open the cylinder and checked the load. "They took us prisoners when Lowery, the one who is the computer expert, turned us in."

She gave it a nanosecond of thought, and her face grew

ferocious. "Then I will kill him first. I am a Spanish woman who never sleeps—I have time to plot my revenge." She stretched her neck and glared at the monastery, a full lightning storm in her eyes, matching the clouds to the west. "Your daughter, you have seen her, she is okay?"

"I've seen Alexia, the housekeeper who is taking care of her. She says Cady's all right."

She nodded. "You are sure the housekeeper, she will not also turn?"

I leaned a little to the side, glancing up the street toward the sale barn where the guard still stood. "Culpepper killed her nephew."

"We trust her then?"

I smiled a sad smile at the plural. "Yep, we do."

"Then we kill him first."

"Well, when you are sure of the order you let me know. In the meantime, I stashed a load of weapons on the other side of the wall near the monastery that I think might come in handy before too long."

"You cannot walk the streets."

"Can't we disguise me?"

"Not sufficiently, no." She looked me up and down, shaking her head, the eyes sparking. "You need to go into hiding, and we will get the weapons and then come and find you."

As much as I wanted to argue, it made sense. "Any ideas where?"

"This place is too open." She leaned closer to me, her lips near my ear as a few people walked by and then glanced up the street toward the sale barn. *"El ratón se esconde en la espalda del gato."*

"Meaning?"

"The mouse hides on the back of the cat." She studied me. "I'm not sure if you've noticed, but no one goes near that round barn."

"Except Culpepper and his cronies. You think something is in there?"

"I don't know, but it is a place you can go and be out of the way. Until they find you are missing, we are free, but once they find out they will begin looking for you and I am not sure there are that many places to hide."

"Agreed."

"Alonzo and I will get the weapons and then come and get you. You will have to see us when we return and somehow let us know where you are."

I gave her a detailed description of where the guns were hidden and then looked to the left where the rock walkway continued around the building. "I'll go to the other side and see if there's another way in, so look for me in that direction when you get back." She started to go, but I caught her arm. "And be careful—I don't know if they know where those guns are."

She nodded and then set her jaw, slipped around the corner and twirled with an arm raised, snapping her fingers like castanets.

Staying near the wall, I drunkenly stumbled up the sidewalk, slowly turned at the far end of the building, and leaned against it as if I were going to throw up again.

The building was actually octagonal rather than cylindrical with stone buttresses and high windows with rounded tops and a tile roof with a large cupola at the apex. The windows were painted black on the inside, which was rarely a good sign anywhere. As I approached it, I could see another door at the rear with another sentinel standing there with his automatic weapon.

Thwarted at both sides, I slipped toward the middle where I saw a mesquite tree that had sprung up under the footings of the adjacent building, filling the small passageway between. It wasn't the sturdiest tree I'd ever seen, but it might give me enough of an advantage to where I could see in one of the taller windows where the painters had run out of either paint or inclination.

I had to turn sideways just to get down the passageway, so nobody was likely to enter it. The branches were low, and I took the first step up, keeping an eye on both sides as I climbed. The tree was surprisingly strong, but the bark was tough and slippery, so I was forced to take my time. The blanket got caught in a snag, so I dropped it and watched as it hung there on the broken limb, drifting like the flag of a lost cause.

About halfway up I noticed that the painters hadn't worked all the way to the edges, and that if I pressed my face close to the glass, I could see a tiny bit of the inside. Like those buildings back in Wyoming, there was a tiered grandstand, but the second-level railing blocked my view, so I climbed a bit more, finally able to see down into the show ring itself and the chutes where livestock usually entered.

There were tables on the first level with what looked to be equipment, and I immediately recognized the cables and the banks of electronics. There were cameras set up, and all I could think was that it was a satellite phone-in, but for what? Lowery had talked about having unlimited internet and communication abilities, but I couldn't figure out why this sort of installation would have been necessary in the sale barn. Possibly to auction drugs?

The Day of the Dead revelries were still going on, and the drums and horns were loud even up here, so I wasn't particularly worried about making any noise and thought that if I'd wanted to, I could've stepped from the tree up onto the roof of the other building.

I looked back down just to check and saw a flashlight beam being cast around the narrow passageway. I hugged the feeble trunk in hopes of not being seen, but the beam fell on the dropped blanket and drew closer.

It was only a matter of time before the light would shine on me, so I figured the roof was probably the best chance I had. Quietly lifting a leg, I pushed off and stepped on the sidewall and then the roof just in time to avoid the flashlight beam. Crouching down, I stayed near the edge in hopes that the flimsy-looking roof was stronger there and waited. There was a ripping sound from below where the guard must've pulled down the blanket, but no more noise and no more light.

I kept a watch on the passageway, aware that just because someone wasn't shining a flashlight didn't mean that somebody wasn't there.

My patience was rewarded when the guard lit a cigar and moved back toward his post—bored, I supposed, at the lack of a target. I waited a few moments and started back to the tree but then, noticing that there seemed to be a lot more foot traffic around the sale barn, moved back onto the roof and scuttled to the front where I could see that streams of people were migrating from the plaza and up the hill toward the adjacent octagonal building where the doors were now open.

Looking down the wall, I couldn't see Bianca or Alonzo but figured it would be nice to know what was going on in the sale barn before we made any decisive moves. If nothing else, the goings-on might provide a workable distraction so that we could get Cady out of the monastery.

I got back to the tree, climbed over, and lowered myself

down to where I could see in the top of the window. The place was packed with people standing in the aisles and stairways as a man stood in the center of the ring holding a microphone that had been lowered from above like a boxing match.

I could hear him plainly, for all the good it did in that he was yowling Spanish and at about a hundred miles a minute. I wasn't sure how much longer my legs would hold out when the man of the hour appeared at the edge of the walkway behind the ring, the spot where the auctioneer usually stood and the only place with room to spare.

Bidarte wore a large pistol at his hip and was calmly watching the proceedings while talking with a group of individuals who were sitting in the exclusive area away from the hoi polloi. They were an odd-looking group but well-heeled and being served from a private bar that appeared to be only for that section.

Again, I thought about climbing down and finding my compatriots, but now I was curious as to what was going on and figured as long as they hadn't discovered that I was missing from the plaza, I could indulge myself and see what the hell was happening here.

The announcer in the middle of the ring kept talking, and I was beginning to get the feeling that that was all there was going to be when Bidarte made a gesture and the man handed the mic up to him. He began speaking, but I still couldn't tell what he was talking about when he suddenly gestured toward a couple of the gunmen who reached back to open the livestock entrance gates.

I was fully expecting a prime steer to walk out or a forklift with a truck skid full of the bundles I'd seen in the monastery when I saw someone being pushed by one of the gunmen stumble out into the ring. He wore a black suit, and his hands were tied together. He was barefoot, and his head hung so low that his chin rested on the wrinkled and bloodstained white shirt that covered his chest.

Bidarte went on talking in a low tone before handing the suspended mic to the auctioneer who began the bidding for this man.

There were varying responses from the crowd when someone shifted and sat in front of me, blocking my view. I moved to the right—the barefooted man still stood at the center of the ring, but now there was another man who walked down the steps and approached him. There were no words between them, and then the man who had come from the audience raised a pistol and shot him in the face.

I crouched there in the tree, unblinking, as the bound man fell backward onto the dirt and lay there. The crowd cheered, and the armed man raised the pistol in mock victory before dropping it on the dead man's chest and spitting on him.

I sat back on a limb, my eyes refocusing in time to see two people below, looking up at me. Clamoring to find my voice, I croaked at them with one of the few Spanish words in my limited vocabulary as I pulled the .38 from my jeans. "*Vámanos . . .*"

"*Vete* is the word you are looking for." They continued to look up at me and then the slightly larger one spoke. "And I'm happy to, but maybe we should give you these guns first?" Alonzo chuckled, and even in the dark I could see his smile, which at least in some small way buoyed my spirits.

Scrambling down the tree, I reached them. "Did you find all the weapons?"

"They must've found the others, but these were buried a little away under heavier rocks so I was able to retrieve them." He held the Dallas Cowboys gym bag out to me. "As you know, they are mostly old handguns, and I'm afraid that's not going to be enough."

I set the bag on the ground, pulled my canvas windbreaker from it, and slipped it on, filling the pockets. "That's all right. I've got some other armaments that I think will do the trick." I turned to look at them. "You guys need to get out of here."

They stared at me, Bianca the first to speak. "Are you insane? They will kill you."

"Maybe, but there's only one way to make sure they don't kill you and that's to get you out of here. Now."

I glanced at the stone wall of the sale barn and decided not to pull any punches. "Look, if this all plays out the way I think it will, then the only way to do this is head-on. I already got your brother killed, and I'm not doing the same to you two." I stepped in closer. "I don't think I have much time, but you can help me by finding some vehicles on the roadway and pulling them out and blocking the way down, disable them so that they can't be moved, flatten the tires, rip out the plug wires, anything. Then wait on the other side for my daughter." I continued before they could interrupt. "If you see anybody else coming, it means I've failed and you should drive for your lives—now get out of here."

Alonzo frowned. "What about you?"

I handed him the bag. "I've got other plans."

He stared into the satchel. "You didn't take any of the guns."

Handing Bianca the .38 she'd loaned me, I shook my head. "I won't be needing them."

There wasn't much room as I peered past the guard that I'd knocked cold.

Carefully sitting him on the bench beside the sales barn door, I pulled his cowboy hat over his face and laid his rifle in his lap. Taking a few sideways steps, I sidled my way through the doorway, and since I was about a head taller than everybody else, I had a clear view into the arena.

Most of the auction sales weren't as violent as the one I'd witnessed, the saddened merchandise prodded forward and then after a few bids, led away by the gunmen. Keeping an eye out, I watched as Culpepper entered from one of the side exits and approached the sales platform where he whispered something in Bidarte's ear.

I ducked my face as he immediately glanced around the building but then turned to Culpepper and dismissed him. Bidarte moved back to the platform, stood there for a moment, and then slowly raised his hand. In the hubbub of the moment, no one saw him, and after a bit he pulled the long-barreled revolver from the holster at his hip and fired it in the air.

The entire building went still, like they were posing for a picture postcard.

"Ladies and gentlemen, I have become aware that a unique opportunity has presented itself. . . ."

I was pretty sure he'd switched to English for my benefit.

"Tonight, we have a very special opportunity, an opportunity which presents itself only once in many lifetimes. Some of you are aware of the troubles I have had in the north, and why it is that I have embraced this place as my home." He paused but then looked around and continued. "But there is a man, an individual who pursues me even here in his attempt to destroy me." There was general grumbling, but he raised his hand. "No, please . . . He is a brave man, but I have given him few choices and tonight I give him only one." He nodded toward the gunmen and they pulled the doors open.

Cady's hands were tied like the others, but unlike them, she held her head high, the nickel-plated eyes flashing around the arena as she stared the hooting crowd down.

One of the gunmen made a move to step toward her, but she backed him off with a look and took three more steps toward the center of the arena. She stood there, turning her head to take the place in before stopping with her attention on Bidarte.

She was wearing my badge, and she looked bored. "Let's get on with this."

The crowd cheered again, and Bidarte looked unmoved. The auctioneer took a step toward him, but he shook his head and held the mic to his lips. "Very well . . ." He glanced around. "Here we have the daughter of my enemy. She is a United States Assistant District Attorney—once again exhibiting the lengths of my vengeance." The smile returned to his lips. "What am I bid for this lovely example of—"

"Four million, two hundred and eighty-two thousand, four hundred American dollars." My voice echoed off the stone walls, and the crowd swiveled their heads as one. "And sixty-two cents."

Pushing my way through the crowd, I kept my hands in my pockets, took the steps to my right, and climbed onto the walkway, opposite but now level with Bidarte.

Cady looked at me, and I couldn't help but wink, to which she responded by rolling her eyes with a ferocious smile—if we were going to die, we were going to die with attitude.

"What, my money's no good?"

Before Bidarte could speak, one of the well-dressed individuals raised a hand. "Four million, two hundred and eighty-two thousand, and five hundred American dollars."

Calmly, the drug dealer raised the revolver and shot the man in the head, spraying his brains across the attendees sitting beside him, before he slumped into the lap of the adjacent woman who pushed him forward onto the floor as if dislodging a cat.

Bidarte turned back to the audience at large to smile broadly. "Any more bids?"

There was silence.

He gestured with his palms up in mock exasperation, still holding the revolver. "No one?"

More silence.

He raised the pistol toward my daughter, and I was about to go over the railing when he raised it even further, again firing it into the rough-hewn rafters. "Sold!"

The crowd cheered, and I moved to the edge and threw a leg over the railing, Cady running to me as I stepped down onto the sandy surface of the arena. I caught her and then slipped a hand into my back pocket to pull out a rusty pocketknife I'd procured from the gym bag to cut her free. "You all right?"

Her eyes widened. "You're kidding, right?"

Turning back to Bidarte, I waited until the noise died down, and he raised his voice. "She is free to go."

He said nothing more, but after a moment he gestured toward the gate behind us and two of his men pushed it open. The crowd moved back, making way as I spoke to Bidarte again. "No tricks."

He shrugged and then gestured with his chin as we started backing away. "But not you."

I nodded and dropped my head in order to speak out of the side of my mouth. "Get out of here, Cady. There's a car waiting for you on the main road—get in it and get the hell out of here."

She gripped me harder. "I'm not leaving you."

"I've got a plan."

"Oh God, no . . . Please?"

"You're overwhelming me with your enthusiasm." I lowered my head to hers. "Get to that car—you won't be able to miss it."

I nudged her, but she stood there looking at me as I mouthed the word. *"Go."*

She slowly backed away, the tears lining her face as she moved through the crowd to the gate. She stared at me one last time as if memorizing my face, and then she was gone.

After any great challenge or crisis, the moment comes when your nerves stop twitching and you settle down to the new condition of things because you feel that any possibility of fresh horrors is used up. You have little choice but to stand back and take in the whole picture. When it's finally too late and you acclimate yourself to that's it and there's nothing left to do, except maybe one thing.

Buy time.

I turned back to face Bidarte. "All right, here I am."

He played with the pistol, even going so far as to try and twirl it. "Yes, you are."

"So do whatever it is you're going to do, abuse me, torture me, or kill me but be done with it, because I'm tired of you and your immorality, brutality, and insanity—you bore me."

Looking down at me, he smiled and holstered the revolver. "No, I am not going to abuse you, torture you, or kill you—you see, Sheriff, I am going to sell you."

The crowd began cheering again, and I took the opportunity to move to the center of the arena, and when the noise died down, I scratched my neck in my best Will Rogers and looked up at him. "I don't think you'll get very much."

"You underestimate your value." He gestured toward the well-heeled ringside, minus the leaking one that his henchmen had hauled away. "Any one of these fine individuals will be happy to purchase your fate, along with a number of others on the phones over here."

I glanced toward the electronic banks, and at the young people now seated there. "You've got to be kidding."

He looked genuinely surprised. "No, not at all . . . You've made a number of enemies in your long tenure as a lawman, some of them very powerful people with very long memories and uh . . . deep pockets." Rearing back, he roared into the microphone. "Ladies and gentlemen, we have arrived, somewhat abruptly, at this evening's main event—the auctioning of Sheriff Walter Longmire."

The crowd roared again, but for the life of me I couldn't hear them anymore; like the whirring of tires on an endless highway, the sound was there, but I could no longer hear it.

I watched as Bidarte drummed them up and even watched as the bidding began. I mildly wondered who were these people who wanted my life so badly. I think some of them even looked vaguely familiar—the swarthy one on the end who might've been related to the drug dealer I'd killed in Philadelphia, the stalwart-looking one who might've been connected to the intelligence officer I'd caused to be killed in Vietnam, the woman who bore a striking resemblance to the rich man who'd faked his own death on the Powder River—any of them could've been connected to the Dead Center Association or to other individuals who had crossed paths with me that had unfortunately cost them their lives.

Backing toward the platform where Bidarte stood, I glanced up at all of them and at the earnest young people on the phones and listened to the bidding rise on my miserable carcass. It had moved so fast that Bidarte had been forced to hand the mic over to the auctioneer.

"*Seis millones cuatrocientos mil!*"

Thrusting my hands back in my pockets, I turned and looked at the screaming people and wondered what could've brought them here in the first place. Some were, no doubt, innocents drawn by the titular attractions of money and power, but the others?

"*Seis millones quinientos mil!*"

It was a pity, really, and when you considered the beauty of the place, it was almost heartbreaking. I glanced around at the structure of the sale barn and thought about the monks and laborers who must've built it and the monastery.

"*Seis millones seiscientos mil!*"

I thought about the things I always thought of when confronted with such spectacular structures. I knew they were built as monuments to God, but I could never help but marvel at the men who had built such things.

"*Seis millones setecientos mil!*"

Ninety-six men died building the Hoover Dam, but contrary to popular belief, none were buried in the concrete. Ninety-six men, and that was with relatively modern construction techniques.

"*Seis millones ochocientos mil!*"

How many lives had been lost constructing the Great Wall of China, the pyramids at Giza, the Taj Mahal, the Colosseum, the Bagan temples, Angkor Wat, or Notre-Dame Cathedral?

"*Seis millones novecientos mil!*"

I guess there were worse things to which you could sacrifice your life, something that would live forever as a testament not only to God but also to the beauty of the human mind and its ability to imagine, design, and construct such things.

"*Siete millones!*"

It is consistently amazing to me that people could disavow the one thing that separated us from so much of the natural world—the ability to think, the responsibility of asking why and what if.

"Siete millones cien mil!"

Never a big one for dogma, I believe that there's more divinity in an idea than in all the prayers in the world.

"Siete millones doscientos mil!"

But here I was, giving thanks for the fact that my granddaughter was safe and that my daughter was climbing into a pink '59 Cadillac convertible and speeding to safety.

"Siete millones trescientos mil!"

Pulling my fists from the pockets of my canvas jacket, I held them up to my mouth, biting on the two pins in my hand, slipping one on my little finger and spitting the other into the sand. It was with a mild sense of satisfaction that I was thankful for those large hands, and more than anything else for what I lifted up in full display.

"Siete millones cuatrocientos mil!"

Two ready-to-explode hand grenades.

12

It had grown remarkably quiet in the sale barn arena as I slowly turned, showing the crowd what was in my hands. Some of them realized what I held, the majority didn't, but all were very aware of the change of tone in the room.

I smiled up at Bidarte.

He shook his head. "What do you think you are doing?"

"Raising the bid." I stared at him. "These look to be two M67 fragmentation grenades. Now, the average man can throw these things about a hundred feet, which means I can pretty much land them anywhere in this building."

He continued to shake his head and gestured toward the gunmen who were now aiming at me. "And if we shoot you?"

"It would have to be a very good shot, and besides, I'd still get at least one thrown. With all this Composition B, these things have an injury radius of about fifty feet and a kill radius of over fifteen with steel fragments going out some eighty feet—so if these things in my hands go off . . ." I glanced around. "Every-body in this building is going to get a taste."

"Including you."

"Yep, but that's the thing—I don't care. Everything I care about is out of your hands now. You no longer have any control over me." I took a few steps toward him. "Do you really think that I wouldn't give up my life to make sure that you and all these other people that wish me and mine harm were permanently removed?"

He placed his hands on the railing. "I don't think you will do it, not with all these innocent people in this arena."

I glanced around. "You know, I'm having a hard time finding the innocent in this place."

He shook his head some more and looked around at his men, probably searching for Culpepper as his go-to guy, but I didn't see him and that was either very good or very bad.

I took a deep breath. "Well, for lack of anything else, I suppose I'll save my own life."

"And walk out of here? Just like that?"

"Just like that."

He smiled. "You won't get very far, out there in the open."

"I'll take my chances." I looked behind me and was relieved to see that Culpepper was still missing. "Have your men open the gates, and I'll just back out—what happens from there is between me and you."

He gave me a good long stare, but without his chief crazy I guess he wasn't willing to take the chance; he'd courted death when he had dragged himself out of the Powder River country with a chest full of lead, and I suppose he wasn't wild about the thought of rekindling the relationship. He made a barely perceptible gesture with his chin, and I listened as the gates squealed open.

Careful not to trip over my own feet, I began backing out, still keeping a wary eye on the gunmen, strategically placed near all the exits. Some of them looked a little squirrelly, but I didn't figure they'd do anything without Bidarte's say-so.

Everyone stayed clear, and I was about even with the

doorway when I pitched one of the grenades back into the center of the arena.

Erupting, the crowd started rushing in all directions and even the gunmen seemed intent on saving their lives by vacating the place as quickly as possible.

With a loud pop, having reached the limit of its four-second M213 fuse, the grenade began filling the arena with a thick, white smoke, making it impossible to see anything. Pulling the remaining ring from my little finger, I threaded it back in the lever and deposited the remaining M67 back in my jacket pocket, truly thankful that Culpepper had been MIA since any veteran of the recent wars would've immediately spotted the blue color on the handle of the smoke grenades.

A majority of the people coughed and stumbled through the thick vapor, and I reached over and took the AK from the guard who still sat slumped on the bench where I'd left him. I had a few more tricks up my sleeves, but I was going to have to meter them out if I was going to survive the night.

Flipping the safety off, I fired a long burst above the building, which caused even more chaos as a lot of the audience fell back inside, thinking the war had begun.

Taking off at a jog, I traced the layout of the tiny village in my mind and set out to the right, circling along the wall toward the monastery where I had more work to do before seeing if I could get out with my hide intact.

I ducked into the plaza and edged behind the giant puppets that had been used for the Day of the Dead parade while three more gunmen ran from the monastery toward the sale barn and all the noise.

Leading with the barrel of the Kalashnikov, I turned into the main entryway and looked down the halls, but there was nobody there. I thought briefly of returning to the radio room but figured with my limited knowledge, it would be a waste of time that I didn't have.

Alexia was on my mind—I wasn't going to leave this place without her, not after the way she'd taken care of Cady, never mind the prisoners who were in the same position as I had been and had just as good of a reason to get out and cause a little mayhem.

I took the steps to the area below and threw open the first set of doors, but there was no one inside. I was beginning to think that anyone who had been down here must've been hauled away to the sale barn for the human auction until I heard a couple of people yelling farther down the hall. I flung the door open to the first cell, but it was empty. I had turned to go when something struck me in the back of the head.

I almost lost the grip on my weapon but managed to re-aim. I stared at my assailant. "Adan?"

He gawked at me, his face attached and perfectly fine. "You!?" He reached out and grabbed my shoulders. "I thought for sure you were dead, my friend!"

"I thought they cut off your face."

He looked confused. "No, they brought a man into the cell and skinned his face to show me what they were going to do if I didn't talk." He thought about it. "He had a goatee not unlike my own."

I rubbed my head where he'd hit me. "I thought for sure you were dead."

"No, alive and relatively well, considering." He glanced past me through the open door. "What's going on?"

"I saved Cady."

"Wonderful!"

"But I'm not so sure about us."

"Ah, but then all we have to do is escape."

Ushering him back through the door, I explained about Bianca and Alonzo. "As far as I know they blocked the road and are on their way down the mountain." I paused. "She saved me."

"My sister?"

"Yep, she saved me."

"She is an amazing woman." He shook his head and thought about how to get out. "The roadblock will not hold Bidarte for long, but if Bianca and Alonzo get a good enough head start they should be able to drive north from Torero and get back to our place."

"Then what?"

"That is according to what direction we use. We will not be able to escape on that road—Bidarte is sure to go that way after us; only the insane will go by way of the canyon and the river, especially since I do not know of any horses or mules here. Mules are really the only form of transport that can navigate those trails."

"Then it's the canyon, but I'm wanting to inflict a little damage before we go."

He followed as we continued to open the doors and release the men who remained. "I assumed as much."

With the help of the liberated prisoners, we were able to dump not only the crates full of drugs, but also the cash from the windows at the end of the hall into the space behind the monastery where the smell of the slag heaps from the sulfur mine and the methane from the decomposing bodies was strongest.

Patting the last man on the shoulder, Adan dismissed him, explaining that anywhere besides with us was probably safer and we stood there in the hallway, alone.

"What good is all this going to do?"

Dumping the last crate through the window, I turned to look at him. "I'm going to set it all on fire."

His eyes widened. "You are going to ignite the mines?"

"I am."

He looked out the window at the caves and the slag heaps that trailed down the rock face, the luminescent yellow of the sulfur even more visible at night. "We have no idea what kind of damage that might do."

"Sulfur doesn't explode unless in a contained environment like those uninhabited caves, otherwise it'll just burn."

"And produce sulfur dioxide gas."

"Yep, but anybody who's interested should be able to move the blockade pretty quickly—then they can all safely escape."

"And if Bidarte and his men attempt to stay and retrieve their money and goods?"

"They die." I looked out at the radiant cliffs. "Only appropriate that the devil should choke to death on brimstone, don't you think?"

"Genius." Smiling, he shook his head. "I only hope the retainer wall is enough to contain the rockslide."

"In the meantime, we need to get out of here and to those mules, because I don't think they're going to react positively to all the pyrotechnics."

With Adan following, I worked my way back down the hall. I was unhappy to hear noises and shouting from the plaza and rewarded the first gunman to come around the corner with the wooden butt of the AK. He wasn't completely out, so I threw him in one of the rooms and blocked the door. Collecting the Kalashnikov from the floor, I handed it to Adan. "Here, we can start up an Eastern bloc gun shop back at your place."

We'd made it to the end of the hallway when I heard the sound of a simulated electronic firefight. Glancing back at Adan,

I lifted a finger to my lips and then slowly pushed the door open to find Peter Lowery in his game chair, back to us as he decimated attacking soldiers on the screen.

He had his headphones on, but the volume was so loud we could hear it from the hallway. Slowly, I brought up the barrel of the 7.62x39mm and fired a few rounds.

The large flatscreen exploded with a great deal of flying glass and sparks as Lowery fell backward onto the floor, the space-age chair spilling him out at my feet as his headphones flew off. The gunfire continued, the sound system evidently not connected to the TV.

I aimed at the computer tower and blew it apart with a few more rounds.

Lowery started screaming. "Shit, shit, shit!"

"Shut up."

He slowly removed his arms from his face and looked up at me. "You're alive?"

"That isn't the half of it." I reached down and grabbed him by the front of his shirt, along with some chest, and lifted him up to his unsteady feet.

"Wait, wait!"

Transferring my hand to his throat, I pulled him in close. "For what?"

"I'm the one that helped you call the cops, remember?"

"And sent them to a restaurant in Mexico City."

"What?"

"Culpepper said you gave them the coordinates for the Taco Garage or something."

"What? Wait, no . . . Culpepper is full of shit, man. He wouldn't know the coordinates of his asshole if he didn't wipe it every day." He tried to dislodge my hand but gave up as I spun him around and put him against the wall, lifting him till he was on tiptoe. "Look, the Feds would know if I gave them the coordinates of the capital of Mexico, honest!"

"Then where did you send them?"

He looked around, the panic writ broad across his face. "Here, I sent them here—goddamn it!"

"Why did you backtrack and rat us out?"

His expression made it plain as he struggled with my hand some more. "So they wouldn't kill me. Jesus!"

I turned to Adan. "Do you believe him?"

The Doc nodded. "I think he's too scared to lie."

"You think we can trust him?"

"As long as we have the upper hand, yes."

I turned back to the computer whiz. "You change sides again, and I'll cut your head off and put it on a stick, you got me?" He nodded, and I lowered him to the ground. "Do you have some other way of contacting the outside world?"

"You mean, besides the computer you just shot up?"

"Yep."

He reached down and pulled up a small, padded vinyl container and unzipped it, producing a smallish cell phone in a hard black case with yellow highlights. "Sonim XP."

"What good is that going to do if we don't have service?"

"It's a sat phone, it'll work anywhere, almost."

"Almost?"

"Inmarsat doesn't work at the North and South poles, but other than that . . . I don't know, sometimes it doesn't work and you have to turn it off and back on again like everything else, but as long as you have power and a clear view of the sky all systems should be go."

I took it from him and stared at its blatant simplicity. "How does it work?"

"Like a cell phone."

"Calling the US?"

"Country code 011 and then 870 and the number."

"Charger?"

"Unless you're going to talk for more than eight hours, you should be fine."

I nodded, stuffing the thing in my pocket. "Now, where do they keep Alexia?"

"Who?"

"The Mexican woman who was taking care of my daughter."

He glanced up. "Second floor."

I shoved him toward the door. "Show me."

Massaging his throat, he croaked, "What about me, don't I get a gun?"

Adan and I spoke simultaneously. "No."

I pushed him out in front as we made the stairwell and moved up to the second floor where the hallway appeared empty.

I glanced at Lowery, and he pointed farther down the hallway to the door on the end. "That one, they were keeping her in that one and the one next to it."

Hustling down the hall, I motioned for Adan to wait at the stairwell, just to make sure no one came up behind us. The accommodations were a little nicer on this floor, the doors replete with regular locks, and I noticed the key sticking out of the mechanism where Peter said they were keeping Alexia, which I found handy. I took the precaution of knocking on the door. "Alexia, it's me, the sheriff."

There was no answer.

I knocked louder. "Alexia, it's me, Walt Longmire."

"Sheriff?" Her voice was faint but still discernible.

I turned the key and pushed the door open to find her on the floor beside a chair. Kneeling at her side, I turned her over and could see that one eye was blackened and swollen to the point of being completely shut and that the skin was broken at the bridge of her nose and at the corner of her mouth. The side of her forehead was scuffed and bleeding where it looked as if she'd been kicked, and her nostrils were clogged with blood. "Oh, Alexia . . ."

"It look much worse than is."

Adan had already returned from the next room with a few washcloths, dripping with water, and gently began cleaning her. "Who did this to you?"

Struggling to enunciate, she spat out the words. "Culpepper. When they come to get Miss Cady I fight with them and knock him down in front of his men."

"Oh, I bet he liked that."

She attempted a smile. "He is very angry."

"Uh huh." I helped her to sit up. "Can you stand?"

"Yes, yes, but where is . . . ?"

I steadied her as she struggled to her feet. "Safe, and on her way out of town—where we should be getting."

She squared her shoulders and planted her feet in the sensible shoes and made for the door like a dreadnought. "We go."

Glancing at the other two, I smiled, and we followed, finally overtaking her in the hallway where I moved to the front and started down the stairs toward the plaza, hoping with all my might that we'd run into Culpepper.

I retraced the route I'd taken to get there, avoiding the crowds by staying along the walls of the square. We hung a sharp left before following the wall to the narrow street a little ways behind the sale barn and the small meadow where I hoped the mules were still grazing as if nothing had happened.

Most of the people who had been at the auction were rushing toward the monastery and the main road, so I wasn't too worried about running into anybody in the dark, but things were calming down and it was just a question of time before they started looking for us.

When we turned the corner of an adjacent building, the four modes of transportation raised their heads to look at us, and I was never so happy to see a team of mules in my life.

Lowery stopped dead and turned to look at us. "You've got to be kidding."

I nudged him forward with the barrel of my AK. "What?"

"I thought you had a helicopter or something." He stumbled forward, looking back at me. "Donkeys?"

"Mules, and if you hurt their feelings you'll have to walk."

Arriving at the animals, he glanced around. "I think I'd prefer it."

Turning to Adan, I handed him and Alexia the leads and pointed toward the precipice where we'd met the patrol. "You two go ahead, and I'll meet you at the rock outcropping on the ridge where we let the kid go."

"What are you going to do?"

I glanced at the wall and pulled the remaining grenade from my pocket, the darkened cliffs looking ominous and the smell of sulfur choking the air. "Light this place up like the Fourth of July."

"*Día de los Muertos.*"

"I sure hope not, but you'll have a ringside seat from up on that ridge." I patted his shoulder and then gave Alexia a hug. I watched as Adan nodded and started off with two of the mules and Lowery in tow.

Alexia sat there on her mule. "I stay with you."

"No." I gestured after the departing two who had paused on the trail looking back at us. Turning and handing her my rifle, I paused a moment to lean my head forward where we touched on the spot where she was undamaged. "I cannot thank you enough for what you've done for me and my family." Lifting my face, I kissed her dark hair with the few threads of silver. "Now let me help you up and hang on to that mule—I don't think he's going to like what happens next."

Watching as she caught up and all of them began threading their way on the trail, I started fussing with the fuse mechanism on the M67 and tried to remember the grenades we'd trained with back in Vietnam. The one I'd tossed in the arena had blown off a few sparks, but I wasn't sure if that would be enough to ignite the sulfur-laden overburden on the other side. I'd heard stories in Wyoming where the heat of a dirt bike exhaust had been enough to light up fields of the stuff, but I didn't want to take any chances.

As I stepped up on the wall's footers, I thought of all the bodies that had been dumped on the other side and reassured myself that they were better off incinerated than lying there rotting.

Adjusting the fuse to the shortest possible time, I was pretty sure that I'd get the maximum amount of spark.

I looked back up the hill and could see in the periodic moonlight that Alexia, Adan, and Lowery and the mules had reached the first cutback and, in a few minutes, would be safely out of harm's way—at least I hoped.

I went through my calculations and figured it would only take seconds for the blue flames to travel up the cliffs and hit the mines, at which point the trapped sulfur dioxide gas would bring at least part of the mountainside down in a monumental tidal wave of blue flame that would look like the wrath of an angry god.

I looked again and was pretty sure I saw my friends' outlines in the full moon at the high point of the ridge about to disappear by the rock outcropping nearly nine hundred yards away.

I pulled the pin on the M67 and turned back to the wall, just drawing my arm up and making to throw, when I heard the distinct sound of more than a half dozen fully automatic weapons being charged, the clacking noise echoing off the wall in front of me.

Turning slowly with the grenade still in my hand, I was greeted by Culpepper and eight of his closest gunmen, the pale, ferocious blue eye focusing on me from below the brim of my hat and above the iron sights of his M16 carbine. "Hey Sheriff, what're you up to?"

I shrugged, gesturing with the grenade. "What would a party be without fireworks?" He motioned for me to step down, which I didn't do, gesturing again with the grenade. "You don't mind if I'm careful with this?"

"What? You worried about smoking us to death?"

That's what I got for trying to use the same trick twice.

He stepped forward, now only a couple of yards away, as the others fanned out. "You the one that dumped all our stuff out the windows back at the monastery?"

"Seemed like a good idea at the time."

"Yeah, well the four dumbasses who were supposed to be guarding it have been maximally demoted." He gestured with the gun again. "C'mon, get down." I did, this time, figuring I didn't have many choices as he lowered the weapon but still kept it aimed at me. "So, anything to say before I demote you?"

"Your boss isn't going to like that."

"Yeah? Well, he doesn't get a vote anymore."

"What's that supposed to mean?"

"Me and my guys, with all this shit-show going on, we've decided to promote ourselves—we're taking over."

I sighed. "Bidarte's not going to like that either."

"Well, like I said—he doesn't get a vote. We've been putting up with his esoteric shit for long enough, and we think it's time for a change of regime."

"With you in charge?"

He smiled some more and then assumed an expression of humility that did not suit him. "You know, I've wracked my brain, and I honestly can't think of anybody better."

"Probably didn't take much wracking."

He nodded. "Well, at least you get the honor of being my first official act." I watched as he raised the barrel of the M16 and centered it between my eyes. "It's been nice knowing you, Sheriff."

Jumping in spite of myself at the sound of the shot, I stood there without moving as seven more rang out and all of Culpepper's henchmen slumped to the ground, the loud ping of an M1C Garand clip being ejected just barely perceptible in the night air—then after a moment, of all things, the faraway spring mating call of the western meadowlark, the Wyoming state bird.

Isidro.

Epitafio.

Culpepper hadn't moved, but his eyes searched the periphery of his vision, as all of his men now lay on the ground, all of them head shots, all of them most certainly dead.

Not sure to what lengths Culpepper's knowledge of vintage weapons ran, I figured it would take at least a couple of seconds for Isidro to recharge the en-bloc clip—but I was willing to take that chance. "If I were you, I wouldn't even twitch." Slowly stepping forward, I reached up with my free hand and took hold of the automatic rifle. Next, I reappropriated my hat, Colt .45, and Henry Standing Bear's Bowie knife. "I think your men just got demoted."

He still didn't move. "Who in the hell?"

"You wouldn't believe me if I told you." I waved my hat toward the rock outcropping on the ridge where I could see four individuals, including the one with the cotton poncho waving in the breeze with his weapon aimed exclusively on us. I put my hat on, turned back to Culpepper, and stuffed my Colt in the pancake holster at the small of my back along with the knife. "Now, what am I going to do with you?"

"I've got a couple of suggestions."

"I'm probably not going to like them." Without any warning, I brought the butt of the M16 stock around and walloped him with it.

He landed on his back and lay there for a second, unmoving—of course, his mouth was the first thing to recover. "Damn . . ." He raised his head a little but then let it drop back. "I don't think I've ever been hit like that in my life."

Taking a step forward, I dropped the muzzle down in line with his chest, and I had to admit that I was impressed that he was conscious, let alone able to speak. "You were right, they are making these stocks sturdier."

He rubbed his jaw, surprised it was still attached, and slumped up on his elbows. "I guess you felt you owed me that one for hitting you?"

"No, that one was for Alexia—the housekeeper you abducted, the one whose nephew you killed, the one whose face you beat."

He thought about it. "Oh, yeah."

I reached down and took the S&W .357 from his shoulder holster and then poked his knee with the M16. "Now, I'm not stupid enough to believe that you don't have a backup somewhere."

He dropped his hand, and I could see where the left side of his jaw was swelling up like a softball. "Small of my back."

"Roll over—you don't get to reach for it." He did as he was told, and I snatched a Glock 9mm and stuffed it in my jeans, letting him roll back and look up at me.

His head must've cleared enough to give it a shot, and he kicked at the rifle with his foot, knocking it sideways, but I was able to get my free hand around his wrist before landing a knee and all two hundred and fifty-five pounds into his solar plexus. His eyes bugged out, and his ribcage attempted to not punch through his spine. I listened as the air rushed back into his lungs like a bellows, and he started coughing like he might bring up some solid organs.

I raised a hand toward the ridge and stopped Guzmán's sniper from scattering Culpepper's brains across the grass. "Just for the record, I don't think I could be more pissed off at you than I am now." Re-aiming the M16, I asked again. "That's it?"

He nodded, still coughing as he lay there.

"Other than your winning personality?" He glared up at me, not all of the fire completely gone. "I've got another question— who killed Vic's brother, Michael, my son-in-law?"

"Not me."

I gestured with the barrel of the automatic weapon. "Who, then?"

"I don't know, that was just Bidarte's deal. I had nothing to do with that."

Pushing the muzzle closer, I pressed the point. "But it *was* his deal."

"All I know is I didn't have anything to do with it."

"He never spoke about Michael Moretti in Philadelphia?"

"Not to me; he keeps his own counsel, Sheriff." He tried to laugh but with his damaged jaw, couldn't. "Look, I'm not saying he doesn't have his dick in every dirty pie on the planet, all I'm saying is that it had nothing to do with me." I considered what he'd just said, and he did a pretty good job of reading my mind. "What are you going to do, Sheriff? I mean, you're not gonna kill me, it's not in your nature. We've established that."

I stared down at him and said nothing.

"I mean if you were going to kill me you would have done it right after you hit me or when I made my play, something that you could've rationalized into a noble deed—but not like this, not when I'm just lying here hurt and unarmed."

"You mean like you were going to do to me?"

He massaged his jaw some more and then sat up. "Different . . . You're not a cold-blooded killer, Sheriff. Believe me, I know." He smiled, and there was blood between his teeth. "I see the predicament. I mean you've got to get out of here, but you don't want to kill me, so how 'bout we make a deal?"

"How about I shoot you in the kneecap and just let your boss do my dirty work for me?"

His eyes widened just a bit. "Oh, come on now, Sheriff. We're just a couple of ol' cowboys here . . ."

"Try again."

His eyes dropped, and I like to think that he honestly did think about what it was that he was asking, and for just a moment I thought I caught a glimpse of the man he'd been or the man he should've become.

"From one soldier to another?" He shook his head, and he sighed as his eyes came back up to mine. "All I want is a sporting chance." He gestured toward the wall. "You're gonna blow this place sky high? Gimme thirty seconds on the other side of the wall before you throw that grenade, and either way, you'll never hear from me again."

My turn to think about it as I used up time I didn't have.

"I know I'm a piece of shit, but you're not."

I glanced back at the cliffs. "Do you have any idea what that sulfur is going to do when it ignites?"

He chuckled a laugh that would've curdled milk. "Gotta be better than a bullet to the head."

"Not necessarily." Running out of time, I stepped back.

He smiled, and there was a lot of blood there now. "Thanks." He slowly gathered himself and gingerly stood.

"You won't be thanking me here in a minute."

He nodded and moved toward the wall, stumbling a little. "I'm surprisingly agile, even with twenty-four bruised ribs."

I watched as he hoisted himself onto the footing and then reached and took hold of the top, dragging himself up and straddling the wall as my conscience got the better of me, just as I knew it would. "Come on back down on this side, and I'll let you go the other way, toward the monastery."

"No, a deal's a deal." This time he laughed wholeheartedly. "I know me well enough to know that if you do that I'll change my mind, get a gun and come after you." He looked down at the other side of the wall, no doubt at all the rotting bodies. "I deserve this, and who knows, maybe I'll make it."

I said nothing but swung his rifle around, slinging it onto my shoulder as I pulled out the grenade again.

He stretched his jaw where I'd struck him, his face completely lopsided now. "Thirty seconds?"

"I'll give you forty-five."

"How 'bout them Cowboys?" With the raising of a fist and a quick nod, he threw his other leg over the wall and was gone.

Pulling my Illinois pocket watch from my dirty jeans, I noted the sweep hand of my grandfather's timepiece and counted the seconds as I placed the ring of the M67 in my teeth and pulled, still holding the lever in place as I reared back.

Against all better judgment, I gave him seventy-four.

In honor of Bob Lilly.

13

Phlegethon.

That was the only way to describe it.

I had heard my grandfather use the word, explaining that it was one of the five rivers of Hades; he had threatened numerous times to throw me in it if I wasn't accomplishing the ranch work up to his expectations. I couldn't help but think of the old bird as I stood there holding his pocket watch and seeing the inferno twisting its tendrils toward the sky.

The air had left the environs with the sudden whoosh, and I'd thought the smoke from the grenade had blown back in my face, but the truth was that the oxygen surrounding the mountain had been consumed. Like spider webs of fire, the white-blue flames had shot through the slag heaps and covered everything like a moving tide.

There was no explosion yet, but the channels of wind that the lack of air had created spun the fire in perfect funnels that danced up the cliffs as if the laws of nature and physics need not apply.

Throwing myself backward, I could feel the heat from the conflagration and watched as the yellow powder burned between melting and boiling temperatures, changing its composition to a lower density but a higher viscosity and forming polymers, the molten sulfur assuming a dark red color, the entire mountain bleeding.

There was no way Culpepper could've made it through all that.

I figured it was time to hotfoot it out of there before the heavy poisonous gas poured over the wall or the mines exploded, sending tons of rock toppling down on me. I started running but slowed to a jog with the effort, climbing after the mule train and hoping I could get enough distance between the cliffs and me.

Making the first switchback, I stopped, wheezing for breath, with my hands on my knees, and wishing I'd kept running with Henry. I took a few deep breaths and turned to get a good look at the strangely illuminated mountainside. A small bank of what looked like ground fog was building on the upslope of the wall and in minutes it would overrun the thing and begin seeping through the empty streets of the mountain town where I could see the eight dead men lying on the grass.

Blowing the pungent smell from my nose, I coughed and thought about what the poisonous gas would be like down there. Looking up at the cliffside at the numerous boreholes, I started thinking that I might've overestimated the effects of the trapped gas in the abandoned mines and that it was possible they were better ventilated than I'd thought; but it didn't really matter, the fire and subsequent gas would do the trick of shutting down Bidarte's operation.

From this perspective, I could see the taillights of the few remaining cars and trucks that were clogging the roadway, but I figured the occupants would make it to safety after moving the roadblock my friends had constructed—I silently thanked the powers that be that they and my daughter were far away.

Winded from the exertion or from the fumes, I covered my

nose and began climbing again, figuring that the sooner we all got going, the better.

I'd just topped the ridge and was only a hundred yards from my companions when I heard the first rumble. I turned in time to see one of the lower mines explode as if by a thousand sticks of dynamite, sending rock shards and boulders cascading down the cliffs and against the wall. A credit to the builders, the structure held until three more of the holes blew out in a chain reaction of destructive power like a planned demolition.

In a matter of seconds the rest of the mines began exploding, and the entire cliffside slumped toward the town in a tide of burning stone. The wall didn't stand a chance against the millions of tons of fiery rock that pushed it aside and filled the streets, herding the deadly cloud of sulfur dioxide ahead of it like one of the ten plagues of Egypt.

The sale barn was destroyed, as were the majority of the buildings to the north of the town, and I noted that the old monastery took the brunt of the landslide and was collapsing onto itself, the rubble being pushed forward and down the hillside and toward the few abandoned cars that were left on the road.

I'd never seen anything like it.

There was a hand on my shoulder, and I turned to see Adan. "God help anyone who was still there. We have to go."

I followed him across the ridge where Isidro stood with the Garand hung over his shoulder. I stuck a hand out, and we shook. "Thank you."

Returning the fingers to his mouth, he replicated the western meadowlark—his "you're welcome."

I patted Isidro's shoulder, and we joined the others. Lowery shook his head. "You cowboys and Indians aren't supposed to work together."

"Watch us." I passed him and walked toward Alexia, who

was looking on from a safe distance, and spoke after catching my breath. "How are you doing?"

She tried to smile, her face a mess. "You did not kill him?"

"Culpepper? No." I glanced back at the collapsed and smoldering massif. "I think the mountain did it for me."

Isidro, predictably, decided to walk, trusting that he could probably go safer and farther in his tire-tread sandals than on our broken-down mules.

The rest of us were comfortably saddled, or as comfortably as we could be, and made our way in the darkness over the ridge, across the open meadows, and toward the drop-off that led to the sounds of the river that seethed below.

The river twisted through the canyon like a rattler intent on biting itself, and in the moonlight, I could make out the remains of a trestle bridge that the old-timers must've used to drive ore wagons across when mining the sulfur.

I could see the flat rim of the canyon and the plateau that would take us back to Adan's home and hopefully a reunion with Cady, miles away. Isidro led on foot, and I pulled up the drags, glancing over the itchy spot between my shoulder blades every minute or so, wondering if Bidarte had gotten away. Anybody who had returned to the monastery was most certainly dead, but he was an escape artist and had gotten out of dire situations before like a black cat with nine lives.

Thinking I'd seen something on the ridge, I pivoted in the saddle and studied the skyline, but after a few moments, figuring it was my imagination, I followed the others over the edge and down the treacherous track that was only as wide as a dining room table.

It was moderately dark, and the path was rough, but the

mules were sure-footed and there were only a few slips as we got to a cornice that wrapped around the canyon wall. Personally, I was going to be happy when we had gotten far enough so that we wouldn't be sitting ducks from above.

I unslung the M16 from my shoulder and wondered what, exactly, the mule I was sitting on would do at the sound of automatic gunfire. There wasn't a lot of room for mistakes on the narrow trail, and if one of them started to run, it was a surefire train wreck to the stony floor of the canyon a good quarter of a mile down.

Past the cornice there was a wide enough overhang where the group had converged, Adan circling back and waiting for me. "I think we made it."

"I'm glad you think so."

Urging his own mule a little forward, he looked back up the trail. "Did you see something?"

"No, just a feeling."

"We have traveled too far, too quickly." He reached down and patted his mount's withers. "And we have the only mode of transportation that can go this way, other than walking."

"I hope you're right."

Nudging past, he joined the others as I caught up with Lowery who, on the mule, looked to be the most uncomfortable person in the world. "Hey, Sparky, I need a word."

He looked at me, puzzled. "What'd you call me?"

"Sparky, it's an old term for radio operators."

"Radio?"

"It was a thing, before your time. . . . Anyway, the coordinates you gave the Feds were for the village?"

"Yeah, why?"

I glanced around for effect. "I don't know if you've noticed, but we're not in the village anymore."

"So?"

"So how are they going to find us?"

"Oh."

Fumbling with my shirt pocket, I took out the sat phone and looked at the cracked screen. "Well, hell . . ." Remembering the code that he'd told me, I punched it in and then dialed one of the only numbers I knew by heart.

There was some buzzing and clicking and then a familiar voice. "Red Pony Bar and Grill and Continual Soiree."

"Henry."

There was some fumbling, and I think for one of a half dozen times in his life, he was taken aback. "Where are you?"

"You wouldn't believe me if I told you. How is Lola?"

"Perfectly safe. There were two men who came up on the Rez asking questions about you and your family a few days ago—specifically about your granddaughter."

"And?"

"They disappeared." There was a long and loaded pause. "No one seems to know what happened to them."

He said nothing more.

"Thank you."

"Where is Cady?"

"Free, and on her way back." I adjusted the thing at my ear as the mules traipsed on. "Look, I'm in the middle of nowhere, Mexico, and I think I'm going to need some help before this is all over."

"What would you like me to do?"

"Contact McGroder's office in El Paso and tell them we've left the village and are heading west by northwest at a pretty slow pace, but that as soon as they can get here would be great."

"They know where this village is?"

"They have the coordinates."

"Consider it done." There was a pause. "Bidarte?"

I held the phone there for a second. "I'll talk to you when I get back." Thumbing the button, I returned it to my shirt pocket.

Slapping my mule in the ass, I headed off after the group and then turned to look up, still seeing nothing but still feeling something.

After another twenty minutes we made it to the canyon floor and a smooth pathway that circled back about a quarter mile between the boulders, leading to the dilapidated bridge. The river was narrow, only about fifty yards across, but the water was fast moving with rapids and whitewater a tainted brown.

The bridge had evidently been built before the use of modern cars and was about the width of a Model T or A, which figured into the life span of the sulfur mines that had been in operation after the consolidation following the Mexican Revolution. The hand-formed stone and concrete abutments held rusted cables and deadheads that had likely been there since the twenties. There was plenty of room for a mule, but we would have to pick our way carefully over the broken planks.

Isidro stood on the bridge as Adan stopped his mount at the short incline.

"I think maybe we should walk the mules."

"I've seen structures that have inspired more confidence, yes."

We all climbed off, and I went over to help Alexia dismount before turning to Adan. "Do you want to try it first, or do you want me to?"

"I weigh less than you."

"Your mule doesn't." I smiled, handing him my lead, and then began lessening my weight by unslinging the M16 and handing that to him as well along with the .357 revolver and the Glock 9mm.

"Jesus."

"Culpepper." Pulling my own Colt from the small of my back, I handed it to him also. "But this one is mine so take especially good care of it."

The boards of the bridge were warped but roughcut to an exact thickness as they had been in the old days, so the four-bys were actually a true four inches thick and stretched all the way across the ten-foot width.

The ramp was on solid footings, but the span was supported by the cables and swung perilously. I could see the river rushing between the abutments after the first step I took onto the planks, but they didn't crack in two. I got brave and jumped up and down on the thing, but it didn't break.

I was starting to get a little more confidence, so I reached out and took hold of one of the guide-wire strands that made up the makeshift railing—it came loose in my hand and dropped into the river where it was swallowed and disappeared.

The Doc stood on the first plank. "I don't think we should rely on the railings."

I called back. "Agreed."

Walking a little farther out, I could see that the weather had done more damage near the center. There were a few planks missing, and the ones that were still there weren't likely to hold the weight of a mule, let alone a mule and rider.

I stepped on one and watched as it split and hung there, one half on one side, one on the other. The next one seemed stable, but then there were two bad ones, and I was pretty sure that bringing the mules across this bridge was going to be an impossibility and a downright disaster.

Turning back to Adan, I shook my head and yelled, "Not possible, not on the mules."

Carefully picking my way back, I figured we could make it walking; we'd have to let the mules go, climb the canyon trail on the other side, and then hike the distance to Adan's place. The only one I was worried about was Alexia, but she was tough and even after what she'd gone through I figured she'd be okay.

I'd almost made it back when my ears picked up a strange sound over the roar of the river. The sound bounced off the canyon walls, so it was difficult to tell which direction it was coming from, but I finally settled on the west, and the rim from which we had just climbed down.

The high-pitched whine of two-stroke motors.

Studying the rim of the canyon headed back toward the mountain village I'd destroyed, I could see headlights playing over the top.

Adan followed my stare. "What is it?"

"Motorcycles. God, I hate motorcycles." I watched as the driver, who had taken out a pair of binoculars, spotted us immediately.

"Damn." I gestured toward the others. "Get off those mules, they're not going to make it and we need to hurry." Moving to help Alexia, I threw a thumb toward the bridge. "We need to get over to the other side before they get here."

Lowery stared at the trail bikes now congregating at the rim. "Then what?"

"I don't know, but I don't want to be here when they get here, do you?"

In answer, he scrambled off his mule and immediately moved toward the bridge as I turned to Isidro, who already had unslung his M1.

Following his gaze, I made a few calculations and figured it to be past the abilities of anybody. "Can you hit them from here?"

He shook his head.

"But when they get lower?"

This time he nodded.

"I'll be back." Moving toward the bridge, I handed Alexia over to Adan as he attempted to give me back the armory. "No, just the M16."

"What are you going to do?"

"Hold them off."

"Once they get down here, you won't be able to make it up without getting shot."

"If we don't slow them down, none of us will make it out of here." I gestured toward Isidro. "Besides, I've got some pretty good help." I pushed his shoulder as he and Alexia started across with Lowery leading the way.

The mules, bless their hearts, stood there looking at me as I carefully pulled off the saddles and halters. Moving to the left, I herded them away from the bridge and then shooed them down the banks of the river toward the north, where they stopped. "Git, go on. Get out of here!"

They moved a little farther and then found a grassy patch and began eating.

Oh well, I was sure they'd figure it out when the shooting started.

Trying to think what our best position of advantage might be, I turned back to Isidro and glanced around at what I hoped was not our last stand. There were large boulders scattered across the canyon floor in a few spots, but what I was concerned with now was finding a path of retreat if that turned out to be necessary.

Touching Isidro's shoulder, I drew his attention from the dirt bikes as they worked their way down the canyon wall a lot faster than we had. "I'm thinking that we should get across the bridge now and set up behind the concrete abutments over there, because that bridge is going to be a no-man's-land when they get in range and I don't know what kind of weapons they're carrying."

He stared at me for a moment and then pointed to himself and then the ground where we stood.

"You want to make your stand here?"

He ignored me and looked back at the headlights of the oncoming motorcycles as they navigated the trail.

"Isidro, there's not enough cover, and if we have to retreat they'll shoot us dead on the bridge."

This time he pointed at me and then across the river.

I shook my head. "I'm not leaving you over here."

He smiled and pointed toward the cliffs, flashing four fingers twice and then pointing toward his antique rifle and flashing the same number of fingers.

"You want to even the odds a little before we cross the bridge?"

He nodded his head once.

"All right, why not?" I looked around again and picked out some pretty good-sized boulders and pointed toward them. "Over there?"

He nodded, and we retreated, setting up on the other side of the rocks just to give us a little protection. Detaching the M16 magazine, I counted close to thirty rounds which was good; at least with the limited range of the 5.56x45mm NATO, I could lay down some suppression fire as the Tarahumara/Apache Indian picked a few of them off.

This was going to be some dirty business.

I looked back up the canyon wall and counted the headlights— there were at least a dozen motorcycles. "Well, hell . . . Maybe some of them will fall off before they get here."

The mules took notice of our hiding place and ambled over to investigate. I hissed at them, and they looked at me like I was crazy and then came closer to make sure we were all right.

Isidro ignored them, and I was pretty sure he was of the mind that when the shooting started, our noble steeds would make a hasty retreat. I decided to move them off. They'd done us good service, and call it the rancher's son in me, but I couldn't stand the thought of them being shot.

The trail bike motors sounded like a swarm of angry hornets as I stepped out from the boulders and moved toward the mules. "C'mon, guys . . . Get out of here. Yah! Yah!"

They stood there, looking at me.

Remembering that they probably only spoke Spanish, I used one of my few words and this time I yelled, "Vamoose! *Vete!*"

They studied me some more.

Not wanting to fire any of the weapons in hopes of not wasting any more ammunition, I picked up a pebble and pitched it at the lead mule, who flinched, and then redirected his large ears toward me.

I picked up another pebble, and they all took a step toward me, curious.

I dropped the pebble, shook my head and rejoined Isidro, who was smiling as he leaned against the back of the boulder.

The bikers had taken the trail away from us in order to get some level land before turning back to make the run at the bottom of the canyon toward us. I was thinking there were at least a dozen of them, which didn't bode well. Even if Isidro tagged eight, that meant four of them could set up camp and take potshots at the remainder of our party.

There just weren't enough of us.

I looked at the mules.

The mules looked at me.

I thought about the story I'd told Bianca, the one about Ambrose Bierce and the counterattack near Brown's Ferry. If my estimations were right, it would be another couple of minutes before the dirt bikes made flat ground and would be bunched up in the narrow pass for the charge.

Smiling at Isidro, who was studying me with a curious expression, I climbed up on the boulder and the mules moved in even closer. Checking the magazine and then slapping it home, I selected full-auto and then pushed the button to close the bolt. Propping the butt of the stock on my hip, I pointed the barrel skyward and addressed the combatants, with all apologies to Tennyson.

> *Half a mile, half a mile,*
> *Half a mile onward,*
> *Right toward the Georgia troops,*
> *Broke the two hundred.*
> *Forward, the Mule Brigade,*
> *"Charge for the Rebs!" they neighed,*
> *Straight for the Georgia troops*
> *Broke the two hundred.*

Squeezing the trigger, I cut loose with a quick burst and watched as the mules spun, bucked, crow-hopped, and then took off at a high rate of speed back down the trail from whence we'd come.

They quickly disappeared around the corner, and I listened to the sounds of shrieking men, screeching metal, and braying mules.

It was with a great deal of satisfaction that I watched as the four mules appeared in quick succession. They were heading up the trail, apparently unhurt, racing up the narrow path back toward the village. I wasn't too concerned about their health, figuring that they would stay in the high meadows where there was plenty of food and water until somebody found them.

Isidro stood, looking at me and shaking his head, finally coming around the boulder and starting toward the area where we'd last heard the motorcyclists.

I followed as he began trotting, and after a couple hundred yards we rounded the corner and took in the devastation. There were motorcyclists everywhere, most of whom had crashed among the boulders, almost all of them unconscious and bleeding, with only a few sitting up, although clearly dazed. There was one man standing in the path holding his arm and turning in circles, trying to figure out what had just happened.

I punched him hard in the gut and then sat him down in the path.

We picked our way through the broken men, gathered the scattered weapons, and checked them for other weapons as we went.

The final rider was trapped under his bike where it had gone off the road and then caught traction and flipped over and back onto him. He was holding a pistol and had it trained on us as we approached. I was hoping it was Bidarte, but we weren't that lucky. His leg was turned in an awkward angle, and I was pretty sure it was broken.

The semiautomatic shook in his hand as he aimed it at us.

I stopped, about three paces from him. "*Hola*. You speak English?"

He spat and then gestured with the 9mm. "I speak with this."

I glanced at Isidro, who had the barrel of Epitafio pointed at the man's head. "If you're not careful, this conversation is going to be over before it starts."

He snorted. "I'm the only one of us who speaks the English."

"Where's Bidarte?"

He gestured with the pistol. "He's never far, gringo."

I crouched down and studied him. "Look, your leg is broken and probably a couple of other things too. . . . Now, we can leave you here under your motorcycle to die, or we can gather you up with the others and put you over against those rocks."

He snorted, studying me with wavering eyes. "Why would you do such a thing?"

"Because I'm a police officer."

He wheezed a laugh. "So was I."

"I was sworn to protect and to serve."

"So was I, but I found something that paid better."

"Though not quite as worthwhile."

He grinned and re-aimed. "It's the things you do, the things you leave behind that matter, and I think killing you will be something worthwhile, yes?"

I nodded toward Isidro, who was now even closer. "You'll never get the round off."

"Maybe, maybe not."

"Where's Bidarte?"

"Are you the one that set the mules on us?"

"I think the mules made that decision themselves, but I might've helped." I waited a moment and then pushed my hat back on my head. "Where's Bidarte?"

He gestured with the gun again, motioning behind us. "We have a saying in our country, that you are permitted in times of great danger to walk with the devil until you have crossed the bridge."

"What's that supposed to mean?"

"You'll find out, gringo." He redirected the 9mm toward me, and Isidro fired, knocking his head back as if it had been kicked by one of the long-gone mules. His faceless body slumped to the side and twitched a few times before lying still.

We disentangled the rest from their bikes and dragged them to the slight overhang, doing our best to make them comfortable using all their supplies except for one wool-blanket-sided canteen, which I kept for myself. One young man looked vaguely familiar, with his American soccer ball cap. "Iván?"

He avoided making eye contact with me.

I nudged his leg with my boot. "Iván, the last time I saw you we made a deal that if we saw you again we were going to stitch your face to a soccer ball."

"Um, yeah."

"What the hell are you doing down here trying to kill me?"

His head shrank down on his neck like a turtle trying to become invisible. "Um, I had nowhere to go."

"How about landscaping in Tucson?" I glanced around. "How about anywhere but here?" I shook my head and pulled out my wallet, snatching a couple of fifties and handing them to him. "Once we get out of here, buy some help."

He looked at the bills. "Is this all you got?"

"You know, I may kill you myself."

Isidro, standing to the side, raised his weapon but I waved him off. "Look, you're the most mobile of the Light Brigade. Hang around for a few hours and then if nobody comes looking for you, take off and get help from one of the towns, okay?"

"Nobody is going to come looking for us." He glanced around. "Maybe I can get one of the local ranchers to come help, but it will take more money."

"So much for the milk of human kindness." I pulled out a

couple more fifties and handed them to him. "Do it, and if you leave these guys down here to die and I hear about it?" I threw a thumb at Isidro. "I'll send him after you, and believe me, you don't want that."

He nodded, glancing at the Indian, who looked like some vision from an Edward S. Curtis photograph, with the exception of the M1C Garand sniper rifle.

"Now, one more thing. Where's Bidarte?"

"I don't know. Honest."

"Was he the one that sent you and your friends after us?"

"Um, yeah."

"When and where was that?"

"At the monastery."

That seemed curious. "So before the avalanche."

"Yeah."

"Then why did it take you so long to catch up with us?"

"Um, the avalanche? And we went down the road because we thought that was the way you went."

"Did you see my daughter?"

"No."

He wasn't telling me everything, so I crouched down there, very close to him, and leaned in. "Did you see a pink Cadillac?"

He avoided my eyes. "Um, yeah."

I reached out and gripped his chin, pointing his face at mine, moving in even closer. "Where?"

"Um, on the road, but there was nobody in it."

14

Even in my agitated state, I couldn't keep up with Isidro.

Maybe it was my age, lack of sleep, the heat, the beating, dragging around bodies or what, but no matter how hard I tried I could feel myself slowing down.

The two of us kept climbing, and I continued to look ahead to see if we could catch a glimpse of the others, but so far there was nothing except the flat, horizontal light peering over the canyon edge like an empty page.

The temperature was rising with the sun, and my energy was playing out as we climbed, but I was a long way from stopping. I wasn't sure how long it took to get to Adan's place, but I hoped that Cady would be there. Maybe the Cadillac wouldn't start—it had shown a propensity. Maybe they'd gotten a ride in a better vehicle more suited for the mountain roads. My mind raced ahead of me on the trail, leaving me in the mental dust.

Looking back, I could see Iván peeking out from under the outcropping, and I was pretty sure that he was simply waiting till we were out of sight to abandon his *compañeros* with my couple of hundred dollars.

Ah, the honor of thieves.

I trudged after Isidro, feeling like a grizzly bear trailing a pronghorn antelope.

I stopped, resting an arm on an adjacent boulder, and adjusted the M16 strap. I wiped the sweat from my face, and when I looked up, Isidro was staring at me from above. "Sorry, not as young as I used to be."

Predictably, he said nothing.

Pushing back my hat, I shook my head. "Who am I kidding, I couldn't have kept up with you in my prime." I started toward him. "Played college ball at USC—I was an offensive lineman. Got my degree in English." I smiled. "That's why I speak it so good." I caught up with him and pulled out the confiscated canteen, which I held out to him—he declined. "Maybe I should've taken Spanish."

He grinned.

Unscrewing the top, I took a swig. "Thank you again, for my life."

He nodded once and then turned to head up the trail as I put the purloined canteen away and started off again—after a while it became obvious that our two paces were not going to match. "Isidro."

From the next switchback, he turned to look down at me. "You go ahead, and I'll catch up at the top. I'm just slowing you down, and I'd rather you be up there with them than hanging around here waiting for me."

He tilted his head in an almost canine confusion.

I pointed toward the rim of the canyon. "I don't want them up there without protection."

He quickly nodded and then doubled his pace, and in a matter of moments his thin legs and tire-tread sandals were out of sight.

After what seemed like a couple of forevers, the added

high-test adrenaline was beginning to peter out, and I was just glad to make it to level ground as I took one last look at the canyon bottom and then walked over the edge into a flat, ochre-colored landscape that stretched as far as my tired eyes could see. It was like a huge, dead beast, leonine in color with ridges resembling desiccated ribs that rose without grace—a carrion land.

Isidro was not there, and neither was anyone else.

I slowly turned in all directions, but all I could see was the heat undulating from the baked surface of the desert like invisible samba dancers. I wished for a sound, but pressed hard against the sky, the terrain gave no answers.

There were a few cactus and sagebrush sprigs to break the monotony, but the tract seemed to go on forever and, pressed here between sky and earth, I could only see the shape and roundness of the earth. I took a few more steps and stumbled over the wash of an old two-track that had grown over. A few of the pieces of sagebrush were bent, and as I looked closer, I could see the imprint of tires in the powdery sand; the tire marks were fresh—off-road truck tires which looked to be pulling on all four wheels. Someone had been here and recently.

I turned around slowly, trying to spot a trail of dust that might give me an indication of where they'd gone, but there was nothing.

I backtracked and moved to my left, where I could see that our group had stood in a bunch and then had either been forced into a vehicle or had driven off in one of their own, but if that was the case who was driving the truck, how did they get here, and why would they leave Isidro and me behind?

I didn't like it, I didn't like it one bit.

And where the hell was my sniper?

There was a strange noise, almost like a chirping, and I

turned in a circle in an attempt to locate it. It was only after a moment that I realized it was the sat phone in my pocket.

I pulled the thing from my shirt, glanced at the further damage it had incurred, and then hit the green button and held it to my ear. "Howdy."

"Now where in the wide world of fuck are you?"

"Hi, Vic." I licked my lips and swallowed. "Henry call you guys?"

"He did, and McGroder and the rest of them are trying to get a GPS positioning off of that satellite phone in your hands, so don't you dare hang up." There was some jostling, and her voice became more personal. "Other than where, how are you?"

"Tired." I glanced around. "I thought we'd gotten away, but I'm thinking something's happened and now I'm not so sure."

"Are you hurt?"

I breathed a laugh. "A little beat-up, but fine."

"Well, this place is a clusterfuck. . . . Did you set off some kind of thermonuclear device in that village?"

"No, I just ignited some old sulfur mines as a diversion."

"Well, it also ignited a panty bunch of international proportions. The Mexican government now thinks there's some kind of military intervention going on on their soil and are refusing to assist."

"I'm never eating Mexican again."

"What?" There was more fumbling. "I don't fucking know. I'll ask him." More fumbling. "Walt, why isn't your phone giving us a GPS positioning?"

"How the hell should I know?" I held the thing out, staring at the screen as if it did me any good, and then put it back to my ear. "Is there a button for that?"

"They say they're not getting anything. . . . "

I glanced around in all directions. "Look, I'm about seven

miles east of the village. Wherever the others are, I've got to find them before we can do anything, so work on the assumption that I'm headed due east by northeast at a walking pace."

"Walt?"

"I've got to go." Punching the button before she could reply, I stepped into the sand and started following the tracks. I hadn't gone far when I saw something standing upright on a flat rock in the center of the road.

I reached down and picked up the gleaming, 180-grain .30-06 round and held it up to the sun, turning it in my fingers until I saw the tiny sign of a cross scratched in the brass casing that Guzman had mentioned a couple of lifetimes ago.

Isidro.

They'd gotten him too, or he'd seen something and hadn't had time to come back for me.

Slipping the calling card into my shirt pocket, I looked in the direction where the road disappeared like the vanishing point of a surrealistic painting and started walking toward the horizon, following the tire tracks and looking for the prints of the Indian's sandals.

The sun was about an hour from reaching its zenith, and I judged the temperature to already be in excess of a hundred degrees. The sweat burst under the band of my hat, ran to the end of my nose, and dropped on the sand, making a slight indentation, which quickly evaporated. It was like walking in a convection oven. I tried to think back to the conversation I'd had with Adan about the layout of the area, and I remembered him saying it was about five miles to the canyon from his place—I could only hope that by following the road, I was taking the right direction.

I'd gone about a hundred yards when I hit a fork. Staring at the dust, I could plainly see that the tire tracks headed slightly south, which was strange, because I could've sworn from the set of the sun that the ranch was slightly north. I looked at the tire marks again, still not seeing any sign of Isidro, and then set off after whatever vehicle had made them.

A vast and prehistoric basin covered with mica, basalt, feldspar, and quartz that reflected the sky like a shattered mirror, a land where ice claws had ripped deep arroyos, wounds that then had been healed by the wash of ancient waters, a land that now thrived with mesquite, cactus, and Spanish bayonet, a place with a snake of low, blue hills at the horizon.

I found the first body an hour later.

Trudging around a rock shelf, I could see something lying in the ditch ahead, a few turkey buzzards picking at it. I ran toward the body, scattering the vultures, and flipped it over, finding the electronic whiz, Lowery, with his throat cut. The desert had greedily drunk up the blood from his almost severed head, the neck cut with a surgeon's precision, the fatal wound looking almost like a wide, lipless, second mouth.

The California kid's dry eyes stared out straight into the burning sun and even in death, the cocky smile still played on his sand-covered lips.

I sat there holding him for a few moments and then dragged him to the side of the road, propping him against the rocks, I'm not sure why. Maybe I was showing respect, maybe I was a lawman used to clearing the road, and then maybe it was just something to do.

I went through his pockets, but there was nothing, and it was only when I eventually stood that I came face to face with a second Springfield .30-06 round standing erect on the rocks. Noting the scratched cross, I stuffed it in my pocket and again glanced around trying in vain to find tire-track sandal prints; then I started off again without looking back.

Unless I'd dreadfully misjudged Isidro, my assumption had been correct. Bidarte's men must have taken the others who had covered for the Indian and me, and when Isidro had gotten to the flat he'd seen a vehicle and had given pursuit in hopes of keeping them in sight, leaving messages for me in the only tongue in which he spoke.

I pulled the canteen up and started to take a swig but then decided I'd better start rationing if I was going to make it to who knew where. Placing a hand at the small of my back, I stretched in an attempt to drive away the muscle cramps.

The makeshift road continued to sweep southeast, and I dragged my feet along the tracks until the surface of the desert changed, becoming harder with less vegetation. The hardpan gave way to the dead south where the tail end of the mountains curled to the southeast, and I couldn't help but think I was headed in that direction toward the Orfanato or Torero and not north to Adan's ranch.

It seemed as if I'd been walking for hours, my legs and back cramping and my throat feeling like the road I was walking on, so I opted for a swallow of water. I unscrewed the top and took a deep slug.

As near as I could tell, I still had a quarter of my water supply left.

I set off again, but the spasms were getting worse. All I could think about was finding a shady spot to rest, of which there was none. I kept moving. Somewhere out there was my daughter, and if they thought I was giving up short of dying, they had another thought coming.

The second body was lying in the road just like the one before. Even from a distance, I could see it was Alonzo, lying on his back, his throat cut from ear to ear. Once again, the blood had poured onto the ground, but here the rocky surface refused the young man's blood and the stuff was everywhere, drawing flies that buzzed around me as I stooped and turned his jaw to look in his face.

His eyes behind the broken, thick lenses were still, but his face held the rigor of a vicious battle. He must've seen how Lowery had gone and decided it wouldn't be as easy to kill him, but he was dead nonetheless, and for the second time that day I dragged a body from the road.

I was panting with the exertion and putting my hands on my knees, took a deep breath and glanced around, still seeing nothing but the endless expanse of desert. The sun was now directly above, and I felt like the flesh was burning from my bones, even with my palm-leaf hat, the light striking the desert and bouncing back up at me like grease in an overly heated frying pan.

Taking the next step, I wavered a bit and used the stock of the M16 to steady myself. A little panic ran through me as my eyes wavered, and I felt my balance giving way again. Finally standing still, I looked at the minimal shadow that I cast, barely covering my dust-covered boots.

There must've been water at some point that had maybe filled the flat distance, but the water was gone now, leaving behind a hardened crust of gray mud that broke apart with the weight of my boots like thin-set tile. I took a step and then stood there looking at the cracks spreading out from beneath my feet; it looked like the entire world was covered with dirty ice, ready to break through and swallow me up.

Taking the second step I looked down and saw a .30-06 round lying on an elevated portion of the dried mud.

I reached down to pick it up, and as I did, I could feel my balance giving way and I crashed into a rut in the road. I just lay there for a moment to catch my breath, watching the dust scatter as I shot air from my nostrils. I could feel the sun on the side of my face where my hat had come off. Finally rolling onto my side, I reached out and took the bullet, placing it in my shirt pocket along with the others.

How many were dead? I couldn't even remember. When had this all started, and how many would be dead before it ended? I had to get up or I would be part of the count, but somehow I couldn't and put my head back on the ground.

Lift up your head and heart.

"I'm tired."

I don't care.

"I can't move."

You can, you simply have to want to, Lawman. Lift up your head and your heart will follow.

Sliding a boot beneath me, I shifted my weight and leveraged the rifle so that I could lean into it. I looked around for Virgil White Buffalo, but he wasn't there.

Taking a few more deep breaths, I gathered my hat and pushed myself up, nearly collapsing from the strain, but my legs held and I stood there pulling the rifle sling onto my shoulder with the canteen.

My hands and feet were swollen, making me feel like I was carrying a weight that was suspended from my arms and legs like the pendulum bobs hanging from the lyre on a grandfather clock. I stepped forward in time, swinging my other leg past in opposition with my arms and found I'd taken a step, then another and another, using the momentum to lurch forward.

I thought about how the seven-foot Crow Shaman showed up in desperate times and wondered if I could summon him up again, for shade if nothing else.

Dropping my eyes, half blinded by the white-hot brass eye of the sun, I looked into the distance and thought I could see some-thing up and to the right. When I got closer, I saw that it was an abandoned vehicle, an old truck from the early 1900s with large metal wheels, solid rubber tires, and steel-plated sides.

Pretty sure I needed shade more even than water, I stag-gered up beside the thing and pulled open the back door, but the wave of heat that greeted me convinced me that trying to sit in the thing was going to be like trying to rest in a stove, never mind the abandoned mud nests that adhered to the roof of the metal structure, the inside coated with swallow dung.

Satisfied with sitting on the lip of the doorway, I looked up at the rounded turret in the rear and the heavy rivets where the monster had been stitched together. Thinking back to pictures I'd seen of Pershing's punitive expedition during the Mexican Revolution, I couldn't help but think that this old fellow had been driven down here and then abandoned—I knew how it felt.

There was a plate inside the door that read THOMAS B. JEF-FERY COMPANY, KENOSHA, WISCONSIN.

You need to get moving, Lawman.

"I know, I just need a second."

She needs you.

I spoke to the dwarf juniper and the candelilla that must have leached some moisture from the shadow of the armored car. "I know, I know . . ."

Now.

I attempted to struggle onto my feet but slumped on the edge of the armored car and just sat there, my breath short. I tried to focus my eyes and looked out across the desert at the cactus and the acacia and suddenly remembered the canteen. I swung it around slowly and unscrewed the top, gulped a few mouthfuls of the warm water and then carefully screwed the top back on.

With a deep sigh, I edged off the metal lip and stood, adjusting the straps of both the rifle and canteen, and then taking a step, then another and another until I'd made the road and started off southeast, farther and farther from home.

I'm not sure when I became aware of the sun being behind me, but it was, drying the sweat that threatened to solidify me into a statue. I'd given up thinking about much of anything as I stumbled on, pretty sure that if I lessened my attention for even a second I was likely to go crashing to the ground again and unsure if I still had the energy to get back up.

I wiped the sweat from my face and opened the canteen but there was nothing there except the leathery dryness.

The land had changed again, but the iron-colored mountains still trailed to my right. It was hard to judge how far I'd come. I was sure I'd been traveling most of the nightmarish day, my legs having turned into stilts that moved like a drawing compass, awkward and stiff. The landscape was a negative photograph of itself, the color washed away with nothing but the creosote phosphorescence flushed with heat.

I watched the tail end of the mountains begin to peter out— I was sure I was as far south as the Orfanato and cast my eyes around looking for it, but there was nothing. Maybe there was nothing as far as I could travel and this was how it ended, alone in a desert. Maybe after all the walking, I was no closer to saving Cady than when I'd cleared the canyon rim at the beginning of this endless day.

There was a low rumble behind me, like drums.

I was in mid-stride when I felt a bit of a breeze.

Turning just a little, I could see the cloudbank that had been building over the mountains, the edges of the clouds shining like platinum, and I could've sworn the temperature had dropped a good ten degrees as more than a dozen dust devils wildly pirouetted through the ironwood and cactus, the smell of the creosote like a tonic as I stood there wavering in the wind.

The world darkened behind me and with the wind at my back I turned toward the Cecil B. DeMille sky with a little more energy, like a light on the road to Damascus.

The drums were still beating, and I could feel them pushing me forward. My boots took on a life of their own, each following the other carrying me along with the low-flying wind. It was flat now, and the road was straight, and I'd found a juggernaut reserve that kept me stumbling forward, my shirt parachuting in front of me.

A lashing skiff of rain sheeted across the desert, a gift from the heavens that cooled my skin and allowed some color to return to the world. It was enough to combat the smell of creosote, but not enough to sustain the land, so the desert lay back down and did what it has done since the beginning of time—it waited.

I cleared my throat as best I could and stayed concentrated on the horizon in front of me when I saw another body lying in the road, saturated by the brief rain, the blue blouse and badge huddled in the center, unmoving.

Every organ in my body flipped, and I found myself running toward her. I fell onto the road and pulled her to me. I held her head up and gently brushed the wet, matted hair away from her eyes to find the face of Bianca Martínez, whom he must have dressed in Cady's clothes.

I hugged her to my chest and held her there, feeling relief that it wasn't Cady but a deep sadness at the loss of such a friend. I held her tighter and suddenly realized that she wasn't cold.

Pulling her back away from me, I looked and was even more shocked by her fluttering eyelids and the violet irises looking up at me.

Her lips parted, and she expelled air from her lungs, saying a single word. "No."

Pulling her in closer, I smiled as best I could and croaked, "You . . . You're going to be all right." I sounded like a mote of dust released from an ancient book.

Her hand came up, brushing my arm. "No."

"I promise, you'll be okay."

"No." She looked away, and I was afraid I was losing her, so I started to scoop another hand under her legs in an attempt to lift her. "No, they . . ."

I'd just gotten her in my arms and had begun to lift her when something struck me in the head from directly behind.

I fell forward and lay across her, now trying to get my arms under me to push off from the caked red sand that stuck to my face. I heard her crying, but then another blow landed on my head and I flopped forward and lay there because that was all I could do.

15

It was a slow process, like a log dislodged from the depths, rolling, tumbling, and finally surfacing, bobbing along in the current. Up from the blind depths, I felt myself rising through the levels of awareness until I was alive again.

There was a hand on my face, and the fingers were cool.

My eyelids fluttered, and I became aware of amethyst eyes looking down at me; I just lay there gazing into them. "Seven Spanish angels . . ."

The eyes smiled. "What?"

"An old song."

"Well, there's only one of me."

I tried to sit up but collapsed back onto her lap. "Cady."

"She is alive."

I closed my eyes and just lay there breathing, grateful for small successes. "Your brother?" She said nothing, and I opened my eyes again to see if she had heard me, the streaks of tears telling me that she had.

She looked away. "Four men it took, four armed men, and he fought them to a standstill, but they beat him senseless. He is up at the house with the women and children."

I glanced around in the mild darkness, taking in the

collapsed stone wall and the rickety hayloft and even the manger where I'd found the AKs. "The Orfanato?"

"Sí."

"Is there anyone else alive?"

"I don't know where the Seer is—all but the orphans, your
daughter, Adan, the housekeeper, and myself are dead."

Finally summoning enough energy to rise up and support
myself with one arm, I craned my neck in an attempt to exor-
cise some of the pain. "Have you seen Isidro?"

"Who?"

"The sniper."

She studied me with a strange look on her face.

"Oh, right—you never saw him." I tried to stand but decided
that could wait. "What happened?"

"Alonzo's ridiculous car wouldn't start, so we took another
that had the keys in it and almost made it to Torero before it ran
out of petrol and they caught us. They got a message that you
were going by way of the canyon, and Bidarte's men were waiting when they came out ahead of you."

"How did they get there so fast?"

"A private plane."

Rubbing the back of my head, I grunted. "Was Culpepper
the one who brained me?"

"Yes."

"How the hell did he get out of there?"

"Just lucky, I guess." We both turned to look at the cocky
man who was on the other side of the broken wall, half his face
bandaged and my hat back on his head. He sauntered around
the low end with my .45 Colt, Henry's knife, an old kerosene
lantern, and a plastic grocery bag. "I gotta tell ya, you are one
tough son of a bitch."

"Praise from Caesar."

"Right, whatever that means." He nodded, sat on the rail of the manger, and hung the hissing lamp on a bridle hook, the grocery bag at his boots. He pulled out his fixings from his shirt pocket where I could see the top of the sat phone. With a bandaged hand he made a show of nonchalantly rolling a cigarette, licking and sealing the edge. "We thought you were dead about four times, but you just kept right on going like the Energizer Bunny."

"You were watching me?"

"Periodically." Pulling a lighter from his pocket that I recognized as Adan's, he flipped it open and lit his acrid-smelling smoke. "I mean, we had to leave a trail for you."

I let that one pass—for now. "How did you get out?"

He touched the bandages that entirely covered one side of his face. "Well now, it wasn't unscathed, if you know what I mean." He took another toke and held the cigarette out, blowing on the embers and watching it glow in the twilight. "That was a hot time in the old town. . . ." He glanced at me. "I told you. You should've killed me."

"Boy howdy."

He smiled. "Climbed up about a hundred yards down the wall and then you threw that grenade and it touched off the sulfur along with the methane." He gestured toward his face. "Caught some of the flash, and it burned off all the hair on one side of my head, but I got over and was able to run away before the whole damn mountain came crashing down." He pointed the cigarette at me. "You did a number on the place, cost a lot of money and product, and really pissed some people off."

"Glad to hear it."

He smiled. "Yeah, well we'll see about that."

"Where's my daughter?"

"She's safe." He nodded his head toward Bianca. "We had to

borrow her clothes just to stop you, you know?" He puffed on the cigarette. "I'll make you a deal, you tell me where that Injun sniper is, and I'll show you your daughter."

"I don't know where he is."

Some of the swagger left him as he glanced out into the darkness.

"But he's out there I'm betting. Somewhere."

Culpepper pulled the .30-06 shells from his pocket. "Where did these come from?"

"I couldn't say, but then I guess you can't either."

He considered me for a long while. "Okey-dokey, then I guess we got no deal." He shrugged, dropping them back in his pocket. "Now, let's get back to business—need to know how you are feelin'."

"Let me see my daughter."

"You'll see her tomorrow." He waved my request away. "Now, I repeat, how are you?"

"What do you care, you're just going to kill us all anyway."

"Not my choice. *El Jefe* has plans for you come daybreak, and I need to assess if you're up to snuff." Carefully dragging a leg underneath me, I ponderously stood, towering over him as he slowly aimed my gun at me. "Easy there, cowboy."

I felt like I was going to fall over or throw up, neither of which would likely intimidate the challenger, so I did as he said and just stood there. "So you two are back together?"

"Like two peas in a pod." He gestured with the barrel toward the grocery bag. "There's food and water in there for the both of you, and there'll be more in the morning, but in the meantime, I suggest you get some rest, you're going to need it."

He stood and walked out, his voice trailing behind him. "I've got some boys of my own here guarding you and out there circling the perimeter, and they'll be looking for that little

Apache prick so if you hear some shooting tonight that's probably them sending the little fucker off to the happy hunting ground." He began whistling Patsy Cline as he strolled off. "Sweet dreams."

I limped toward the crumbling wall where he'd disappeared and could see two men standing by the corral. Beyond them, the moonlight was gleaming off the aluminum skin of a twin-engine Beechcraft. I was coming around to the thought that having my old Doolittle Raider boss, Lucian Connally, on this trip might've not been such a bad idea.

After a moment, I felt Bianca standing beside me. "I'm assuming you have a plan?"

The food was good, but the water was better. We sat under the unforgiving light of the thirties kerosene lantern I'd just repumped, a less than romantic mood having settled in with the hiss, as we took stock of what our options were. "What do you think Bidarte has planned?"

"Something dramatic—it's what he does." I finished munching on the tortillas and swallowed some more water, feeling a little better. "I'm wondering where they've got everyone. There aren't that many places where they could have them. There's only the main house and this place, so unless they're on the plane out there . . ."

"Do you fly?"

I entertained the thought for a nanosecond. "I think we'd all be safer facing overarmed, psychotic drug dealers than climbing into a plane with me at the controls."

"Then what?"

I walked back to the manger where Culpepper had been sitting and flipped open the hidden drawer where I'd found the

AKs I'd taken with us to the mountain. The space lay empty, the Zapata estaba aquí! message in chalk mocking me. "Well, whatever we're going to do we're going to have to do it unarmed."

"What about your friend, the Indian with the rifle?"

I shook my head. "I honestly don't know where he is or if he's even out there." I limped back over to the wall. "It's you and me." I turned to look at her. "How many men does he have with him?"

She came over, joining me in watching the two men at the corral as they smoked and watched us back. "Maybe a half dozen."

"That's not very many. With one or two out checking the area and with someone with the old woman and kids and Adan and Cady in the ranch house, it's possible that they'll leave only one man to guard us through the night." I glanced down at her. "What vehicles are there?"

"There is the SUV they took us in at Torero and then an old school bus that belongs to the Orfanato."

"Yep, well, I don't think that thing has run anytime since Truman was a tyke." I sighed and then thought about it, remembering what Adan had said. "Your brother, he said they drove it every day into Torero, but I'll check the Escalade first—I doubt they left the keys in it, so unless I can get them off of someone . . ."

"Then we will take the bus, and I'll disable the Cadillac. If they were to chase us with the Beechcraft what are they going to do, bump us with the tires? You can't exactly break the windows out of those things and shoot at us, and if I have my way I'll have something to shoot at them; in my experience civilian aircraft don't respond well to incoming fire. Besides, you're worrying about disaster one hundred and forty-seven before we even get to number one."

I glanced at the two men, and her eyes followed mine as her fingers twined around my arm. "You're going out there?"

Adjusting the lamp, I glanced at her. "I think I just might."

It was later, much later, and we'd turned the lantern way down in hopes of indicating to the guards that we were going to sleep and to let our eyes adjust to the dark.

Crouched by the lowest end of the wall, I watched and decided that these two jaybirds obviously had more cigarettes to smoke and things to discuss than any other two men in Mexico.

Bianca lay out of the way, gently breathing as she slept, and I was about to give up the ghost and get some sleep myself when one of the men said something about *cigarrillos* before walking off toward the main house.

Evidently, they had finally run out of cigarettes.

There was a small area under the manger where the rocks had given way, and it was possible I could get out that way, but just as I started to move, the one guard who remained stepped to the side to look at us and I feigned sleep.

After a moment, I heard him crunching back across the roadway and turned to find Bianca looking at me and whispering, "Now?"

I crawled toward the opening, pausing only once to look back at her. "Remember, fifteen minutes." She glanced down at the pocket watch I'd given her and nodded, and I was off.

Elbowing my way through the dirt and cobwebs, I came out in what would've been the old compost heap, which added an odiferous quality to my already sartorial splendor. Dragging myself up near a rickety fence, I glanced around but could only see one light on somewhere in the ranch house. If I were to make a bet, I would be willing to wager that Bidarte, Culpepper, and maybe one or two of the others would be availing themselves of the comforts on the plane rather than the run-down cottage.

The barn blocked the one guard from observing me, but I was now in plain view of the ranch house and could only hope anyone there was otherwise occupied.

The first thing to do was see if we had any way of escape—I thought I'd check the SUV before the run-down bus, on the offhand chance someone had left the keys in it.

Staying low, I moved across the road toward the far end of the corral, away from the guard and where the Cadillac sat. Moving around the hood of the black Escalade, I crept up the side to look in the window for the key and then realized the thing had keyless entry and start. There really wasn't any way to see if the keys were in the thing without opening the door and alerting the entire ranch.

I couldn't even tell if it was locked without pulling one of the handles.

Hell.

Shaking my head, I moved toward the lawn ornament of a bus manufactured by Mercury in 1959 and found the bifold doors hanging loose, and the key with a bottle opener chain hanging in the switch. How many pumps and cranks would it take to get this piece of crap running, and then how long would it run?

Double hell.

I was going to have to commit, because there wasn't going to be any time to play musical vehicles when we were trying to get out of here. As much as I detested the thought, the safe move was to disable the Escalade and hope the old bus would start.

Pulling the key from the vehicle, I moved back over and used the pointed end of the opener to try and stab one of the Escalade's tires, but it would only go in so far. Giving up, I took off the cap and used the point to gently push in the valve, slowly letting the air out until the tire was pretty well flat. I wanted to flatten another, but I knew I was running out of time, that at any moment Bianca was about to start our planned distraction, and then all hell was likely to break loose.

I moved toward the house and circled behind, taking up a post beside the steps that led from the back screen door.

The kerosene or maybe propane light was on in the kitchen, and I could see a couple of men drinking cans of beer at a table with their feet up, the crushed remains of the evening celebration scattered across the floor.

There was a door to the right, and I assumed that was where the women and children and Adan and Cady were. Slipping past it, I worked my way across the back of the house to another window where Alicia, the solemn little girl whom I'd met here when we'd gotten the mules, was looking at me.

I froze and slowly raised a finger to my lips. I looked at her and then the window sash. It was about then that she simply raised the thing up and leaned out to look at me.

Alexia's broad face appeared beside the child's, and I held the finger to my lips again. "Is Cady here?"

She shook her head. "No, she is on the plane with the bad men."

I sighed, staring at them as more tiny, grubby faces joined us in the window. "What about Adan?"

She glanced behind her. "He is on the floor; he is badly hurt."

"Let's try and get him to the window, and I'll carry him."

She shrank away from my outstretched hands. "The children."

I glanced past the faces, searching the room behind them. "Where's the old woman?"

"They killed her. On the porch, with the children watching."

I stood there shocked for a moment and then lowered my forehead on the sill. "Lord have mercy."

Alexia's voice was solid. "Yes, with all the saints of heaven, He watches over us. We take the children with us, yes?"

Breathing the dust away from the sill, I suddenly felt tiny hands patting the back of my head and raised my face to look into Alicia's dark eyes. Feeling like the world had been pulled out from under my feet and sturdily placed on my shoulders, I raised my arms, picked her up, and lifted the first of many through the window.

The kids were actually better than the two of us at keeping quiet. Playing as if it were a game, they began scurrying across the open ground like church mice and carefully climbed aboard the old bus. I helped Alexia get the unconscious Adan up the vehicle's stairs and was about to turn when I heard someone yelling and looked over to see flames licking the rafters of the half-collapsed barn.

"*Fuego! Fuego!*"

Evidently Bianca and the kerosene lantern had done the trick, and the entire barn was doing a pretty good job of lighting up the place for a hundred yards around.

I had two more passengers to pick up, so I told Alexia and the children to stay in the bus and to keep down away from the windows; then I circled around the back where the first guard was running past toward the ranch house.

Realizing an opportunity when I saw one, I threw a leaping body block into the much smaller man, crushing him into the sand and dirt, my weight squeezing every bit of air out of him as I grabbed what turned out to be the M16 carbine I'd been carrying.

I swung the butt of the weapon and knocked his head

sideways like the return carriage on a typewriter—if he wasn't out cold, he was at least down for the count. I swung the M16, checked the magazine, and flipped it to auto—things were starting to even up.

Limping across the road, I saw Bianca racing for the vehicles and presumed she'd figure out it was the bus or nothing when she got there. Logic dictated that most of the men would head for the fire, but I knew Bidarte would leave at least one to guard Cady, and I knew which one I hoped it would be.

I trailed behind the corral and inched toward the plane, which still sat there, the interior lights flicking on as more than a few people scrambled out of the fuselage door down the abbreviated stairs.

Just to add a little confusion, I screamed in my best Spanish accent, *"Policía! Policía!"* And then sprayed the sky with a few rounds just to reinforce the ruse. The two men running from the house threw themselves to the ground when I fired, and I drifted another series of rounds across the yard, stitching the terrain with small geysers of dirt and rock.

Somebody else fired, but I was pretty sure the shots were coming from the other side of the ranch house, so I continued around the wide tail assembly and came up on the door. Slowly rising, I saw a man I didn't know on the other side, kneeling on something wrapped in a blanket. He was holding a strange-colored Glock 9mm and looking out the window.

Ducking back down, I figured I'd try at least one trick to see if I could save my daughter the anguish of watching him get sprayed across the interior of the Beechcraft. Standing just to the side of the door, I shouted inside. *"Fuego, fuego amigo!"*

Evidently, he was only waiting for an excuse to vacate the plane, because he came barreling out with the 9mm held high and was met with all the force I could put into the butt end of the M16. He dropped, and if he had any nose left, I really couldn't see any evidence of it.

Snatching his sidearm and stuffing it in my jeans, I raised the M16 up to a firing position, stepped on the stairs, and checking to make sure there weren't any other gunmen on the plane, lodged myself in the doorway. I stood there for a few seconds, still not taking my weapon from him as he lay there on the floor unmoving, when I heard a small voice from somewhere inside.

"Daddy?"

Charging down the aisle, I swiveled my head in search of her, finally stopping at the row of seats where the gunman had been kneeling and where I could see a mop of reddish-blond hair and a set of nickel-plated eyes peering up at me.

"Oh, God . . ." She was crying, pushing off the seat and climbing up to me as I grabbed hold of her with the firm intention of never letting her go again.

"Are you all right?"

She sobbed and nodded her head. "Yes, yes I'm fine, but where did—"

"We've got to get out of here." I scooped her up with one arm and checked each window before climbing down through the doorway with the barrel of the automatic rifle leading the way.

The gunman hadn't moved, and I stepped out and turned back to her, noticing for the first time that she was wearing Bianca's flamenco dress and was barefoot. "You don't have any shoes?"

She swiped her fist to clear the tears, and her eyes glinted. "Don't worry about it—you lead, and I'll follow."

Swinging down the fuselage and around the tail section, I

could see that the barn was a full-blown inferno, the dry hay in the loft swirling flames into a massive bonfire with orange sparks carried away in the vortex of its own heat.

"C'mon." I half carried her across the roadway toward the vehicles just as I saw some of the men moving back toward the house and another one running toward the front of the plane. "We haven't got much time . . ."

Cutting through the corral, we climbed the rails on the other side, and I ushered her toward the old bus. "Get in there with the others, but if I get this Caddy going, everybody needs to pile in it posthaste, got it?"

Glancing around at the moldering mode of mass transit, she sighed. "You've got to be kidding."

Bianca reached down and took her arm, pulling her in. "That's what I said."

Threading my way around the front of the SUV, I reached the driver's-side door and yanked on the handle, which did not give. I pulled again, but it was, indeed, locked. "Who the hell locks a car door out here in the middle of the damn desert?" Rearing back, I slammed the butt of the M16 into the glass and watched it bounce off.

Hell.

I was running out of time, so I headed back to the bus and leapt onto the sprung seat. I handed Cady the rifle, and she stood with Bianca where Adan lay on the floor. Glancing back at more than a dozen eyes, I focused on Alexia. "If all the saints of heaven ever answered collective prayers, you need to beg that this hunk of junk starts."

Pushing in the clutch and pumping the gas pedal for all I was worth, I hit the starter and listened as the motor gave out with a herniated grinding that lasted only a few seconds—and then nothing.

I hit it again—nothing.

Slowly becoming aware of a skinny boy speaking in Spanish standing beside me, I glanced back at Alexia, who translated. "He says the flywheel a few teeth is missing, but if you keep pumping and grinding she will catch."

I did as the waif said, and on the fourth try the old V-8 sputtered to life and finally roared through a truncated exhaust, and I was ready to believe in saints. Reaching over, I grabbed the handle for the door and came face to face with the guard I thought I'd knocked out on the plane.

He stood there in the doorway with a mashed nose, the blood covering his face as he smiled and spat and raised an AK, having rearmed himself.

Figuring Cady wouldn't be fast enough and unsure if she even knew how to operate the M16, my hopes lay with the Glock in my waistband, and those hopes didn't shine too brightly.

He raised the Kalashnikov, aiming it directly at my face. I watched as, smiling a bloody grin in the half-light, he tightened his finger on the trigger. I'd just about made my peace with all those saints when the right side of his head exploded like a pumpkin, the fine red spray of his blood shooting out and coating the glass pane in the bifold door. He dropped like a sack of rocks, the AK fire ripping up through the roof of the old bus as I dove to the side for cover. Catching my breath, I glanced back where everyone still stood in an unmoving tableau. "Sit down and hang on!"

Sawing the wheel, I popped the clutch, lurching the bus forward only to stop for a moment and reach back for the M16 in Cady's hands. "Give me the rifle!" She did as I asked, and I leveled the thing one-handed through the open doorway at the Escalade, opening fire while dropping the clutch again.

Sparks flew off the sides of the Cadillac as we lurched forward around the corral and lumbered back toward the main road that led toward Torero, but not before I careened across the opening long enough to throw a dozen rounds into the back of the Beechcraft as a few shots flew our way along with a lot of yelling.

I turned the wheel to the right, and we bumped over the berm and took a lesser road heading northwest as I fumbled to find the light switch. I finally did, and a feeble, yellowish glow emitted from the front of the old bus as I hit second, wallowing the decrepit four-by-four down the washed-out sand flats like a johnboat slipping off a high wake.

Turning back, I yelled to be heard over the engine. "Everybody all right?"

They looked around at each other with Bianca translating for me, and then the collective heads nodded, and we were on our way.

I looked back but couldn't see any approaching headlights, so maybe I'd done enough of a job on the Escalade to knock it out of the game. I was also pretty sure they wouldn't risk taking off in the bullet-riddled Beechcraft in the dark, at least I knew I wouldn't.

I'd just hit third gear when I thought I saw something to my right, something bounding through the stunted junipers and cactus like a pronghorn in full gallop.

Cripes, the old Mercury couldn't even outrun an antelope.

Finally making out the familiar figure who was holding pace with the bus unlike anything human, I slowed and watched as he matched my speed and moved closer, finally leaping onto the landing and grabbing the rail, the M1 Garand pointed back down the road toward our would-be antagonists.

He climbed up the steps as I flipped the safety on the M16, handing it to my daughter again who sat behind me. I gestured toward the wild-looking individual in the ratty cotton poncho. "This is Isidro; he's not much for conversation, but boy can he shoot."

Fortunately, the gas gauge on the bus read half full—unfortunately, we'd been bumping over the washboard road for at least an hour before I saw the old abandoned armored car where I'd rested.

I knew the bodies of my friends were out there, but there was no way I could take the time to pick them up. Turning right at the fork, I headed in the direction of Adan's ranch, figuring that if we got that far there would be reinforcements enough to allow us to escape north.

Cady slipped forward, flipping down a jump seat near the door and attempting to steady herself by grabbing the chrome bar and the dash. "Not that I'm ungrateful, but what the hell?"

I cocked my head and raised an eyebrow. "All according to plan."

"And what was that plan?"

"Saving you. Henry, Vic, and the rest of the posse are tied up in legalities, so I jumped the gun and decided to go freelance on this one."

She glanced back through the bus. "You're liberating orphanages, too?"

"Only as a sideline."

Cady chin-pointed toward Bianca and Adan still lying on the floor. "And who are they?"

"My medical staff."

Her eyes became more thoughtful, and she was silent for a bit. "I thought I was dead and gone, Dad."

I glanced in the oversized rearview mirror that gave a

panoramic view of the bus's interior where I could see Isidro at the back aiming through one of the busted-out corner windows. "I would never let that happen, Punk."

She breathed a laugh, reaching over and touching my arm as she gazed out the windows at the black desert. "Well, you've got to admit that this is a little outside your usual line of work."

We rode quietly for a while, and I noticed that most of the children were stretched out, attempting to sleep on the bench seats.

"The Texan, the one who kidnapped me?"

I turned and looked at her. "Culpepper."

"Yeah . . ." Her eyes stayed out there in the darkness. "He said he was the one who killed Michael."

I watched the road.

She looked at me again, and I could see that she was crying. "I want him dead. That's horrible, isn't it?"

"No, honey, it's not. It's only natural."

"Do you want him dead?"

I thought about it, trying to find the truth in my next statement, but settled for a formula instead. "I could've killed him earlier, and maybe I should've."

"He kept calling us—the two of us—weak. He said that's why they always win, because we show kindness when we shouldn't. Do you think that's true?"

"I think it's twisted." I tried to explain as best I could. "There are so many things worth living and dying for, but only a few things worth killing for, and maybe the two are intertwined—I don't know. I can almost forgive Culpepper—he's just a killing animal—but Bidarte made it personal by going after my family and friends." I glanced at her. "All I know is that I'm not going to let him kill anyone else important to me."

"Headlights!"

I looked in the rearview mirror and could see that Bianca was standing in the center of the bus. She was looking out the back where a set of modern LED headlights bounded over the road, gaining on us fast.

16

Trying to keep the top-heavy Mercury in the wallows of the
rutted desert road, I turned to my daughter who had learned to
drive on my grandfather's 1948 8N tractor and shouted, "Can
you drive this thing?"

She nodded. "If I have to!"

Allowing the old bus to slow a bit, I stepped out of the seat
and gave her room to jump in and take the wheel. "Just keep
her steady and stay on the road."

She mashed the gas and leaned forward, staring through the
dusty windshield. "What road?"

I staggered, snatched up the M16 from the front bench seat,
stepped over Adan, and worked my way back past the terrified
children to Bianca and Alexia, who made room for me so that I
could sit across the aisle from Isidro and gauge the situation. They
were gaining on us like we were parked. They were a good quarter of a mile away, but they would be right behind us in no time.

"It's them?"

I turned to look at Bianca. "Move the children forward."

She and Alexia did as I requested. Isidro, who had taken off
his poncho and folded it on the sill of the missing window, leveled the .30-06 on the approaching headlights. "If we need to,
can you hit them from far out?"

He shrugged a shoulder as we bumped along.

"How many rounds do you have?"

He held up two fingers.

Boy, I wished I had those three rounds in Culpepper's pocket.

Sitting in the last bench seat on the opposite corner, I disengaged the magazine on the M16, counted the rounds at around fourteen, and slapped it home. "This Armalite is not going to have the punch that that thirty-ought-six has, so I'm going to have you shoot the front of that SUV when it gets up here."

He glanced at me.

"I know it's not your specialty, but we don't know how many of them there are in that thing, and the easiest way to stop all of them is by killing the car either by shooting the radiator or the engine."

He studied me, and I wasn't sure my logic had convinced him.

I gestured with the automatic rifle in my hands. "After you fire your two rounds, believe me, you can have this one."

He turned back to the advancing target, and I assumed we'd reached terms.

The Cadillac was gaining even faster now that we'd hit a straightaway, but although the road was straight, its condition was even rougher, which actually gave us a bit of an advantage as the Mercury bus was so antiquated it had a higher clearance and a longer wheelbase.

Even so, the Escalade was only about a hundred yards away. It surged forward, and Isidro fired, the battered wood stock kicking against his shoulder like it had grown there.

We both peered into the oncoming headlights but couldn't see that the bullet had had any effect. "Throw another one into it." Isidro took aim and fired again.

Nothing. The big SUV roared forward, gaining considerable

ground, and slammed into the back of the bus with tremendous force; the Mercury swerved in the ruts.

We scrambled to get back into position. I shouted to Cady. "Are you all right?"

"I'm okay!" She corrected the drift in the slippery sand and then recorrected, keeping the bus at a straightforward speed of about fifty, which appeared to be its limit.

When I turned back, the SUV was making another run at us, and even more alarming, the sunroof was opening and someone was attempting to get through it with what looked to be another Kalashnikov rifle.

Gesturing toward the hard-charging Escalade, I took the Garand from Isidro and handed him the M16. "Do what you do best."

Staring at me for a second, he studied the automatic rifle as if it were an Atlas rocket and then threw it onto his shoulder in time to level it at the individual clamoring out of the roof just as it slammed into the rear of us again.

The force of the impact caused the bus to swerve sideways, this time clipping the tops of the ruts before Cady could turn the wheel, and I could feel the Mercury leaning up on one side in an attempt to roll over. Steering into the drift, Cady got the thing back under control, but we'd slowed to the point that the Cadillac was only a few feet behind us. I could even see that Culpepper was in the passenger seat, grinning as he fired at us with my Colt that he held out the window.

I looked back at the roof, where the gunman had repositioned himself and was raising the assault rifle to his shoulder. I glanced at Isidro, but he was already aimed up and had his finger on the trigger. He squeezed, but nothing happened.

AK fire ripped across the back of the bus, and we all dove for whatever cover there was. I yelled at Bianca and Alexia, doing my best to be heard above the general mayhem. "Get those kids further in the front of the bus!"

They scrambled to do as I said, and I turned to look at Isidro, who held the rifle out to me with a confused look. Reaching across the aisle, I flipped the safety off just as another volley ripped through the sheet metal, and we threw ourselves to the floor again.

The bus swayed but not as bad this time, and both Isidro and I scrambled to get back to the window, whereupon he leveled the M16 over the edge and took careful aim.

Looking through the cracked glass of the other corner, I pulled the Glock from my belt and watched as the turret gunner in the Cadillac attempted to keep the front sight of the assault rifle on us while at the same time battling the swales in the desert road himself.

We'd just found a sweet spot of a straightaway when he lifted the Kalashnikov, only to be answered by a brief burst from Isidro, the M16 fire climbing like an antiaircraft gun, a standard mistake by those unfamiliar with automatic weapons.

Even so, the sunroof shooter's head snapped back with the first round, and he tumbled into the Escalade only to be quickly replaced by another shooter with another AK, along with the driver, who was hanging a pistol from the side window.

Stuffing the semiautomatic back in my jeans, I reached across, taking the M16 from Isidro and crowding him to one side. "My turn."

Taking quick aim and switching to single-shot as they swerved and rushed forward, I fired into the windshield, watching it shatter as the SUV leapt forward again, hitting us even harder than before, the replacement gunman in the sunroof slamming forward, throwing a few rounds up at us before losing his gun as it slid onto the hood and then over the side.

The Mercury lurched again, this time the extended period of two-wheeled travel seeming to last forever as Cady tried to correct the oversteer and then climbed the berm only to crash back onto all four wheels, swerve again, and climb the other side, sliding to a sickening stop, most likely high-centered.

The Cadillac smashed into the corner of the bus one last time and then veered to the left before gliding to a stop at a crazy angle, lodged in the sand itself.

Looking forward, I could see all the children on the floor. Cady gunned the engine, but the bus didn't move. She threw it into reverse, but the results were the same. "Get those kids over to the right side of the bus!"

Just as I finished yelling, another strafe of fire stitched its way across the length of the Mercury, Bianca and Alexia grabbing the children and huddling on the far side.

Leaning forward, I hung my arms out the window and unloaded the M16, watching the rounds blister the side of the Escalade. Pulling back in, I slumped against the rear door, ejected the mag, and dropped the Armalite onto the floorboard.

Looking at Isidro, I shrugged and pulled the Glock from my jeans. "Well, we are now officially out of rifle ammo."

He stared at me, his eyes unmoving.

I reached toward him and watched as he slumped forward, the blood covering his back; I caught him and held him, feeling his neck for the pulse that wasn't there. With my breath stuttering in my chest and throat and feeling the anger that I'd fought against my whole life, I sat there holding the young man.

You find that kernel of madness at an early age, and if you're lucky you start building up a callus around it, a tough layer of humanity that holds it at bay, because it's just too dangerous to allow to escape. Your family can't ever see it, your friends can't ever see it, no one must ever see it—but it's there, waiting to burn the protective covering away that has taken a lifetime to build and burst open like a volcanic canker of maniacal emotion.

Carefully laying him to the side, I stood. There were a few rounds of pistol fire striking the bus, but I didn't care. I strode forward, the bullets chasing after me as I walked down the aisle to the front of the bus, stepped over Bianca, Alexia, Adan, the children, and my daughter, and pushed the handle, opening the bifold door.

Curled on the floor mat, Cady uncovered her face long enough to look up at the unfamiliar me. "Daddy, what are you doing?"

Swinging on the chrome bar, I stepped down the stairs and landed both boots in the powdery sand and turned as a few more rounds pierced the side of the Mercury.

The driver stumbled past the hood and fired again, this time toward me but wide to my right. I raised the Glock and shot him dead center in the chest.

As I walked across the rutted road, another round flew from the Escalade, and I focused on the muzzle flash at the back window as the shooter opened the rear door—it took two rounds to stop the gunman, and he fell out and planted face-first in the roadway.

I turned to aim at the front passenger-side door as it slowly opened wide. It hung there revealing Culpepper, covered with blood and still caught in the shoulder belt like a broken marionette, my hat on his head and my .45 dangling in his right hand.

At first I thought he was dead, but then I saw the half grin as he watched me approach. "Jesus, you play rough."

I cased the rest of the vehicle until I was sure the others were dead and then put my full focus on him.

He tried to move but then coughed up more blood onto his shirt and laughed. "I don't think I'm going to make it."

I stopped about a grave's length from him. "Probably not."

The blood drooled from his lips as he tried to lift his head with a laugh. "I get that little Aztec fucker?"

I wasn't going to give him the satisfaction. "No."

He glanced up at me from under the brim of my hat. "You're a liar."

"Raise that pistol of mine and find out." He didn't move, and I kept the front sights of the 9mm on the one eye that I could see. "I'll ask you one last time, did you kill my son-in-law?"

He laughed some more, ending it with more coughing, more blood, and more lies. "Yeah, I killed him—back in Philadelphia— shot him in the back and then rolled him over and shot him in the face." He smirked the smile that I'd most certainly had enough of. "He cried like a bitch."

"You're a liar."

He continued grinning the death's head smile, and the one eye stayed on me. "All right . . . The boss did it himself; he likes doing his own dirty work when it's personal. He says when that hot rod of an undersheriff of yours shows up, he's going to do her, too. Do her slow." His head shifted. "Right after he does you."

"Where is he?"

"Out there. Somewhere."

I took a breath, maybe the first since I'd exited the bus. "Well, as much as I've enjoyed our conversation . . . We need to get going, and I want my hat, gun, and Henry's knife."

He turned my Colt in his hand, the dark metal glinting in the cold, soulless moonlight. "I'll give you the gun, all right."

"Don't."

"Oh hell, Sheriff . . ." He began lifting my .45 very slowly. "At least I'll be killed by an American."

When he'd almost gotten it at eye level, I fired.

His head snapped back and his body followed, bouncing off the upholstery before slumping forward in the belt, hanging there lifeless. The blood poured into his lap from the hole where his remaining eye had been.

I took another breath and stepped forward, picking up my hat and putting it back on my head before stooping to pick up my sidearm. I found Henry's Bowie on the floorboards. Looking up at Culpepper's ruined face, half of it still covered by the bandages, I could see he had died with the smirk he'd carried laughingly into hell.

Standing, I checked the Glock, found it empty, and tossed it into the Cadillac. Slipping out the magazine of my Colt, I found it also empty, the only round left the one in the pipe. Sighing, I fed the mag and then walked around the Escalade in order to gather up one of the Kalashnikovs and as much ammo as I could carry.

When I got back to the bus, Cady, Bianca, and Alexia were using their hands to dig it out, scooping double handfuls of sand from under the old Mercury. Bianca turned to look up at me. "Isidro's dead."

"I know."

She glanced toward the drug dealer's SUV. "And them?"

I gestured with the collected armament. "All dead."

Cady dusted the sand from her hands and then assisted Alexia. "I think it'll move now."

"No one else was hit?"

"No." She shook her head and stepped toward me, the streaks from her tears washing across her dusty face like war paint. "We wrapped him up in his poncho and placed him on the floor."

I nodded and glanced at the faint glow on the eastern horizon, feeling the energy leaving me as if I'd opened a valve. "We need to get going; the sun will be up before long." I glanced at the rust and powder blue bus and barely got the next words out. "And I'm not sure how good the air-conditioning is in this thing."

She stepped forward the rest of the way and wrapped her arms around me, and it felt better than anything I'd felt in quite a while.

We dislodged the Mercury and got enough traction to allow it to drag all four weather-checked tires back onto the roadway, the first rays of the sun digging gorges in the flat, volcanic terrain of the desert.

With the sun rising it was almost as if a strange world were erupting around us, a ruinous, unrelenting planet of rock and fire that was enhanced by the internal combustion of the old bus that chugged along.

The gas gauge read a quarter tank, and all I hoped was that we would be able to get somewhere where there might be gas enough to get us to the border.

My tank on the other hand had long ago reached the critical stage of no reserve. We were now angling east, and my eyes were closing, and I wasn't sure if it was because I hadn't slept in years, the accumulated beatings I'd taken, or if I'd just had enough of staring into the sun.

Cady and Bianca were quietly talking in the seat behind me. They were ministering to Adan, but Alexia and the children were asleep, and if there had been any way in the world, I would've joined them.

It seemed like we'd been driving for hours when I thought I could see something far in the distance, but I honestly wasn't sure what it was, or if it was really there. In the simmering yolk of the sun, there was something with wings, great wings that in my imaginings spread, sending undulations of heat across the surface of the desert.

The phoenix is the legendary bird with a brilliant plumage and a wondrous voice that rises from the pyre of its own ashes only to regenerate itself and fly to Heliopolis in Egypt to the Temple of Ra, the Egyptian god of the sun. A symbol of immortality and an allegory of resurrection, the thousand-year-old female bird was there in the road in front of us, and all I could think was that it was like the sun that figuratively dies each night and is every morning reborn.

I slowed the bus and looked around, but the only thing that my red-rimmed eyes saw was the unforgiving terrain of Mexico, unyielding to this tired Mercury, every bit the mythological match for the obstacle that blocked the road in front of us.

I sat there for a long moment, looking to my left and right before cutting the ignition and allowing the engine on the bus to die.

Cady's voice behind me was just above a whisper. "Oh my God."

There is a lie in all fiction, a fabrication that says that when the critical moment of your life arrives you will be rested, clean, composed, and prepared, but you won't be. I guarantee it. You will be exhausted, scattered, dirty, and wounded. But with this comes one miraculous strength.

You. Won't. Care.

Lumbering to a standing position, I turned and looked at the three women and the wounded man, who had regained consciousness and was now sitting up and looking back at me with a bloody face.

"Don't go out there."

Looking past him, my eyes rested on the children and particularly Alicia—and then I turned. "Close the doors behind me, and no matter what happens, don't any of you get off this bus."

I opened the folding doors and slowly stepped down the stairs onto the hard-boiled surface of the road, and pulling the .45 with its one round from my jeans, I turned to look at the Beechcraft twin-engine, the gleaming aluminum sides sparking with the light of the rising sun.

Walking forward, I gazed out into the desert where a number of men were scattered, standing about fifty yards from us in all directions, their automatic weapons pointed at me and the bus.

Taking a deep breath, I focused on the sun, the plane, and the man standing in the road as the sweat began building under the band of my bloodstained hat. I began walking toward him, pretty sure that if I raised my hand with the .45 in it, I'd be dead before I hit the dry ground.

"Welcome."

I stopped at the sound of his voice, then registered what he'd said and attempted to assemble a response. "Get out of our way."

He stepped forward, and I could see that his knife was in one hand and some sort of red cloth was in the other. "Still following your moral compass?"

"If you don't get out of the way, I'm going to kill you."

His head cocked a bit in mock surprise. "Ah, Sheriff, perhaps your moral compass does not encompass situations such as this—a place where justice is helpless."

I gestured, ever so slightly, with the Colt in my hand. "Hardly helpless."

Studying me from under the brim of his hat, he clarified the situation. "You could shoot me, but then my men will shoot you and then they will kill every living soul in that bus behind you."

"What do you want?"

He moved slightly to the left, studying me still. "It is time for this to end, this thing between us." He glanced around. "This is not as I had planned, but then again it is perhaps as it should be."

"So how do we end it?"

At first he didn't move but then quickly unfurled a long, red, Basque sash, the *gerriko*—the material lying in the road like a fresh wound.

"So you want me to hang myself?"

He breathed a laugh. "You have your friend's knife?"

"I'd rather use this Colt."

Shaking his head, he took another step closer. "Somehow, I do not think that would be fair."

Considering all my alternatives, I tossed the .45 into the sand at the side of the roadway and pulled Henry Standing Bear's stag-handled Bowie from the small of my back. "I don't suppose we could just duke it out?"

He flipped the end of the twelve-foot sash toward me. "I am afraid that in that, you would also have the advantage."

Stepping forward, I stooped and picked up the end. "And you don't have an advantage with this?"

He shrugged. "Perhaps, but it is mitigated by your superiority in size and muscle—shall we see who is victorious, skill or strength? One last bullfight to determine the sacrifices to the altar of justice, even if there is none?"

Wrapping the thing around my fist with a vicious yank, I drew his arm forward as he positioned himself sideways with the foot-long stiletto poised at shoulder height like the curled tail of one of those scorpions.

I circled to the left, he countered by moving right, and I watched his careful foot placement—he was like a picador, waiting for the bull to be distracted for even an instant.

Henry's heavy-bladed knife felt good in my hand, and I attempted to awaken all my senses, knowing full well that if I didn't do that quickly, there would be no reason to bother.

I felt like the bull that was reaching the final act, bleeding and bowed, just waiting for the final blow that would pierce its tired heart. I moved in a half circle and could see Cady and all the others crowded in the windshield of the old bus. They watched with the horror of the situation written across their faces, and I wanted to smile or say something that would assure them.

And that's when he struck.

The only thing I felt was a tug at the front of my sweat-soaked shirt and the popping of one of the snap buttons as it came loose.

I hadn't even seen him move—he was that fast.

Passing underneath my outstretched arm, he must've gone completely by me only to turn and regard me with an impassive expression. "The *acoso y derribo*, a test of the spirit before the true fight begins."

Using my knife hand, I brushed the back of it against my abdomen and looked at the fresh blood that was smeared there. There was no pain—the cut wasn't deep, just enough to let me know that it could've been and that he could've ended the fight with a single move.

A slight chill traveled across my skin like electricity as I was just starting to understand what I'd let myself in for.

"So you don't enjoy the bullfights, Sheriff?" He still watched me and changed directions, raising the blade again. "The *cambio*, of which we will have many before this fight is done, my friend."

I felt the anger rising in me. "Are you enjoying yourself?"

"I shall attempt to educate you." He continued circling, and I countered. "My greed overtook me in my attempts to auction you, but this is better, more personal—and all justice, remember this in your last moments, is personal."

He feinted to his right and dipped in as if to attack again, and I went for it, stumbling a little on the uneven road as he pulled back and studied me, taking in another weakness.

Pulling in the opposite direction, I grabbed another handful of the sash and wrapped it, figuring that if I could get him close I'd have an advantage in size and weight, but he simply danced to the side and raised his blade again.

"The *embestida*, or charging of the bull."

Sensing an opportunity, I swung wide, but he carefully stepped back and then sliced through the unprotected shoulder of my knife arm, almost causing me to drop the thing.

He came around behind me, but I had circled and swung again, this time barely catching him on the forearm as he withdrew. "The *parado*, the bull tires but retains his cunning." He watched as I stretched my shoulder, felt the alien stitch in the movement, and now knew I was impaired. "There is no shame, Sheriff; however, there is a price."

I stood there on wooden legs and figured I had maybe two more lunges before I collapsed, but I was at least going to make those two lunges count. If I was going to die, carved up like a beef roast, I was at least going to make sure the devil got his due.

Spreading my arms to their outermost reach, I circled opposite him but then changed directions, yanking the sash toward me. I charged again, but he slipped to the side and ducked under my arm, slashing my thigh and roping the cloth between my ankles causing me to trip and fall.

Scrambling up the berm, I limped onto my wounded leg and

spun to face him, but he was watching at the full length of the sash again. "The *suerte de varas*, the first act of the kill."

Breathing heavily, I looked up at my daughter's horrified face as I felt the blood in my body along with any energy seeping into the sand at my feet. Time to regroup. I shambled my way to the right. He'd taken a few steps, but then spun in with a backhand that slashed across my face before I could get out of the way.

Swinging hard, I caught something as the blood sprayed from my jawline. I stopped and turned, blind in my left eye, but could see him standing there, looking down at the blood seeping onto the torn side of his shirt.

His face rose, but there was no panic in it.

Swallowing, I wiped my eye on my shoulder and was alarmed by the amount of blood. It was still in its socket, but I was essentially half blind.

Stopping with his back to the bus, I watched as he raised the stiletto above his head again, shifting his weight to one side and then the other so that I was unsure of which direction the blade would come.

I could almost read a sadness in his face for my incompetence, but then he slipped to the right and when I followed him he spun to the left again, passing under my arm and bringing the eight-inch blade up between my ribs.

Everything in my body froze as I unconsciously rose up on my toes in an attempt to escape the thin blade, but it remained there in my body as I rested my arm on his shoulder, my grip loosening as Henry's knife slipped from my fingers.

Unable to breathe, I looked up at my daughter and could see Alexia and Bianca holding her as she screamed, but there was no sound, other than Bidarte. "*Suerte de matar*, the final act."

My arm dropped beside his in a pathetic movement signaling

utter defeat at the hands of a master—but then I closed my bloody hand around his as I seized him with my other arm like a horn and held him as I turned my face to look at him with my one eye.

With a crushing grip, I took his knife hand and slowly began pulling the stiletto from me like a scabbard. The dread in his face heightened as he struggled to free himself but couldn't.

I finally pulled the stiletto from my ribcage and held his hand around the switchblade, the point of which I had lifted to the underside of his chin where it pushed an indentation in the skin.

As he looked into the nickel-plated, apocalyptic pause in my eye, I could now see the panic in his. "You're wrong, not all justice is personal—but this is."

Hammering it upward with all my remaining strength, I plunged the blade through the soft flesh under his jaw, through his palate and into his brain, and his eyes widened and then slowly, with an agonizing stillness, gazed into a distance beyond.

I held him there for a moment to make sure of the deed and then released him. He slid from my arms and fell to the sand where he lay, gasping like a landed fish with his mouth opening and closing before lying there, very still.

Hunching to the right in an attempt to lessen the pain from my wounds, it was all I could do to keep from following him to the ground. I leaned over and attempted to catch my breath, but either because of exhaustion or the amount of internal damage, I couldn't. Finally pushing what little air there was from my lungs, I inhaled and tried to stand upright but still couldn't, standing hunched over like that for I didn't know how long.

I slowly became aware of boots standing around me and was finally able to raise my face enough to look at them through my one eye.

There were about a half dozen of them there backlit in the

sun, the men from the desert with the automatic weapons now drooping toward the ground as they first contemplated Bidarte's corpse and then me.

They spoke in low voices, and even though I couldn't understand them and the voices seemed to be coming from a long way away, I marveled at the beauty of the language. A spasm overtook me, and coughing, I brought a hand up to clear my eye, but there was too much blood and I finally gave up, concentrating on keeping on my feet as a wave of nausea hit.

Glancing around, I was suddenly aware that the boots weren't there anymore and that I was alone.

Unsure of how much time had passed, I suddenly became aware of a roaring noise and looked up as best I could to see the phoenix rising again, screaming rhythmically and taxiing around, blasting me with dirt, grit, and sand as it moved away, faster and faster until it slowly lifted into the sky, headed for Heliopolis in Egypt to the Temple of Ra, or Mexico City—whichever came first.

My legs collapsed under me, and I sat in the middle of the road, cupping a hand at my side in an attempt to stanch the bleeding. After a few seconds the nausea struck again, and I felt the need to just lie down, so I did but perhaps not as gently as I wanted to.

Lying there on the ground, I watched as the phoenix circled and glinted in the sun-scorched sky, aware of its impending death and resurrection, rising from the ashes *con moto* to a beautiful song that rang in my ears as I slowly slipped away, hoping to be reborn.

"Daddy, Daddy . . ."

EPILOGUE

When I finally came to the first thing I was aware of other than only being able to see out of my right eye was that I was clean and not sweating. The second thing I became aware of was that sitting in a chair at the foot of my bed was Tomás Bidarte, smiling and sharpening his knife.

I jolted and tried to sit up, but when I did my vision blurred and hurting, I fell back against the pillow. After a moment, I opened my eye again, but he was gone and I was alone in the room.

A warm wave overtook me, and I stared at the textured paint on the pale-as-death ceiling that looked like skin. Everything was fuzzy, and in the distance I heard someone speaking Spanish in a murmuring voice. There were other sounds, but they were nondescript and mechanical and try as I might, I faded away into the soft warmth.

When I woke up again, I didn't want to open my right eye for fear that I would be back in the desert, dead, staring up at the sky, so I opened my left eye, and didn't see anyone or anything, only an absolute darkness, which was a little worrisome in itself.

After a while I decided to open my right, desert and death be damned, and could see the hospital room again and a nice-looking nurse who had come in to adjust what felt like bandages on my head. She prepared a syringe and smiled at me.

When I blinked, she disappeared without a word.

I nodded in and out for days, which was fine with me since the Mexican government had a lot of questions, which explained the two suited men sitting at my bedside. "How do I know you guys are real?"

They showed me their Federal Ministerial Police badges.

"We don't need no stinking badges."

They stared at me.

I attempted to sit up, but the pain in my side caused me to gasp and clench my eye shut. I waited for the spasm to pass and slowly opened my eye again, but by then they were gone. "Well, this is getting tiring."

The nurse came back with food, which I ate, and I decided that that was how I was going to determine if people were real, whether or not they brought me food. The two agents from the FMP came by again.

"You guys have anything to eat?"

They looked at each other and then were gone again, but at least I had the satisfaction of watching them go.

"Evidently it is not okay to waltz into a foreign country and give the big *adiós* to a couple of dozen men no matter how much everyone agrees that they deserved the big *adiós* and then head back across the border with a hearty hi-yo Silver." Glancing around the room, a battered Adan Martínez now sat at the foot of my bed. "Doc?"

He smiled or did his best to. "Yes."

"You're here in the hospital, too?"

"Yes."

"Do you have anything to eat?"

He studied me through the bandages on his own face. "Would you like me to speak to someone?"

"No."

"Are they not feeding you in this hospital?"

"They are, but I've decided that the only way I can tell if people are really here is by having them bring me food or stick a needle in me."

He placed both hands on the footboard. "I will remember that for my next visit."

The next day the nurse, who I had decided was real, wheeled me into a small garden between two of the buildings where a hunchbacked man in a porkpie hat sat without legs in another wheelchair—he didn't look at me.

"Are you really here?"

He turned toward my voice, his sunglasses reflecting the flowers.

"You have lost your mind in this place?"

"Maybe." I waited a moment and then spoke again, studying the man across from me for fear that he might disappear. It truly was like that with the Seer, if you didn't pay attention, he drifted away and you were left with nothing but your own thoughts, something I was desperate to avoid, although they crowded in on me anyway. "Your nephew, Alonzo . . ."

He nodded, but it was impossible to read his face behind the large sunglasses. "Father Rubio helped me to light a candle for him earlier today."

"I'm so sorry."

He nodded some more and then lifted his face so that the sun gently struck him—at least I think it was the sun in that I wasn't taking anything for granted lately. "This garden is pleasant, no?"

"Yes."

"Have you spoken to any of the others?"

I chortled a laugh without much humor in it. "That's the problem—I've been talking to everyone." I glanced around, considering the two FMP men seated near the door. "I think I'm under house arrest."

He smiled. "Your friend, the government man, your government, hopes to see you soon, but he told me things to tell you."

"McGroder?"

"Yes."

"My daughter?"

"Has returned home to your granddaughter, along with the large Indian who terrifies everyone."

"Henry."

"Yes, and there is a blaspheming woman who loiters near the hospital."

"Vic."

He nodded. "She is in contact with Señor Guzmán—a bad influence."

"On whom?"

"Both."

My turn to nod. "What about Adan, Bianca, Alexia, and the children?"

"You are lucky that they did not kill the doctor, and he was able to bring himself together enough to save you." He adjusted his porkpie hat and for the first time, smiled. "They have all joined forces and moved the Orfanato to Adan's ranch."

"Will they be safe there?"

He nodded. "With the attention you have brought to Monasterio del Corazón Ardiente, and the fact that the mines are still active, the government is now concerned, and I do not think the narcos will be doing business there any longer."

"So Alexia is planning on staying here in Mexico?"

"It would appear."

"Looks like my daughter lost a friend." I glanced toward the door where the two men had started talking to each other, both looking down the hallway. "I suppose there is no reason for her to come back to Wyoming." Rolling my wheelchair forward just a bit, I reached out and placed a hand on the stump of his leg just to make sure—and the leg was solid. "It seems to me that everyone involved in this fiasco has lost someone—everyone except me."

His head dropped, and if he had been able to see, he would've been looking at my hand. "You almost lost yourself, no?"

"It was kind of touch and go there for a while."

"But you are still here."

"Yes."

"And he is gone."

"Is he?"

The Seer paused, and I couldn't help but feel a slight panic as he slipped off the sunglasses for only the second time since I'd known him and stared at me with the milky-white, opaque pupils. "You doubt your own abilities?"

"Like a cat, he seemed to have lots of lives."

He slipped the sunglasses into a shirt pocket, and we sat with the weight of silence smothering us. "Have you ever been to the bullfights, my friend?"

I stared at him. "What?"

"The bullfights, have you ever been?"

I took a breath. "That was what Bidarte asked, when he came to the cell in the monastery, and then later on the road, he asked me if I'd ever been to the bullfights."

"And have you?"

There was a noise down the hall, and I noticed the two Mexican Feds were gone. Gesturing to the Seer and then realizing he couldn't see me, I spoke. "I'll be back in just a minute."

Wheeling my chair toward the hallway, I rounded the corner, but no one was there. I could hear loud noises coming from the interior of the hospital and a lot of shouting, but I figured that wasn't anything with which I needed to be involved. Sighing, I turned my chair and rolled back to the garden where I discovered that the Seer was gone.

"I really need to get a grip on myself." Sitting there for a few minutes more, I suddenly decided to stand. I locked the wheelchair and carefully placing my bare feet on the stone path I steadied myself and rose, kind of hunched over, to a semistanding position, the pain keeping me from straightening all the way up.

I went back inside and caught my breath, and my eye followed the black and white tiles down the hallway where I could see that one of the glass doors at the end was hanging half open, an incredible light flowing through the tempered glass. I took another sweep of the hallway with my one good eye, but just as before, the place was completely empty.

I turned back and discovered Alonzo adjusting his thick glasses and smiling the goofy grin. "You should go."

"What?"

"The door is open, and you should go through it."

Looking back at my wheelchair, I shook my head. "I'm not moving very fast these days."

"Take your time."

Staring at the glow still shining through the glass doors, I placed a hand against the wall, sliding it along as I moved, very slowly. "Your uncle was just here." I couldn't say the next part without dropping my eyes. "Alonzo."

"Sí?"

"I'm sorry. I'm sorry I got you killed."

He shrugged. "Everybody dies."

I stopped there, my head hanging down. "Everybody around me."

"You save many."

I took a deep breath and tried to straighten, slowly standing upright until I thought the pain was going to split me in half. "We did."

I looked up, and he was gone, too, but in his place someone else stood backlit in the open door. Sliding along, I tried to focus my eye but it was like I was back in the desert, staring into the unforgiving sun.

Predictably, he said nothing.

Considering the circumstance, neither did I.

I turned my head to the side and stared at the bushy-haired, wild young man still dressed in the cotton poncho, the M1 rifle still hanging off his shoulder. I could feel the light, almost as if it were burning its way through the door. After a moment he gestured, extending his arm with his palm up, bidding me to exit or enter whichever it was.

"I'm not so sure I want to go through that door, Isidro."

He held the other hand out to me and through no volition of my own, my hand crept out to him and he guided me the rest of the way as he stooped and the amulet fell forward from around his neck on the thin chain—Riablo, the trickster devil that attempted to keep the balance of the universe with sacrifice.

The bas-relief of the imprinted metal glinted in the bright light. "You giving me up to the powers that be?"

I stumbled forward with my eyes closed against the brightness and fell, the pressure from the impact robbing me of my breath. I rolled sideways and felt someone pulling me up to a sitting position.

I opened my eyes to tarnished gold ones that exploded with tiny flakes in layers of lighter colors and a mouth that covered mine with tender but insistent lips, capturing what little breath I had left. Her hair formed a dark shroud around my face, giving me relief from the scorching light. "What took you so long—this is a getaway, you know."

"Vic?" I studied her. "Are you really here?"

She pulled back and smiled. "Boy howdy, are you fucked up."

Glancing around, I could see I was seated in the familiar, cavernous backseat of the pink 1959 Cadillac convertible with my undersheriff leaning over the front seat.

"With the bullfighting . . ."

I turned so that I could see the Seer, who was sitting in the backseat alongside me.

"What the hell?"

I was about to amplify my question when a large man in a black cowboy hat, an impressive mustache, and a hospital gown ran down the alley toward us. He was barefoot like I was and gave all of us a prodigious mooning as he threw himself into the driver's seat, cranked the ignition, the big V-8 of the Caddy roaring like a poked panther.

He first looked at Vic, and then threw an arm over the seat where I could see his plastic medical bracelet that read GUZMAN. He looked at me with a wink. "It would probably be in our best interests to get the hell out of here right now."

He yanked the Caddy into gear and floored it, blasting down the alley at mach speed, scattering trashcans, a few pedestrians, and finally some white-coated hospital orderlies, the massive steer horns leading the way.

The Seer, shouting to be heard, yelled in my ear. "As I was saying, with the bullfighting, every once in a great while . . ." He leaned in, his porkpie hat flying from his head and his sunglasses reflecting my image through a glass, darkly. "The bull, he sometimes wins."

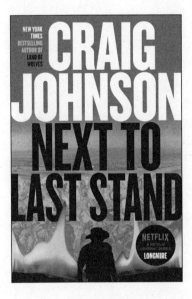

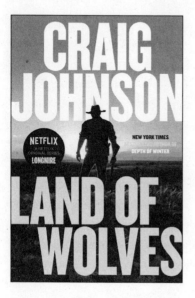